Somebody's Gotta
Be On Top

Also by Mary B. Morrison

He's Just a Friend

Never Again Once More

Soul Mates Dissipate

Who's Making Love

Justice Just Us Just Me

Somebody's Gotta Be On Top

MARY B. MORRISON

Dafina
Books

Kensington Publishing Corp.
http://www.kensingtonbooks.com

DAFINA BOOKS are published by

Kensington Publishing Corp.
850 Third Avenue
New York, NY 10022

All Kensington Titles, Imprints, and Distributed Lines are available at special quantity discounts for bulk purchases for sales promotions, premiums, fund-raising, and educational or institutional use. Special book excerpts or customized printings can also be created to fit specific needs. For details, write or phone the office of the Kensington special sales manager: Kensington Publishing Corp., 850 Third Avenue, New York, NY 10022, attn: Special Sales Department, Phone: 1-800-221-2647.

Dafina and the Dafina logo Reg. U.S. Pat. & TM Off.

First hardcover printing: August 2004
First trade paperback printing: July 2005
First mass market printing: June 2006

10 9 8 7 6 5 4 3 2

Printed in the United States of America

Dedicated to a group of phenomenal women . . .
"The Girls":

Felicia Polk
Carmen Polk
Vyllorya A. Evans
Michaela Burnett
Koren McKenzie-John
Barbara Brown
Marilyn Edge

And in loving memory of
Sandra D. Chavis

PREFACE

Soul Mates Dissipate, Never Again Once More, He's Just A Friend, Somebody's Gotta Be on Top, and my next three novels are intertwined. I recommend, if possible, reading the series in order. Hopefully this brief background will help the reader better understand the connections. To preview an excerpt of each novel, visit www.marymorrison.com.

Soul Mates Dissipate is, for now, the beginning. This page-turning drama takes you on a journey with Jada Diamond Tanner and Wellington Jones, *aka* . . . soul mates. Wellington's mother, Cynthia Jones, who has a history of her own with her sister Katherine, friend Susan, and ex-lover Keith, invites a sexy, single woman, Melanie Marie Thompson, to live with Wellington, with the hopes of sabotaging Wellington's engagement to Jada.

Never Again Once More, the sequel to *Soul Mates Dissipate,* spans twenty years into the lives of Jada and Wellington. Darius Jones, Jada's son, is born and matures to twenty years of age and by the end of this story he's climbing to the top of his mother's corporate structure and on top of her four female executives.

In *He's Just a Friend,* Fancy Taylor is a beautiful but not so brilliant woman on the move to conquer a rich husband by any means necessary. Along her journey she'll meet several friends, some of whom become foes, and eventually Fancy meets Jada's son, Darius Jones.

In *Somebody's Gotta Be on Top,* regardless of the situation, Darius Jones is always on top. His motto, "If it doesn't make money, it doesn't make sense," includes the women in his life. That is, until he meets Fancy Taylor.

Nothing Has Ever Felt Like This is an upcoming release. Will Fancy Taylor outsmart Darius Jones for his money? Or will Fancy fall in love with Darius? What happens when two people love so deeply, they're willing to die for, with, and because of one another? Darius and Fancy will learn the true meaning of love.

If you've read each novel, you know that Cynthia Jones has a history so moving, trust me, her story, *Our Little Secret,* is worth the wait. Cynthia's story creates the beginning and concludes the end of my seven-book series. After Cynthia's novel, I promise not to keep you waiting for *Kiss Me: Now Tell Me You Love Me,* a chilling drama about Harrison and Angela Gray.

ACKNOWLEDGMENTS

With every beat of my heart, I thank God for every breath, every day, every word, everyone, everything. Thanks to the soldiers and civilians who have dedicated, and some instances lost their lives, serving in the United States of America armed forces.

To my loving son, Jesse Byrd, Jr., I'm proud of you, keep reaching for the stars, they're always there, even when you don't see the light. Jesse, your intelligence on and off the basketball court will serve you well. Stay focused. Keep God first. And remember ladies think eight-to-ten steps ahead of most men. Make wise decisions.

Special thanks to my editor, Karen Thomas, my agent, Claudia Menza, and my entire Kensington family for your continual support. My siblings, Wayne, Andrea, Derrick, and Regina Morrison, Marge Rickerson, and Debra Noel, I'm grateful and blessed to have your love and support.

To my author friends, Gloria Mallette, Mary Monroe, Brenda L. Thomas, Toshia, E. Lynn Harris, may your cups runneth over. Mr. Carl Weber, *aka* Prince of Drama, number one best-selling author of *Playa Haters,* owner of Urban Books Publishing, thanks for paving the way for me and so many new writers. Carl, may God continue to bless you to others.

To Felicia Polk, of Felicia Polk and Associates, thanks for launching my career and being a true friend. To L. Peggy Hicks, of Tricom, thanks for arranging my tours. Endless love and thanks to all the booksellers, readers, radio hosts, sororities, fraternities, and book clubs. Last but never least, thanks to my man Black, I love you, Daddy.

Somebody's Gotta Be on Top

Stop!
Somebody's Gotta Be on Top
How much are you willing to pay
To live another day

What are you afraid of . . .

Money isn't keen
It's the realization of a dream
In the color green
Envy
Slime
Slipping
Tripping
Through time
Exchanging hands
Yours
Mine

What are you afraid of . . .

Wishing
Wanting
Never daunting
Taunting
Your faith
Or taking a risk
Or waiting for break
To take a piss

Shit!
Piss on
Those who sing
Piss off
Those who scream
I'm living my dream!
Stop!
Somebody's Gotta Be on Top
How much are you willing to pay
To live another day

What are you afraid of . . .

Success
Achieving your best
Willing to live with less
In order to attain more
Are you afraid to open the door
Before you knock
Or maybe you're content
Shoulda
Coulda
Woulda
Only if . . .
You'd spent
Time Time Time
How much are you willing to pay
To live another day
Frivolous chatter
Doesn't matter
Settling
Meddling
Gabbing
Back-stabbing

Shattering hope
Slippery slope
Walking a tightrope

What are you waiting for . . .

An invite
When the time is right
Not tonight
Tomorrow
Sorrow
Today
You'll borrow
Someone else's
Money
Honey
Hopes
Dreams
Anything
Sign an IOU
Promise to repay
In dismay
That which you haven't earned today
Belongs to someone else
Isn't that funny
Yesterday is gone
You're sitting at home
On a diminishing throne
Of hopes
Dreams
Envy
Green
You scream
Money ain't a thing!

That's a lie
Can't miss what you never had
Lad
Your slice of the pie
Is on someone else's table
You're able
But . . .
Unwilling

What are you afraid of . . .

Stop!
Somebody's Gotta Be on Top
How much are you willing to pay
To live another day
No pain
No sweat
No blood
No tears
Just fears
Who cares
What's new
What are you really going to do
Successful people are the same as you
Living with fears too

What are you afraid of . . .

How much are you willing to pay
Today
Or Not
Regardless
Somebody's Gotta Be on Top

PROLOGUE

In life you must choose a path. Not setting goals or making decisions is the same as choosing. You occupy space that overlaps in time. With time. Emotions evolve. Emotions that are yours but at the same time, not. Is possession a form of ownership if nothing lasts forever but everything has a price? A value. Hopes. Dreams. Love. Loneliness. How much are you willing to pay to live another day? Turn the pages and take a look, if you dare, into the life of Darius Jones. Reading about his life may change your own.

CHAPTER 1

Monogamy wasn't natural. Monogamy was a learned behavior that Darius couldn't be taught. When would women realize, sex wasn't a bed partner of love? Besides, who could teach Darius how to be faithful? Jesse Jackson? Bill Cosby? Willie Brown? Bill Clinton? His dad, the ménage à trois king? All the men he respected, all the men he knew, were men. Fornicators. Adulterers. Players. The distinction of a real man was that a real man kept his family in the foreground and his females in the background. Like backup singers. Once the song was over, their job was done. Thanks for having made him cum. Now go. With Darius, not many of his lovers deserved an encore.

"Ha!" Darius laughed, then said aloud to himself, "You a fool boy." His office was quiet all morning. No constant phone calls or welcomed interruptions by his sexy secretary, Angel.

Any woman who wanted Darius Jones had to commit to him and only him. His woman had to have a job.

Not any job. A high-paying job. Preferably her own business. So what if he had enough money to take care of her. Her mama. And her grandmamma. A woman without a steady income was venomous. A woman with too much idle time was lethal. No piece of ass was worth his millions of dollars. He was the only heir to his mother's empire and one day would split his father's fortune with one of his stepbrothers who was barely four years old.

Darius flipped through the Los Angeles *Times,* pulled out the sports section, then slid the rest of the newspaper to the edge of his desk. He'd read the business section next. Darius bit his bottom lip in disgust. On the front page, another brother handcuffed, this time a football player, charged with allegedly raping a groupie. "Stupid-ass athletes. That fool was so busy trying to get laid he couldn't see that trick was tryna get paid. Now his ignant ass might end up broke and in jail. Trick was probably smiling the whole time she was fucking dude." Darius learned observing his mother how a woman could be a man's best advocate and his worst enemy at the same time.

Scanning the other twelve pages, Darius thought, *that would've never happened to me if I had gone to the NBA.* Those broke leeches in thongs, jiggling their asses on beaches or benches, at the bus stop, were the ones who were constantly plotting and planning—pregnancy, rape, battery—on how to become rich off of a man. For sex. For real. Any wealthy man would suffice. Mike. Kobe. Deon. Including him. Bullshit conniving tricks. They weren't privy to suck his dick.

Fed up with the media favoring the woman's side, Darius traded the sports section for business. While he'd slept, the value of his stocks increased. Money made Darius think about how rich pussy like the Vivica As, and Mary Js, Halles, and Janets of the world needed stroking too. But they also had reputations worth protecting. To them, lawsuits translated into bad publicity. Lost revenue. They'd end the relationship before bringing forth charges. That's the type of women Darius wanted. And if Darius ever caught one of his women cheating, she didn't need to waste his time explaining because he'd personally dismiss her. Immediately!

Thinking about women brought his number-one lady to mind. Darius smiled, picked up the phone, and pressed sixty-nine on his speed dial. His lungs expanded. The warm air escaped his nostrils, grazing his smooth upper lip. Darius removed the elastic band holding his ponytail. Three-hundred sixty-two black pencil-width dreadlocks fell slightly below his shoulders. Darius mastered and measured everything about his body. Dick: nine and three-quarters of an inch long, and four inches thick. Body fat: six point seven percent. Pimples: none. Birthmarks: two. One faded abstract image on the right side of his ass. The other was a black spot on the back of his left earlobe beneath his princess-cut two-carat diamond earring.

"Hey, you," she happily answered.

Her voice penetrated his soul. Chill bumps invaded his skin. The hairs on his arms stood tall. Darius wasn't cold. He swallowed the lump of air clogging his vocal cords then said, "You packed yet? I can't wait to see you tonight. Make sure you arrive two hours early at the airport." Darius deepened his voice then emphasized, "You'd better not miss your flight this time."

Unbuttoning his collar, Darius rolled his burgundy leather high-back chair until his abdomen pressed against the edge of his glass-top desk, creating a crease in his brown Versace jacket. Slowly he placed his finger over the photographic image of her naturally pink-colored lips. Thin and seemingly oh-so-very soft. She looked righteous—not as in holy, as in fine as hell—in the family picture they'd taken a month ago at Thanksgiving dinner with his parents.

"Are you still in the office?" she asked.

Darius's hand traveled from her temple and traced the outline along her straight black hair, which cast a strikingly beautiful contrast against her nearly white complexion. His eyes fixated on hers. She was always nice and polite with a caring-Cancer demeanor other women despised. She was perfect marriage material. She was the ideal woman to rear his kids.

Loving someone more than himself, more than life, more than making money, was absurd and not what Darius had planned. But this special woman—naw, she was more than a woman, she was a lady—had stolen his heart. First she'd become his platonic childhood playmate. Now she was his best friend. With the exception of his boy Keenan whom everyone called K'Nine, she was Darius's only other friend.

The honeysuckle scent of her hair, the subtle movement of her hips when she walked, the provocative melody of her voice each time she innocently laughed while calling his name, the gentleness of her touch whenever she groomed his dreadlocks, the taste of her words lingering on his palate as he gasped into the receiver consumed his thoughts. Nervous energy rumbled in the pit of his stomach. Consciously he erased his boyish grin. She evoked feelings Darius swore he'd never possess for another woman after having been betrayed by his ex-fiancée.

"Of course I'm still in the office, woman. And my

staff too. Just because it's the week between Christmas and New Year's doesn't mean the entire week is a holiday. They're not entitled to leave early but I might let 'em go at three. Maybe. Now answer my question." Darius began rearranging the few items on his desk.

"Don't worry. I packed last night. And my dad is dropping me off in a few. I'll call you when my plane gets into LAX." She paused, then whispered, "I miss you, brother."

Why did she keep calling him brother? He was more like a play-brother. Everybody in California claimed relatives that weren't blood related. Play cousins. Sisters. Aunts. Uncles. Mothers and fathers too. His birth parents weren't hers so technically they weren't related. And since Darius's mom was remarried to Wellington Jones, the man his mother should've married instead of marrying Lawrence, Darius felt Ashlee and he were two consenting adults capable of making their own decisions.

Darius remained silent. He rearranged his gold-and-crystal triangular clock to the left side of his nameplate then moved his in-and-out baskets to the opposite end. The shuffled newspaper, cordless phone, notepad, and gold-framed photo were neatly positioned on his spotless desk.

Although Darius spoke with Ashlee every day, three-to-five times each day, he'd practically forgotten about the incident with her dad. Darius hadn't seen Ashlee's father since the day, almost two years ago, when he'd beaten her father for abusing his mother. In retrospect Darius understood Lawrence's frustrations with his mom. After Lawrence's black eye and bruises healed, Darius's mother gave him the shock of his life. Since that day, Darius's feelings for his mother numbed his compassion toward women even more. If his mother were a liar, then every other woman was too. Except his lady on the opposite end of the phone. But the feasibility existed so he couldn't completely trust her either. *What a fucked-up world to live in,* Darius thought, when the only person he could trust one-hundred percent of the time was himself.

Forgetting about her dad and his mom, Darius massaged his erection through his pleated slacks, hoping she'd continue talking but hopefully not about her dad. Anticipating the sound of her voice made his dick harder. She had him so turned on he wanted to make love. To her. For years. *Say something. Anything. Please.* His dick urged repeating her tone in his mind. *I miss you.* He'd missed her too.

She finally broke the silence. "Did you hear me?" Lightly she articulated, "I said, I miss you."

Ashlee's delayed response made Darius believe she was also thinking about him. The cordless phone slipped from between his ear and shoulder so Darius quickly activated the speaker. "Of course I heard you. I just wanted you to repeat it. That's all." He placed his fingers against his thick chocolate lips then laid the same two fingers atop the glass frame over her mouth.

She inhaled then softly said, "I miss you. I miss you. I miss you. I miss you. I miss you. How's that? Turn on your cam so I can see you."

No way, Darius thought, staring at the flat-screen monitor on the glass-top L-unit connected to his desk. Kimberly's nude layout changed from covering her tits with sand on Venice beach to clenching a lollipop between her vaginal lips with a caption that read, "Sweeter than candy." Darius unzipped his pants and squeezed his head, suppressing the pre-cum trying to escape his hard-on. He imagined what Ashlee looked like in the nude. Although they'd visited one another for more than ten years, he still had no idea if her nipples were lighter or darker than her breasts. If her pubic hairs were curly or straight. If her clitoris was small or large. Would Darius care for Ashlee the same if they lived together? Would he love her if he married her?

"Hey, lady. I've gotta run. I'll see you later." Darius stood. He secured his relaxed muscle into his black silk boxers, then watched the tiny metal clamps overlap until the last one reached the top.

His lungs suctioned in the much-needed oxygen for his brain when she exhaled an intoxicating, "Bye."

Darius waited until Ashlee hung up, then removed his coat and tossed it onto his chair. He entered the private rest room connected to his office and vigorously rinsed his face with cold water. While staring at his reflection in the mirror, Darius wondered why his mother had lied to him about his biological father. Why she'd waited twenty years to reveal the truth. Why didn't his biological father, Darryl Williams, Sr. display the same love for him as he did for Darius's two half-brothers, Kevin and Darryl, Jr.? The relationship Darius's father had with Darius's half-sister didn't count because daughters were naturally closer to their fathers than sons.

Darryl was a former NBA all-star whom Darius idolized most of his childhood, including the four years Darius started on the varsity basketball team in high school. Darryl was his college basketball coach at Georgetown, which explained why Darius's mother never came to any of his college games. His mother apparently had had an epiphany when her mother died and decided it was time for a damn confession. A truth that mentally scared Darius. Possibly for life.

"Fuck Darryl Williams!" Darius's fists swung fast. Hard. Hitting nothing but air. "Darius Jones don't need anybody but Darius Jones." Darius's anger resurfaced each time he relived the day his mother told him the truth. Tears swelled his eyes. Darius squinted and sighed. His beloved grandmother, Ma Dear, the only woman that never lied to him would've said, "Don't waste time disliking people who don't like you when you can appreciate the many people who do love you." Regaining his composure, Darius knew Ma Dear was right but after his grandmother died, disappointment and resentment befriended him.

Although sometimes Darius drowned in waterless tears, real men, when their hearts ached with sadness and their souls suffocated from failure, didn't show signs of weakness. Darius remembered because Ma Dear's husband Grandpa Robert, whom she'd joined in heaven, told Darius when Darius was four years old, "Boy, looks like you been crying. Crying is for girls and sissies. Remember that." Darius never forgot. Tears. Confessions. There was no way Darius would ever let down Grandpa Robert by displaying a wimpish attitude. Sensitivity belonged to losers like Rodney, the undercover bisexual brother who infected Darius's ex-fiancée with HIV. Darius thought again, *what a fucked-up world to live in.*

Buying his three-story office building and loaning him a million dollars was just another one of his mother's ways to compensate for her guilt. And Darius had every intention of making his mother suffer for the next twenty years or at least until he felt she'd repaid her debt. Everyone was indebted to something or someone. But if his mother hadn't married Lawrence, Darius wouldn't have met his number-one lady. So perhaps he should've been grateful, but gratitude required expressing feelings.

Shifting his thoughts back to his lady, Darius smiled in the mirror, running his fingers over his locks. He gathered each strand back into a ponytail then admired the sweet brown succulent flesh that hundreds of women had enjoyed feasting upon. Ashlee's flight would arrive at ten o'clock tonight. What would she wear to his parents' New Year's Eve ball? Hell, it didn't matter. Possessing the same qualities as his mother, his stepsister always looked great. Just like his ex-fiancée, Maxine. Ladylike. Feminine.

Darius returned to his desk wondering why was his childhood so gullibly innocent and his adult life so cynical? As a child, if Darius had done wrong, he was easily forgiven. Women adored him. Fantasies of having his own family. A loving wife who'd only love him and he'd exclusively love her. At one time Darius believed that was possible. Until those two fifth-graders told him he could have both of them or his boring girlfriend. She wasn't boring. She was quiet. There was a difference. But two were definitely better than one. Darius had once believed marriage was sacred. Until he witnessed his mother divorcing Lawrence for no apparent reason other than she wanted to marry Wellington.

Why did grown-ups simply lie about shit? Santa. Where babies came from. The Easter bunny. Who was this dude Cupid? Someone who was supposed to make Darius believe he was in love? Most people weren't. Most people were lonely or afraid of being alone so, good or bad, they clung to the familiar. Not Darius.

CHAPTER 2

Darius walked out of his corner office, one flight down the back exit stairway. The heavy fire door squeaked as he entered the second floor. "How's it going, Randy?" Darius asked his accountant.

"Not bad," Randy said. "Not bad at all to say you've only been in business almost two months. If you seal that big deal next week, things will be great."

"Not if, Randy. When," Darius replied, walking away.

Standing over his newest employee inside her cubicle, Darius folded his arms high across his black long-sleeved cashmere shirt. Quickly she clicked on the minimize box at the top of her computer screen and the card game vanished.

"Naw, put the screen back up," Darius insisted, staring over her shoulder. "I wanna see how good you are because obviously you're no good for my company." Darius waited. "You've got ten seconds. Ten. Nine. Eight . . ." He always counted backward so when he stopped, he was at number one because he was number one. Confidently self-proclaimed the best at business, politics, economics, sports, and sex. Especially sex. Darius's eyes focused on the digital clock at the bottom of the seventeen-inch flat-screen monitor. Ten A.M.

When the screen came into view, Darius pointed toward the door and said, "Pack your shit and get the hell out of my office."

"But, it's the holidays and there isn't any work to do. I can ex—"

"Don't waste any more of my time or my money." He'd warned her in the orientation last month not to use his company's equipment or services for personal reasons. At the top of the items listed on the acknowledgment form by his human resources director was the computer followed by the telephone—both cellular and office—supplies, credit card, and so forth. "What's my mission statement?" Darius asked, watching the woman hesitantly remove his company's cell phone and credit card from her purse.

She mumbled, "If it doesn't make money, it doesn't make sense."

"So, what? You thought I was joking?"

"But, I can ex—"

"Explain what! Explain why I'm paying you thirty-five dollars an hour to waste my electricity!" The back of his hand slapped into his opposite palm repeatedly "Occupy my space! Drink my coffee! Eat my bagels! And play games on my computer!" Darius threw his hands in the air. "That doesn't require an explanation. The only thing I want to know is how your playing a sorry-ass losing hand of three-card draw," his pointing finger landed next to her score, "solitaire made me money? Prove that and you can stay."

The twenty-two-year-old recent college graduate,

who was a year older than Darius, silently stared at Darius, then said, "But everyone in the entertainment business is on vacation except us."

Darryl his biological father hadn't accepted him, and Darius unleashed his misdirected anger. "That's right! And you should be studying the screenplay I gave you yesterday because I specifically told you I need to hand this to my inside contact at Parapictures and give a copy to Morris Chestnut first thing Monday morning. Am I supposed to pay you and someone else to do your job? Huh! Answer, me!" Forget Darryl.

Calmly she replied with a frown, "Why are you so upset? You're the one who said your mother's best friend, Candice Morgan, wrote the screenplay so obviously Candice will select you as her agent. What's the big deal?"

"I don't care who wrote the damn script! Unless I secure the best deal possible before anyone else . . ." Darius shook his head. "You just don't get it. You may have graduated cum laude but you sure as hell flunked basic comprehension. Damn, it's hard to get good help." Darius paged his first-floor front desk security person from his mobile phone and said, "I need you to escort my new employee out of my building. Immediately." Then Darius trotted upstairs to his office.

How in the hell was he going to maintain an advantage over the other five companies that were also given a non-exclusive right to shop the hottest screenplay on the market? As much as Darius wanted to attend his mother's New Year's Eve ball, he had no choice. He had to stay home and work. Darius speed dialed his mother's number.

Candice and his mother had lost favor when Candice produced an unauthorized biography of his parents' love life including all the graphic juicy details his mother had shared with her best friend. That's what his mother deserved for telling all of her business to her so-called trustworthy girlfriend. Women. They all spent too much time analyzing every damn thing, talking too damn much, and complaining all the time. Any man who believed he could keep his woman happy was crazy. Women were definitely responsible for fucking up men's lives and screwing up the world. First, Eve. Then Darius's ex-fiancée. And of all women, his mother.

Sighing heavily, Darius greeted her. "Hi, Mom."

"Hi, baby. I'm glad you called. I was just thinking about you." His mother whispered, "Stop, Wellington. I'm on the phone with Darius." Returning to a normal tone, she asked, "So what time are you and Ashlee coming over?"

"Hi, son!" Wellington's voice cheerfully resonated in the background.

Wellington Jones, although he wasn't Darius's biological father, was the only male man enough to raise Darius from birth until now. When Darius's mother revealed the truth, Wellington had said, "You are my son. A very brave man stepped up to the plate and raised me as his own." Darius recalled how Wellington had shared his adoption history. "I don't wish this type of devastation on any person. Honestly, I'm disappointed in your mother. But God wants us to learn the importance of forgiveness. You have every right to be mad. Just don't let your anger destroy you . . . I love you no matter what." Darius wondered how Wellington could be so compassionate without losing his masculinity.

"Sorry, Mom. I'm not gonna make it to the party tonight. Gotta work. Something important just came up." Darius couldn't dare tell his mother her life was the greatest story roaming throughout the industry because his mother was livid with Candice, while Wellington thought how wonderful if another black person could join the ranks of becoming a millionaire. His dad felt there was no direct harm to them. Wellington's only request, which Candice claimed she'd consider but hadn't agreed to honor, was that Candice change the names.

"Darius, you work too hard. You just started in this business. Give it some time, honey. You'll get the next movie deal and I bet it'll be a more lucrative contract."

"Mom, you don't understand. There's no such thing as working too hard." Darius rocked back and forth in his executive chair. "If I get this deal, my reputation will soar internationally. Mark my words. Darius Jones will instantly become a household name because this is a script all nationalities can relate to. Mom, somebody's gotta be on top. There's those who do and those who don't. And those who don't never come out on top. Gotta go. Gotta work. Happy New Year, Mom, and tell Dad I said the same."

"Well, honey. If you insist. But before you go. How's your proposal coming along?"

"Not as well as I thought. That's why I can't come. I just fired the person assigned to put together my presentation. The meeting for selection of an agent is in four days. Every interested agency is going to pitch to represent Candice. I have a meeting with my inside contact person at Parapictures on Monday. And if I'm lucky, Morris will show up as promised to the meeting on Tuesday." Why was his mother so stubborn? She could forgive Candice, and Candice would happily let him represent her.

"What about Ashlee? Is she coming to the party? I

can send my driver to pick her up from your house around eight o'clock."

"Ashlee's not coming either. She volunteered to help me with my proposal."

"Okay, baby. But I think I should let you know that your father invited Candice and that guy, Tony, from Parapictures who you want to co-produce the film. Tony RSVP'd saying he'll stop by for a drink or two around ten then he'll have to move on to other parties."

"And Candice?"

His mother sighed. "She'll be here."

"Mom, why didn't you just say that at first? You know I'mma be there now."

"I just wanted to see if you'd come this year for me. Last year you couldn't get a flight out of Dulles or BWI. A few minutes ago you said working on your proposal was more important. Darius, after all I've done for you, you never consider me first."

"Mom, trust me. It's not like that," Darius lied. For twenty years she'd lied to him. There was no way Darius could possibly even the score. But he wasn't finished trying. "I . . . I mean we, will see you tonight, Ma."

"Okay, sweetie. Now, I've got to go. Your dad is trying to . . . never mind. I'll see you tonight. I love you."

"Yeah, Mom. Of course you do. Bye."

Darius turned off his computer. He stood, spun around, and danced on his plastic floor mat. Dancing out of his office, he locked his door then called Ashlee from his cellular phone.

"Hey," Ashlee answered.

"Start getting ready. We're going to the ball tonight." Darius entered Angel's office. Rhythmically he moved his shoulders side to side. His secretary smiled.

"But—"

Darius interrupted Ashlee. "I know. Don't question me. You know how slow you are so just start getting ready. Bye." Darius ended the call, spun around in front of Angel, clicked his oxfords together, and then said, "Tell everyone they can go home."

"You must have received great news because it's not eleven o'clock yet," Angel said, quickly typing the e-mail. "You sure you want me to send this?" Her finger paused above the enter key.

"Happy New Year, Angel. Whatever you do tonight, be safe. Send the e-mail." Darius winked as he glided out the door toward the elevators.

Darius hadn't seen his mother's four top-level executive staff since his mother fired him from her company over a year ago. Zen would more than likely be accompanied by her husband. Zen had the best Asian pussy he'd stroked. Miranda, the sexiest Latina in California, had unforgettable breasts. Heather, now that white girl gave the greatest blow job he'd had. Miranda and Heather were working for another company but would probably be at the party. Ginger, she was his favorite African-American spice. Darius wondered if those two brothas were still fighting over Ginger. Darius didn't care. Ginger couldn't resist him. No woman could.

CHAPTER 3

Darius tuned his slow jams CD to *You Don't Know My Name* by Alicia Keys, placed a plastic cap over his locks, and then stepped into the steaming shower. He lathered his towel with shea butter soap. Vigorously Darius scrubbed from his neck to his toes, then re-washed his private parts several times. Rinsing with hot water, then lukewarm, then cold last to re-tighten his skin, Darius stepped out of the shower.

Generously Darius massaged his muscular body with baby oil, toweling off the excess. His skin felt silky, smooth as a baby's. Easing into his black wing tip shirt, black designer suit, and square-toed shoes, Darius smirked at himself in the mirror. Neck ties and bow ties were for squares. Darius didn't own either. After having taken an African-American Studies class in high school and learning life-altering facts about slavery, Darius refused to voluntarily tie a noose around his neck. Darius unlocked his jewelry case. Internally flawless diamond rings, earrings, cuff links, watches, bracelets, and several loose solitaires were displayed. Like having multiple women, acquiring the finest things in life was part of Darius's African heritage.

"Damn, a brotha lookin' good. Sho nuff gon' seal the deal with Candice, secure a verbal commitment from Tony, then celebrate and get deep in some pussy before I leave the party tonight."

Heather would do if she was willing to give lip service. If not, Ginger. Or maybe he'd catch a lonely self-employed female—divorced, single, her marital status was irrelevant—all dressed up with no man to hug, willing to toast him in for the New Year. Darius opened his top drawer, removed three condoms, and placed them inside his back pocket.

Fastening his emerald-cut diamond cuff links, Darius knocked on Ashlee's bedroom door. "Ashlee, hurry up!" Ashlee had her own bedroom at both of his homes, Los Angeles and Oakland.

"Give me a minute. I'm almost ready."

Women. What had Ashlee done from eleven o'clock until eight P.M. that she wasn't ready? Nine solid hours. "Hurry. I don't want to miss Tony," Darius said, knocking again. "Let's go."

Sounding annoyed, Ashlee replied, "Alright, alright. I'll be out shortly."

Click. Darius heard Ashlee lock the door. While waiting for Ashlee, Darius decided to relax and burn the log in the fireplace. He removed his jacket and sat in the family room. African drums and statues were scattered amongst his hundred-plus basketball trophies. Paintings by black artists mounted in huge Kenté cloth frames decorated each wall. Darius walked over to the MVP trophy wall and smiled. Zooming in on his greatest high-school accomplishment, Darius flashed back to the day he won the Most Valuable Player award at the SoCal State championship in Southern California.

Forty-eight points. Four slam dunks—a tip, an alley oop, a reverse, and an unforgettable two-hander. Twenty-two rebounds. Eighteen assists. With twelve-point-eight seconds remaining in the fourth quarter, the score was tied seventy-four. Making the basket and drawing the foul, Darius scored an and-one, giving his team a three-point lead. His teammate K'Nine, a six-nine guard who had committed to attend Texas State University, was fouled with six seconds remaining on the clock. K'Nine scored the first basket, giving their team a four-point lead.

All season it was like Darius and K'Nine read one another's minds. Darius sensed K'Nine wanted to end their senior season with an unforgettable moment. And Darius was right. K'Nine intentionally bounced the last shot off the edge of the rim, rebounded, dribbled between his legs for three seconds, then alley ooped to Darius. With both hands Darius slammed the ball with a mighty force. His legs swung in the air. The buzzer sounded. As Darius came down from the rim, the backboard shattered. With zero seconds remaining. Glass chips were everywhere. The fans went wild! Roars! Cheers! Wellington's fists waved in the air. His mom screamed. Everybody rooting for his team danced, jumped, and yelled.

Why had his mother ruined his chances of making it to the NBA? Owning his own business was good, but basketball was his passion. A highlight tape of his basketball career, designed by Robert Lang Video, included Darius's greatest moments in sports. Darius's sex videos, which were professional enough to sell, were personally recorded and reserved in his private collection, exclusively for his pleasure. And just in case a female wanted to cry rape, Darius filmed her giving an oral statement saying her participation was consensual. Since Darius preferred older women, jailbait wasn't a concern, but for reassurance he carded every woman like a bartender would, checking driver's licenses before serving alcohol.

Darius's brows lifted and his eyes widened when Ashlee entered the room. "Wow, you look nice." Darius cupped his mouth, leaning his thumb against the side of his nose to control his sexually stimulated flaring nostrils. If Ashlee weren't so conservative, Darius would've ripped that gown off and sexed her in front of the fireplace. Darius stood and raised Ashlee's hand above her head. "Turn around. Let me see you." She twirled in a circle. Ashlee pinched her candy red velvet dress, lifting the bottom above her sparkling red rhinestone open-toe shoes.

"You like?" Ashlee asked, lowering her dress over her red toenails.

"You bet," Darius answered, putting on his jacket. Kissing Ashlee on the side of her mouth, Darius opened the front door. "Let's go."

The limo driver opened the car door and waited for Ashlee and Darius to get in. A few minutes and a half a mile later the driver pulled into Darius's parents' long driveway. Limousines, Town Cars, and stretch Hummers were parked in front of his parents' home.

Darius said, "Look at all the people on the deck. It's a good thing I did decline Mom's offer to have her driver pick us up. You know how many people her driver has to chauffer?" Darius hated wasting time waiting on anyone.

"Mr. Jones," the driver said, "What time would you like for me to pick you up?"

Wrong. The driver was mistaken if he thought he was going to be on Darius's dime shuttling other people around, then have Darius waiting on him. "Just wait out here. I'll call you on your cell when I'm ready. And when I say I'm ready, I'm ready."

Ashlee frowned but knew better than to question Darius. Darius escorted Ashlee inside, nodding as they bypassed the host manning the entrance. The fresh scent of pine stemmed from two giant Christmas trees trimmed with lace bows, gold ribbons, and porcelain Afrocentric ornaments which stood in the foyer, on opposite sides of the doorway. Red carpet runners veered to the left and right. The hardwood staircase leading up to the second floor was sealed off with a thick green velvet rope.

Cheerful conversations projected from the family room. Darius directed Ashlee toward the quieter crowd in the living room. "Wait for me in here. I'll be right back." Darius left Ashlee to see who was in the family room. Noticing neither Tony nor Candice nor Ginger nor anyone else, Darius left the room, ducked under the green velvet rope, and disappeared upstairs. The two guest bedrooms were unlocked as well as his mother's exercise and meditation rooms. Either bedroom would suffice to get laid for the New Year. Darius closed the door as he hurried back downstairs to Ashlee.

Darius shifted his eyes toward his parents conversing with guests on the opposite side of the room. He whispered in Ashlee's ear, "If we weren't at my parents' house, I'd introduce you as my woman. But since everyone here knows us, even if we don't know them, I have to treat you like you're family. And you need to act like I'm your brother. But just until the party is over and we get back to my house. You know what I mean?"

"Darius, stop trippin'. Nobody is watching you. And even if they are, they don't know how we feel about one another," Ashlee said, touching his dreadlocks.

Darius held Ashlee's hand. "You can save that for later."

"Hey, Jones. Happy New Year." The unmistakable voice of Tony Briscotti. Tony was the only person that called everyone by their last name.

Darius smiled, turning toward Tony and extending his hand. "Tony, my partner. Surprised seeing you here. You're a busy man."

"Not as busy as you're going to be, Jones." Tony's grip tightened as he slapped Darius's back. "Nice cuff links. Look, Jones. My time is an investment. Remember that. When someone as important and affluent as Wellington Jones invites me someplace, I show my face. Even if I only stay a few minutes. You secure that agency contract with Jordan yet?"

"I'll have everything under control later. Candice will be here tonight."

"Well," Tony patted Darius on the back, "if you get the deal, count me in as co-executive producer." Tony spotted Wellington across the room and waved. "Hey, Jones! Thanks for the invite." Tony turned to Darius. "See how I made eye contact across the room. Now, I'm leaving but your dad knows I came. So if I should happen to need to talk business with him, I don't have to go through you. Call me as soon as you sign the contract. Not before."

Darius quickly distanced himself from Ashlee, who stood by his side the entire time Tony spoke. Darius touched Ashlee's bicep and said, "Wait here, I'll be right back," then he followed Tony to the door. Darius stopped in the foyer. Entering the house was Ginger Browne.

Stunning. Gorgeous. Younger-looking. Sexier. Ginger's hair was tucked behind her ears and curled upward at the ends. The shimmering tangerine-colored gown dipped below Ginger's navel. An amethyst brooch complimented her cleavage. Long wide sleeves shaped into a V-cut covered her hands. Whoever gave Ginger that makeover at thirty-five made Ginger look ten years younger. The tall slim guy with Ginger wasn't either of the dudes Darius remembered. Darius waited near the door beneath the mistletoe.

Ginger handed the host a gift bag. "This is for Mr. Jones and Mrs. Tanner."

Darius spread his arms wide enough for Ginger to see the imprint of his dick, smiled, then asked, "What's for me?"

"A rich mama and daddy," Ginger said with a bright smile. Her embrace was short. Ginger smelled edible, like warm sugar cookies. "This is my man, Lorenzo."

Nodding upward, Darius said, "What's up?"

Looking up at the mistletoe, Lorenzo said, "Sorry, dude. I'm not kissing you. Ginger, let's go."

Ginger winked at Darius. "Don't pay daddy any mind. Lorenzo is always protecting me. Good seeing you again, Darius." Ginger kissed Darius's cheek.

Dude hugged Ginger's waist so tight, it looked like she could hardly breathe. Yeah, Lorenzo was insecure. But if dude made another smart remark, he had to go. No doubt Lorenzo realized Darius could have Ginger if he wanted her. Consumed with thoughts about Ginger, Darius almost didn't notice Candice and her husband, Terrell, entering the doorway.

Darius blocked Candice's path. "Hey, Candice. Just the person I need to see." Darius hugged Candice, then shook Terrell's hands. "Hey, man. Lookin' good." Darius gave Terrell a compliment and a lie at the same time. Terrell was an aging actor trying to stay young by wearing twists with a tuxedo.

Candice smiled. "Hi, Darius. I'm not talking business tonight so don't ask me any questions about the screenplay. Have you seen Ciara?"

"Who?" Darius asked.

"Ciara. Ciara Monroe."

"I don't know Ciara. But I do need to ask you a question about the contract."

"You don't know her, *yet*. No questions. Not tonight. Call me next week." Candice walked away.

No Candice did not walk into his mother's house acting like she was running things. Darius mumbled, "That's cool," then he returned to the living room to find Ashlee sitting next to a woman with cantaloupe breasts.

Sitting between Ashlee and the woman, Darius extended his hand. "If we're this close I should introduce myself. Hi, I'm Darius Jones."

The plunging V-neckline commanded Darius's attention. If she'd perm that afro, her high cheeks and full lips would look softer.

She extended her manicured hand that was disproportionately small compared to her plus-size figure. "I'm Ciara."

"Monroe," Darius said at the same time.

Ciara smiled then gave him one of those quick scans that women do when checking him out. "Why, yes." Ciara looked him down then up, again.

"So you're Candice's friend?"

"Not exactly. But Candice did invite us. That's my man, Solomon, over there talking with Terrell."

"Well, have you met my," Darius hesitated then said, "friend, Ashlee."

"Nice meeting you, Ashlee." Ciara stood. "You too, Darius. Any relationship to Wellington?" Ciara asked.

Darius smiled at Ciara's partially exposed double-Ds sandwiched together. "That's my dad. Can't you see the resemblance?"

"Honestly? No," Ciara replied before walking over to Solomon.

Had Ciara noticed Darius didn't look like Wellington or was she being sarcastic? Women. Darius glanced around the room. No other prospects. Everyone worth pursuing was paired off. Thinking of being paired off. Where were his parents? Darius hadn't seen them in over an hour. Knowing them, they were probably upstairs fucking or as his mother called it, making love.

Darius removed his cellular phone from his pocket. Thirty minutes before midnight. The party was boring. He dialed his driver's number. "I'm ready." Darius looked at Ashlee. "Coming to this party was a waste of my time. Let's go."

CHAPTER 4

Sunday morning. New Year's Day. Darius awoke on his family room floor with Ashlee sleeping beside him. Leaning on his elbow, Darius stared at Ashlee. Dark thick eyebrows. Slender nose with low cheekbones that blended smoothly down to her rounded chin. Yeah. Ashlee had been special to Darius since the day they'd met. On the first day of kindergarten his mom stood face-to-face talking with Ashlee's dad while Darius bragged to Ashlee about attending Duke University. Early in his childhood Darius's mother often talked about him going to college. At five years old, Darius didn't care about college. He had more important things to think about, like how soon was recess so he could take off his navy blazer and swing from the monkey bars on the playground.

When Lawrence married his mom, Ashlee's mother moved to Texas and took Ashlee with her. That was the day Darius thought he'd lost his friend. Almost as sad as the day his mother's eyes stopped shining when she

saw his face. His mom became sad after Wellington had
met Simone. Darius realized early in his life that a man
could control a woman's feelings. For years Darius pretended he didn't miss Ashlee. Now they were grown
and Ashlee was celebrating the beginning of another
new year with him.

They'd fallen asleep hours ago, around three o'clock
in the morning, on a white down comforter pallet covered with blankets. The log in the fireplace burned to
ashes. Kemistry's CD played so low that if Darius hadn't
recognized the melody he wouldn't have softly sung
the lyrics "In your love I will bring my dreams to life."
A pleasant coolness floated around his face. Two empty
champagne bottles lay on the white carpet next to
empty flutes.

Still staring at Ashlee, Darius's eyes signaled his
brain to sample her lips. So he did. But first Darius
cupped his hand over his mouth, huffed into his palm,
and then inhaled. Not bad. Darius flossed, brushed, and
rinsed his mouth with Listerine three times a day. He
licked his lips and watched Ashlee's eyelids as he
moved closer. Darius was ready to take their relationship to an intimate level. This time he wouldn't have to
use his fingers to press against a photographic image.
Darius softly kissed Ashlee. As her eyelids fluttered, he
kissed her again, this time sliding his moist tongue over
her closed mouth. Ashlee tasted cotton-candy sweet.
Probably the sugary residue from the champagne.

Darius moaned, "Umm. Your lips are so soft. Kiss
me, Ashlee."

Wiggling from underneath him, Ashlee sat up,
pushing Darius away. "Darius, what are you doing? We
can't do—"

Ashlee's mouth opened wide enough for Darius to

slip his tongue inside. He held her close. All the years he'd wanted her, Darius refused to stop his pursuit. He hugged her tight until Ashlee's black spaghetti straps fell below her shoulders. Gently Darius bit her bottom lip. Ashlee moaned. Her petite body quivered in his arms.

"Don't fight the feeling. I want you, Ashlee. And I can tell you want me too." Darius's mouth searched for the vein behind Ashlee's ear, traveled two inches down, then suddenly he sank his teeth into her neck. Darius applied a little more pressure, then stopped but didn't release his bite.

"Ummm." A quick sharp breath entered Ashlee's nose as her body stiffened. "Umm."

Lowering his head, Darius bit Ashlee's nipple through the silk negligee. Squeezing both breasts, Darius softly gnawed on Ashlee's other nipple. Desperately Darius craved Ashlee's lips caressing his hard-on. He felt pre-cum oozing from the tip of his caramel-colored dick, wetting his silk pajamas. Ashlee's mood might change if he nudged her head toward his waist, so Darius leaned Ashlee back onto the blanket then buried his face between her thighs.

The tip of his tongue circled Ashlee's clit. "Ahh," Ashlee moaned so Darius spread her lips, exposing her shaft and smothering her clit with kisses. Ashlee's butt tilted upward as her hands rubbed the doo-rag covering his locks. Ashlee pushed his face closer to her pussy. Her thin thighs suctioned, covering his ears.

Darius lapped his moist tongue over her opening, then drank Ashlee's juices until he brought her to the verge of cumming. Just when Ashlee's back arched, Darius stopped. He removed his pajama pants, and straddled her face, pushing his dick toward her mouth.

Ashlee's mouth shifted to the right so Darius moved his dick to the right. Ashlee turned her face to the left so Darius pushed Slugger to the left. Ashlee dodged his erection until his dick went limp.

What the hell? She enjoyed him doing her but she refused to do him. Bump that. The one thing Darius hated was a selfish lover. Darius slid his hand underneath his pillow and grabbed his condoms. Ashlee pulled the spaghetti straps over her shoulders then slid the gown below her waist. Did Ashlee intentionally keep her breasts covered? Forget it. If he wasn't getting laid, he didn't need to see her titties. Darius's mouth curved to one side as he tightened his lips and shook his head. His dick started growing again, pointing toward Ashlee's lips. Before he became angry at Ashlee, Darius left Ashlee lying on the floor, went into his bedroom, and locked the door.

Ashlee didn't have the only pussy in the world but she'd have a lonely pussy if she expected Darius to sexually pursue her again. Picking up his cell phone, Darius dialed 3-1-0 . . . and waited for an answer. "Please be home, mommy."

"Hey, daddy! Happy New Year!"

"Happy New Year to you too, man. How's my girl?" Funny how Kimberly didn't mind when Darius called her man but would get pissed when he called her Kim. Some dude from her past must have had another woman by the name of Kim or something.

"We're fine. I just finished her daily grooming," Kimberly said then laughed.

Kimberly was Darius's number-one piece. Kimberly's body was always immaculate. Nails manicured and pedicure. Pubic hairs flawlessly trimmed into a heart shape. Legs shaved. Marriage couldn't separate Darius from

Kimberly's tight pussy. He still paid the monthly bill on the Visa Darius held in Kimberly's name. He kept her happy because she kept him satisfied. Kimberly created no headaches. Started no drama. And, with the exception of using her credit card, had no expectations of a committed relationship.

"Good. Have my pussy ready and waiting. I need to see you," Darius looked at the digital clock on his dresser, "in an hour."

"We'll be waiting for you, poppie."

Darius nodded. "That's what I'm talkin' 'bout. I'm on my way."

"Bye, daddy." Kimberly hung up the phone.

Darius had to have sex. Masturbation wouldn't suffice. He could've been at Kimberly's house sooner but Darius needed to talk with Ashlee before he left. Darius hung a pair of black slacks, a black pullover sweater, and his tan collarless leather jacket next to his dressing-room mirror. Darius showered. Shaved. Dressed. Dabbed on Mark Jacobs cologne, grabbed his wallet and keys, then unlocked his bedroom door.

The house was quiet. "Ashlee," he called out. No answer. Darius searched the family room, living room, dining room, and kitchen. No Ashlee. He tapped on her bedroom door. "Ashlee."

Ashlee yelled, "Go, away!"

"Go away," Darius replied. "This is my house."

When Ashlee didn't respond he said, "Look, it'll be okay. I'm leaving. You can have your space." Darius knew, right or wrong, he could make Ashlee feel guilty.

Ashlee opened the door. "Where're you going?"

Darius hunched his shoulders. "Out. To clear my head." *Heads* is what Darius thought. "Maybe get a drink."

"It's too early to drink. Don't leave. Let's talk about this."

Whatever Ashlee was thinking or feeling at this point was pointless. "I'll be back. Cook something for dinner." Darius walked into the kitchen, out the door, into the garage, and started his Bentley.

The light traffic made the drive to Long Beach pleasant. Darius pressed the number two garage button in his car and parked next to Kimberly's red Beemer. Scented mango and coconut oils greeted him as he unlocked the door.

Darius inhaled. "That's what I'm talking 'bout. Ambience."

"Hey, daddy," Kimberly said, wearing a smile, a long fiery red wig that covered her breasts, a pair of clear stilettos, and a black sheer thong. Kimberly's hands slid under Darius's jacket, down his shoulders, and removed his coat. "You won't be needing this." She removed his shirt then tossed it on the dining-room table beside his jacket. "Or this." His slacks. Silk boxers. And socks. "Or these." Kimberly squatted in her heels. She scooped Darius's dick in and out of her hot slippery mouth and said, "Oh, daddy. But I do need this."

Darius led Kimberly to the garage and pressed her plump breasts over the hood of his car. The air was cold. His body was hot. Darius rubbed the head of his dick against her shaft until Darius felt Kimberly's pussy become engorged. Her clitoris shaft was hard. Full. Stroking his penis, Darius rolled on his condom then eased his head in and out of Kimberly's wet pussy.

"Spread your ass for me, so I can give you this dick."

Kimberly looked over her shoulder at him, slid her

long red nails from her waist to her ass, and spread her cheeks wide. "This pussy is for you. She missed you. She needs you. She wants you so bad, daddy. Fuck her good."

Darius fucked Kimberly real good. An hour later they were still fucking in the garage. Darius slapped Kimberly's ass and said, "Get the shower ready for daddy. I gotta go."

Kimberly kissed his lips, caressed his jaw, then said, "Anything for you."

Kimberly was heaven sent but she wasn't marriage material. Darius showered, dressed in the dining room, grabbed his keys, and left. The drive home was relaxing.

"Whooo, that's what I'm talkin' 'bout. A brotha getting his dick sucked and getting headache-free pussy from a woman on the regular."

Ashlee would change her mind about being my wife eventually, Darius thought, parking in his garage. But before becoming his wife, they had to have sex. The smell of garlic and onions greeted him as he entered his kitchen. Ashlee stood in front of the countertop tossing a salad.

"Smells great. What are you cooking?"

"Sautéed shrimp, scallops, and calamari with garlic pasta."

"Sounds good. I'm hungry." Darius smiled as he lifted the top off the pot. "Fix me a plate." The aroma followed Darius into his bedroom. He hung his jacket in the closet and tossed his clothes into a dry cleaners bag for the maid to pick up on Monday. When Darius returned to the dining area, the table was set. The arch tier held burning black candles. Steam rose from the platters of seafood, spinach fettuccini, and fresh mixed vegetables. The salad was topped with black olives, croutons, and cherry tomatoes. Pork was not welcomed on his table or in his stomach.

Darius sat at the head of the eight-party rectangular onyx wooden table. "Smells good."

Sitting to his left, Ashlee bowed her head, then waited for Darius to say grace.

"Dear Lord, please bless this table. Bless Ashlee for time and love she dedicated to the preparation and completion of the great meal. Jesus, let this food strengthen our mind, body, and spirit to do Thy will. Amen."

Ashlee said, "Amen," then looked at Darius and said, "I understand what you meant earlier when you said, 'We're good for one another.' But I'm struggling with my emotions. The problem I have is that this can't be morally right. At least I don't think so . . ."

Either Ashlee's words trailed off or Darius had become consumed with his own devious thoughts. One sure thing, in all of her talking, Ashlee hadn't agreed to consummate their relationship because that would've gotten his attention. But more importantly, she hadn't disagreed. Watching Ashlee speak while he ate, Darius realized that with Ashlee's support he could accomplish anything. Darius needed a woman like Ashlee to support him no matter how badly he fucked up. When he was wrong, Ashlee didn't agree with him. And that was good because it was never what Ashlee said. It was how she said it. Sweetly. Caringly. Lovingly. And most of all, without judgment.

CHAPTER 5

The first Tuesday morning of a new year, Darius lay awake under his royal blue suede comforter reflecting on the past year. The main reason Darius had moved to Washington, D.C. was to distance himself from his mother and to make her feel guilty. The first six months Darius didn't call his mother, answer her phone calls, or return any of her messages. The sight of her face made Darius so angry he tossed her pictures—the ones of his mother at his games, his birthday parties, with Santa, the Easter bunny, school events—and all of his photos they'd taken together in storage boxes and mailed them to her in Los Angeles. Darius didn't write his mother. *Click. Click. Click.* He deleted her e-mail messages without opening a single one. She had a choice. She chose wrong. Material gifts—cars, clothes, jewels, money— couldn't replace the years he'd missed growing up without his real father.

Taking a deep breath, Darius gazed at the ceiling and massaged his dick. His morning erection shifted his thoughts. Darius smiled then said, "Boy, yo' dick is always on swole. You ain't never gon' be faithful." Darius had tried being monogamous in the Chocolate City with this Virgo sistah he'd met. What a joke. She truly loved, damn near worshiped, him. Their relationship survived six months. Sex with Mary was magnificent. Frequent. Two, sometimes three times a day. Within fifteen minutes of his request, she'd break for lunch, come to his office, and sit on his dick. Suck his dick. She probably did the same for her other man. Men. Stripped off her clothes. Danced on the desk. If she weren't cheating, eventually she would so Darius pursued new pussy, which ultimately ended their relationship. Tired of spending holidays, birthdays, and special occasions without his mother, Darius moved back to Los Angeles.

Hypnotized by the flames from his bedroom fireplace shadow dancing on the white walls, Darius took another breath then clamped his hands behind his head. No other woman had given him a greater level of security and comfort than Ashlee. Except, at times, his mother, and of course, Maxine.

How was Maxine? Health wise. Had she lost weight? Was she still beautiful? Was she still a national spokesperson for the Centers for Disease Control? Was Maxine happy? How could she ever be jovial again living with a terminal disease ticking inside of her like a time bomb waiting to explode? Boom! Rodney was already dead.

"Fool one day you gon' be dead too." Darius answered himself, "True dat. That's why I'm fuckin' every day for the rest of my life." That was for at least another sixty, seventy, eighty years or more. Did Darius really have that much control over women? Enough influence to make someone do something they'd regret for the rest of their life? Darius didn't feel sorry for Maxine, she shouldn't have given up her pussy.

Darius leaned forward, glancing at the digital alarm clock on his entertainment center. Fifteen more minutes. Kimberly had fucked him so good again last night, Darius wanted to stay in bed. He nestled into the over-king-sized black silk pillow.

"Ahh, life is grand." Darius added, "For a man."

Darius squinted then shielded his eyes from the sunshine creeping into his twelve-hundred-square-foot master bedroom overshadowing the dancing flames. He loved living in The Valley. His neighbors were movie stars, athletes, or other wealthy celebs. Slipping his naked body into his robe, Darius smiled. "This is it, boy. The day you've waited for. Do the damn thang."

Darius brushed his teeth then stood outside Ashlee's bedroom door. The door was ajar. He peeped inside. Ashlee's head rested on the lime-green pillowcase. Eyes closed. Knees bent. A silhouette of her figure curved into an S-shape under the matching sheet. Darius's toes tipped barefoot along the cold hardwood floor. Quietly he eased to the edge of her bed. Ashlee slept like an angel. X-rated thoughts swept his mind. Kiss her. Kiss her. Darius longed to feel the sensation of Ashlee's lips once more. Lowering his face to hers, he pressed his moist lips against her temple.

"Huh. Oh. Good morning." Ashlee yawned as she secured the sheet inches above her breasts. Her nipples grew larger, soliciting Darius's undivided attention.

"Good morning to you. I came to get a pre-victory hug. I know I'm going to get the contract," Darius said as his butt balanced on the side of the king-sized mattress next to Ashlee's hips.

"Come here," Ashlee said, opening her soft slender arms. "You know you worked hard and you deserve this." The comfort of her limbs, doused with the Victoria's Secret Velvet Luxe Crème he'd given her, embraced then drew him close. "As soon as the meeting is over, I want you to call me. Regardless of the outcome. Call me, first. Okay?" Ashlee insisted. Her large brown eyes stared directly into his.

Darius loved how Ashlee understood her womanly place was to support him and wished other women would stop trying to emulate his manly God-given qualities. No woman could ever tell him when to come home. When he could go out. Or how to handle his business. Ashlee never competed with or challenged him.

Darius's arms drifted around Ashlee's waist. The nectar of her perfume and softness of her flesh lured him closer. He sniffed behind her ear. Damn. His dick went from limp to hard in seconds. The pounding of his heart thumped against her firm breasts. The only thing between them was the sheet and thankfully his black flannel robe.

Think, Darius, think. Let her go. Shrink, Slugger, Shrink. His manicured nails rotated in her spine slightly above the crack separating her cheeks. *Let her go.*

"Okay," Darius replied. The left corner of his mouth curved. "I got this deal on lock. When I call you, get dressed so we can celebrate. Make a reservation at Alex on Melrose and reserve our usual table."

Slowly Ashlee's grip loosened. Her lightweight fingers rested on his collarbone. "You'd better get going. Call me later."

"You're right." Darius stopped massaging then tickled her obliques.

"Stop!" Ashlee jumped and howled with laughter. "You know I'm ticklish."

Ashlee's infectious laughter triggered Darius's laugh. They shared a similar joyful spirit whenever they reflected on their childhood. Running away from Lawrence's Malibu home to his guest house outback, protesting their parents' marriage, days before the wedding in Los Angeles, had gotten both of them in big trouble. Darius was relieved his erection subsided. The slippery silk folded beneath his armpits when he stood. Releasing the sheet then tying his belt tighter, now he knew.

Ashlee gasped. The happy sound became trapped in her throat.

"Oh, damn." Darius re-tightened his belt because he couldn't think of anything else to do. He definitely enjoyed the view. Slowly, reluctantly, Darius turned toward the door.

"Just go," Ashlee said cupping her breasts then grabbing the cover. "I'll make the reservation for three."

"Make the reservation for the two of us at three o'clock," Darius clarified.

"Of course. That's what I said."

That was what Ashlee meant but clearly not what she'd said. Returning to his bedroom, the snapshot image of her breasts was etched in his memory. "Ooow, yes." The steamy shower pulsated against the nape of Darius's neck down the center of his back. Side to side Darius's head tilted to each shoulder. His right hand wrapped around the opposite side of his dick. Twisting up and down his shaft, Darius moaned, "Ashlee."

Darius visualized his chocolate dipstick sliding between two plump white peaches with golden-brown raisin-shriveled nipples. "Damn. Nice tits." The flow of white semen washed in waves down his inner thighs and slid into the tiny metal holes. Darius whispered, "Um, um, um. One of these days. Whew." Repeatedly Darius washed the crack of his ass, twirling the tip of his finger inside for extra cleansing. The first time his mother discovered a shit stain in his Superhero underwear she gave him a graphic speech on how to thoroughly cleanse his ass. Darius never forgot.

"Yes!" Darius danced in front of the three-way mirror inside his spacious dressing-room closet, inspecting his dripping wet body. He yelled, "You da man dawg," tightly curling his fingers. *Thump! Thump! Thump!* Darius pounded on his muscular chest and said, "This mutherfuckin' proposal is gon' hit boy-ie!"

Darius flexed, admiring what all his women loved. Him. His exotic locks. A handsome face with chiseled jaws and a manly squared chin. Two muscular mounds of chocolate garnished a chest so appealing that whenever he wore wife-beater T-shirts or swam in his boxer trunks on the beach, men stared too. Darius's "I'll beat your ass if you make a pass at me" look kept the strays quiet. A six-pack of abdominal muscles rolled like waves washing upon the ocean's shore as Darius swerved his entire body like a snake's. Thighs hard as steel but smooth as butter. Flawless skin. No woman was allowed to leave fingernail tracks on his back. Darius didn't tolerate that "let me brand you" mentality "so I can prove to all the other women I was with you." Darius Jones knew he was undoubtedly the sexiest and most arrogant man alive.

Darius retrieved the fifty-page leather-bound proposal from his solid oak, six-drawer dresser. Flipping to page ten, his lips landed against his film production chart.

Title: Soul Mates Dissipate
Status: Filming in the Future
Production Start: September 17th
Studio: To be determined
Location: Oakland, Los Angeles
Primary Actors: Morris Chestnut, Lela Rochon, Kendra Moore, Boris Kodjoe, Diahann Carroll, Loretta Devine, and Cedric the Entertainer

The list of potential financial backers Ashlee had suggested, along with the proposed motion picture companies, producers, directors, casting companies, and a signed commitment from Morris along with Morris's filmography, were enclosed.

Glancing at the clock, Darius slipped into his new tailored black single button-downed suit. Dabbed on cologne. Slid into his customized platinum-colored Bentley with the initials DL engraved in the headrests, dashboard, steering wheel, and floor mats. He cruised to the most important meeting for his company.

"Those amateurs are going to flip when I walk through the door and announce that Morris has accepted the part."

Darius valet parked in the adjacent lot, tossed his keys to the attendant, and then strutted into the lobby of the forty-two-story downtown building. His left shoulder slightly dipped with each step as he strolled through the congregating crowd and onto the elevator.

"Wait! Hold the door!" a woman's voice pleaded.

Darius adamantly pressed the close button while the

other passengers pretended not to watch. Between the disappearing crack, the biggest breasts he'd ever seen, attached to a woman exquisitely dressed in winter white from her hat to her boots, vanished. Frantically Darius searched for the open-door button. Accidentally he pressed the inward arrows again as he watched her lips tighten. The elevator moved quickly and quietly, stopping several times. No one said a word until Darius uttered, "Damn. Oh, well."

Despite arriving twenty minutes early, Darius was apparently late. "Mr. Jones," the receptionist pointed, "the conference room is down the hall on your left. We're waiting for two more representatives before we start."

Darius stepped into the freezing room. It seemed colder than the fifty-degree temperature outside. Candice sat at the head of the table draped in a crimson-colored cape with a navy turtleneck blouse crinkled under her chin. Ten attendees were gathered around the conference table mumbling and perusing documents. The only available seats were at the opposite head of the double-wide black leather-top table.

Darius assessed his competition. Bunch of losers. Wasting his time. Closing his eyes, his thoughts drifted back to Ashlee. He'd bought her an engagement ring after their trip to Cannes last year. When the time was right, he'd ask the question hoping she'd proudly wear the internally flawless five-carat emerald-cut solitaire set in platinum.

Darius's eyelids fluttered. Glancing toward the door, he partially closed his eyes. Quickly he looked again. The woman in winter white he'd seen in the lobby took a seat beside him at the table. Ciara Monroe. A closer look in the well-lighted room confirmed that she wasn't as stunning as the woman to his left. Long silky legs crossed under a short black tweed Scottish pleated skirt. White thigh-high boots with black laces. An alluring fragrance hovered about his nostrils, awakening his already starving sexual appetite. Almost twelve hours has passed since the last time Darius had had sex. That was ludicrous and far too long. Darius craved sex every day. Unbeknownst to the woman in black, if she was as horny as most of the busy businesswomen he'd met, his charm, fine dining, and a couple of martinis would invite him into her bed before midnight.

Shifting his thoughts, Darius bit his bottom lip. Damn, he should've gotten to the meeting sooner. Who were all those people? Darius's eyes drifted toward Ciara. Another woman entered and sat beside her. Darius waited for but didn't receive an introduction.

Ciara turned to the woman next to her and said, "Glad you could make it on such short notice. Thanks." Slowly she leaned those huge breasts on the table, reached for a glass, and proceeded to fill it from the frosty pitcher of ice water.

"You move rather slow for someone with a nice athletic build," Ciara said as her pierced tongue extended, curving under the rigid crystal rim, causing his saliva glands to overreact. Darius watched the water roll onto her tongue, over the silver ball, and disappear beyond her tonsils as she eased her neck back.

Damn, her mouth was pleasantly wide. Redirecting his blood flow, Darius replied, "Who, me?" One drop of water escaped her tongue and clung to her juicy glossy lips. Ciara suctioned the drop into her mouth. Darius fantasized her teasing his balls with her tongue then slurping the cum from his dick. If sex was his addiction, Darius had no plans to attend meetings or counseling.

A mischievous grin accompanied her mesmerizing hazel eyes that were the exact color as his mother's. She didn't blink or fluster. "Yes. You. Mister . . ."

Darius smiled at the sinister tone when she pronounced, *Mis-ter.* Overlooking her confident curtness, Darius replied, "Hey, what can I say. I'm immune to women who yell." Darius despised women who attempted to belittle men. "Next time, to avoid getting a strike under my strike-three policy, try saying something sweet."

Ciara sipped then whispered, "I am the sweetest." Her wet tongue swept her upper lip. "Black." Her tongue traced the water back to the other crevice. "Sexiest." This time her tongue completed a full circle without losing a drip of fluid. Pouting, she perched her lips. "Sole owner and operator of Ciara Monroe Casting Agency and I'm about to spank your tender ass with my new contract. I don't have to be sweet. I have a man because I want one, not because I need one. And you are not God's gift to me. I'm God's gift to you. Pray the black woman never gives up on you, brotha."

Heads synchronized, turning toward them. Silence. Complete silence filled the room. Darius shifted in his seat to adjust his subsiding hard-on. "Casting?" She wasn't a threat. Her casting company wasn't even on his list. Maybe he'd hire Ciara if she improved her bad attitude. "Smart move to get in on the action early. But just so you'll know," Darius whispered, "no one spanks my ass without my permission."

Sporadically, people resumed their conversations.

"Hum," the woman in black said, lifting her brows

in his direction. She peeped behind his back down to his butt. "May I?"

Have these successful sistahs no shame? Darius was definitely bumping her head against the headboard. Maybe she'd learn to use discretion. Darius focused on Ciara's afro. Too masculine. Her stern demeanor accompanied a five-foot-five frame after subtracting three inches for her heeled boots. With so much clothes and a bad attitude, Darius couldn't visualize Ciara nude. But those titties were so unbelievably swollen he had to bury his face in them at least once. If he could bite Ciara's nipples right now while spanking her ass, he'd teach her how to be submissive. Please smile. Laugh. Do something to brighten up the atmosphere.

Ciara flipped open a shiny gold metal case and removed a pen. Darius frowned. Real diamonds and rubies? Couldn't be. He stared. Yep, unlike the owner, the jewels were genuine. Ciara winked at Darius. The woman seated to his left uncrossed her legs, then rubbed her shoe against his shin. Hell, he'd almost forgotten about his fuck buddy for tonight. Easing his business card in front her, he said, "Hi, I'm Darius Jones."

Her lips invitingly gapped wide enough for Darius to picture slipping in a finger or two. Women belonged in the bedroom, not the boardroom. Females were a constant distraction.

"Hum, um, um." Candice's attorney cleared his throat. "We'd like to thank each of you for coming."

Darius thought, *cumming. Coming. The women should go. Leave. Stop competing with men.*

She whispered, "Crystal. My name is Crystal."

Crystal. Lips. Water. Glass. Ciara. Titties. Darius nodded.

"Hum, um." The attorney stared at Crystal then continued. "We've canceled the agenda this morning. Since most of you, as requested, submitted your proposals in advance, we made a selection this morning. We know the purpose of this meeting was to discuss the various proposals, however," he paused, "after much consideration, we decided before the meeting to accept what we consider the most outstanding package. Truly impressive."

What request? No one had asked Darius to submit his package in advance. Darius's knees shoved the rolling chair backward. He had to win this contract. Darius stood tall. Holding his leather-bound papers high in the air, Darius confidently said, "You don't want to make that decision final until after you've reviewed Somebody's Gotta Be on Top's proposal. Morris Chestnut is on his way. And he's signed a commitment to accept the lead role."

Oohs and *ahhs* filled the room. Leather against leather, Darius's package swished across the table. "Top that."

The attorney's long black fingers restricted the pages' movement. The attorney covered his mouth and started whispering in Candice's ear.

What? Is Candice crazy? She's shaking her head. Darius shook his head.

The lawyer continued as if no one had spoken a word. "Candice Morgan is proud to congratulate," he paused then looked at Darius. The left side of Darius's mouth curved. "Ciara Monroe Casting Agency is awarded the exclusive. Candice and I thank each of you and your lawyers for expressing interest."

Darius's mouth leveled. His eyes narrowed, barely leaving enough space to see Candice's glowing face.

Stupid. Dumb. Women. Wait until Darius told his mother about the pre-selection.

Candice beamed. Stood. "Thank you for your interest. I know you've dedicated lots of time in hopes to represent me. I'm writing another screenplay so there will be future opportunities. This meeting is adjourned. Ciara, I need you and your attorney to stay."

Ciara happily replied, "Thank you, Candice," then winked at Darius.

Darius firmly said, "Candice, I need to speak with you in private for a moment."

"Sure, Darius. If you wait a few minutes. I need to speak with Ciara first. This won't take long."

Won't take long. Who in the hell did Candice think she was talking to? Darius looked at Ciara. "Let me be first to congratulate you." Begrudgingly he extended his hand to Ciara's. "May I borrow your pen for a moment?" Darius stalled, praying Morris would walk through the door any moment.

"Thanks. I can tell you're new to the movie biz. Give it some time youngster, you'll find your niche. It took me four years before I decided to specialize in casting. This industry is very political. I'm so excited. This is my first major deal. And it's sad but true. I still have to demand respect from my male counterparts. Can you believe that? This is my good-luck pen. My parents gave it to me specifically for signing this contract. This priceless hand-crafted gem has been in our family for generations," she said, carefully sliding the pointed tip between Darius's long fingers. "I don't know why I'm trusting you. But I am."

Trading stares over their shoulders, Ciara and her attorney watched Darius. Darius wrote a few frivolous notes as Candice said, "Ms. Monroe," motioning for Ciara to come closer, "I'd like to introduce you to my attorney. The two of you will work closely with Mr. Brentwood."

Walking toward Candice, Ciara turned, and then winked at Darius.

Yeah, she was interested in a brotha. Maybe Darius would have Ciara in his bed tonight instead of Crystal. Bad idea. Fuck Crystal tonight. Save Ciara for later. Darius ignored Ciara's wink as she made her way to the opposite end of the room.

Ciara smiled wide, flashing all her pearly white teeth, then said, "Mr. Brentwood, your reputation proceeds you. Congratulations on winning the Pickle case."

Good networking. Darius observed how Ciara was apprised of his background. Or perhaps Candice prepped Ciara before the meeting. Women. Always plotting and planning.

Mr. Brentwood laughed hysterically in harmony with Ciara, her attorney, and Candice.

Darius slipped the pen inside his jacket pocket, closed the case, placing it in Ciara's view, and then quietly tipped out of the room. He'd call Candice later to arrange his private meeting. Without her pen, Ciara would have to contact him eventually.

Darius drove back to his office. What did Ciara know about the industry that he didn't? She must have had a staff of men prepare her contract. If Candice wouldn't change her mind, how would Darius get next to Ms. Monroe and steal her contract before the ink dried? He still had the best actor for the part and Candice knew it. Ciara wasn't wearing a wedding ring and he had her family's precious little pen. The one thing Darius knew well, was women. No matter how successful, every woman needed a man. Or at least a good dick. He'd have to use Kimberly to seduce Solomon in Ciara's presence, then make Ciara his woman.

How could Darius have Ashlee at his house and take advantage of Ciara at the same time? Ashlee had to go. Darius parked on the black asphalt lot behind his office building in the space marked PRESIDENT. He turned off his engine, dialed information, then programmed the number for Ciara Monroe Casting Agency into his cellular.

Darius entered his office building through the rear, hurried up the stairway to his office, and called Ashlee. "What time is our reservation?"

Ashlee gasped. "Oh, no. You didn't get the contract. What happened?"

"I don't want to talk about it right now. I'll explain over lunch. But after lunch you've got to go home. I need to be alone." Darius placed Ciara's pen on his desk.

"That's rude, Darius. But I need to go home anyway. I do have a job."

"Yeah, but . . ." Picking up the pen, a closer look revealed the stones were fake. Man-made rubies, emeralds, and sapphires. That was okay. He'd play Ciara's game. "It's not the job you should have. You know I want you to run my finance department. Seriously. So," Darius emphasized, "on your way home, I want you to think about my job offer."

"Darius, are you okay? You know when things bother you, you have a tendency to hold them in."

"I'm fine."

"I'll think about accepting your offer. But if I do, I have to find a place to live."

"Nonsense. You already have a place to live. With me. I insist. I gotta go. I'll see you in a few."

Ashlee knew Darius well. But talking to her about his problems wouldn't help resolve his issues. Darius needed time to think. Not talk.

CHAPTER 6

Ciara Monroe wasn't the prettiest woman but her sharp wit, big tits, confidence, voluptuous lips, and financial security attracted some of the finest men in the world. Roaming around her quaint Brentwood house, Ciara debated with her only sibling, Monica, who owned a contemporarily decorated home next door but spent most of her spare time at Ciara's place.

Ciara talked openly to Monica about everything from dollars to dicks but what Ciara enjoyed most about her older sister was Monica's candor.

Sitting in her cozy lavender oversized—too big to be a chair, too small to be a chaise—seat across the living room from Monica, who was stretched horizontal on the plum-colored couch, Ciara lamented, "Sis, the more money I make, the more I attract these fine-ass, broke-ass, act-like-they-can-give-me-the-world type men that I end up taking care of."

Maybe if Ciara were less independent and stopped feeling as though she had to pick up the tab or deal with men—wealthy, middle class, or Hollywood wannabe actors in between jobs—chasing her ass or acting as though they were entitled to some gratuitous pussy, Ciara could chill and let a man be the man and pay the bills. But her father had taught Monica and her not to submit. "If a man can't deal with my daughters being successful black women who own and run their own businesses, then y'all don't need 'im." Daddy was partially correct. But Ciara needed a steady sperm donor in her life. One with a strong back, a big dick, and lots of stamina. The three-bedroom house. The Mercedes S600, G55, and CLK 55 AMG convertible. Traveling abroad twice a year. That was the easy part Ciara handled herself.

Ciara was always more popular than Monica. Ciara had countless associates, the majority of them males. A few ex-men were sprinkled amongst the group. Those were the ones suitable to fulfill her womanly needs while she was between relationships or when Ciara required a last-minute escort to private functions.

Growing up, Ciara's mother had preached, "The only true friends the two of you have are each other. Everyone else is an acquaintance. And you shrewdly determine how well acquainted. Never tell anyone all of your business. And never reveal anything personal. If you wouldn't say it on national news, then don't say it at all. If you have to disclose a secret, tell one another and no one else. Ever."

Now, Monica replied, "I told you you can't handle dating a man who's successful before you meet him. You can make a millionaire but you can't marry one. If Solomon didn't depend on you, you wouldn't want him. You've been like that since high school." Five-foot-six and a perfect size nine wearing low-rise jeans, Monica stretched her long legs, flexed her bare feet then said, "I sure could use a pedicure. Remember that senior, what's his name that played—"

Ciara sipped her brandy. "Yeah, yeah. I bought his basketball shoes—"

"Yeah. And his warm-ups, and his sweat suits, and anything else he asked you for." Monica's brandy and cigarette balanced in one hand. "Then you'd complain to me and turn around and buy him some more stuff. And he still ended up getting some other girl pregnant."

"Sis, we were sixteen. I was working and he wasn't. Better her than me single parenting a baby that's half my age. That's crazy. And besides, it's only money. I can't take it with me and as of right now I don't even have an heir." Kids, two or maybe three, were part of Ciara's future plans. But having a husband was definitely a prerequisite.

"So, what's your point? You're thirty-two. Divorced twice. On the verge of a third. I hope by now you've learned a lesson. Before you say 'I do,' get to know the guy first. That's one plus for Solomon: he's been around a couple of years. And no, you don't have any kids. But that still doesn't mean you have to spend your money on men. Spend some of that money on me. My house needs a new roof. And I could use a new Prada purse."

Engagements were a waste of Ciara's time. What was the point in waiting a year or two or forever? To save money? Ciara had money. To decide if love was true or to wait for someone to make a mistake to call off the engagement? Who really knew the person they were marrying, until after they said "I do?" Ciara learned that a marriage certificate empowered and altered the partner who brought less—income, savings, property, possessions—to the union. Men changed like women changed.

The tip of Ciara's tongue poked between the upper gap in her teeth. "In case you've forgotten, sweetheart, I just took you to Venezuela. Remember?"

"And I took you to Amsterdam," Monica replied, bucking her almond-shaped walnut-colored eyes.

"See, that's pathetic. We're dating one another. You don't have a man and I have half of a man. Kind of." Ciara sank deeper into the cushion.

"I don't need a man. I can have one any time I choose. I could have Solomon if I wanted him. That's how trifling he is. But you can't see his shortcomings because his dick keeps poking you in the eyes."

Poking. Stroking. Forget Monica's manless butt. As long as Solomon provided sex on the regular, Solomon's big dick kept Ciara a very happy virtually stress-free woman. Ciara pressed her lips together, unsuccessfully trying to hold in her laugh. "Girl, you crazy."

"You know it's true." Monica laughed.

"Well, that's all about to change. And don't think I missed your remark. I'm thirty-one. I'll be thirty-two on Martin Luther King's birthday and I promise you Solomon will be history before then."

"In less than two weeks. Yeah, right. What happened to 'I'm not taking my relationship with Solomon into the New Year'?"

"I was not showing up at a New Year's Eve party without a date. Trust me. Solomon is on his way over and in fact, I'm not going to wait. I'm going to terminate this relationship as soon as he gets here."

Damn, the way Solomon worked his magicstick was sinful. Fuck him first. Dump him afterward. Solomon's muscular biceps. Triceps. Flat stomach with an inner navel that had a slightly darker line that led down to his luscious thick dick. Six-feet-four inches. Weighing two-hundred thirty-seven pounds, Solomon had easily swept Ciara off her feet. Ciara fanned herself and patted her breasts.

"Look at cha. Your pussy is drippin' just thinking about him." Monica pointed. "And look at your nipples."

"Sis, these used to be introverted, now super protruding nipples, are courtesy of Solomon constantly tightly twirling these babies between his thumb and pointing finger before and during sex. Thank you very much." Ciara bowed in her seat.

Damn, Solomon's thumb. The thicker one he'd stuck inside Ciara's pussy last night while maneuvering his middle finger in her ass at the same time, smothering her clitoris with subtle kisses while drinking her coconut body fluids . . . Ciara shivered. Who could top that? It wasn't like she was seeing anyone else. Or had the time to find a replacement. And that youngster, Darius Jones, whom she'd just met earlier, who was probably still breast-feeding and figuring out how to return her pen, was tempting but wouldn't know what to do with an experienced woman. Ciara pictured herself teaching Darius all of Solomon's tricks.

"There you go again," Monica interrupted Ciara's thoughts, "trying to convince yourself with your sporadic decision-making. You damn near 'bout to cum just thinking about Solomon. I'll bet you a day at the spa. And, if you date that arrogant brother who lost that fat-ass contract to you, I'll throw in a trip to anywhere in the world. Bet you won't follow through. Deal?" Monica walked over to Ciara. Her pinky finger curved into a C.

"Deal." Ciara's little finger latched onto Monica's then pulled apart. "And, speaking of contract, I'm going to need your company to help me out with this one. Either you or that fine-ass brotha. The requirements are more demanding than I realized."

Monica's forehead wrinkled. "I know that look. You're frowning. What is it?"

"Darius fell for the expensive family jewel pen trick. He darn near broke his neck sneaking out of the conference room. I pretended not to see him."

"You are so crazy. Always playing games. How many of those cheap pens did you buy?"

"A dozen. But it works every time. Like the rest, Darius kept the pen because he wants to see me again. By the time he finds out the pen is fake, I'll have him trying to feel these babies." Ciara held her titties.

Ding dong.

Saved by the ringing doorbell, Ciara quickly stood. Brushing past Monica, she said, "That's Solomon. Call me in fifteen, naw make that thirty minutes." Ciara opened the door to let Solomon in and Monica out.

Solomon graced the doorway wearing a black long-sleeve pullover sweater. The darkness of the night faded into Solomon's onyx complexion and blended with his clothing. His smile showed teeth that were slightly crooked but brighter than the stars crackling like pop rocks in Ciara's uterus.

"Hey, baby," Solomon said, gripping a handful of Ciara's cheeks. His lips smothered her mouth as his tongue parted and eased into hers, suctioning softly. His abs flattened her breasts as he pulled her booty closer. His pulsating dick greeted her stomach.

When Solomon stepped back, Monica's eyes lowered then widened. "I'll make that reservation. First thing in the morning."

Ciara replied, "Thirty minutes," then closed the door and turned the top lock.

Ciara's thoughts moved toward her cervix and stopped between her thighs. Breaking Solomon's renewed grip, Ciara pulled away. "Hi, baby." She went into the kitchen and poured two glasses of brandy. Returning to the living room, Ciara extended one snifter to Solomon and resumed lounging in her favorite seat. Solomon sat where Monica had been, clamped his hands behind his head, leaned back on the sofa, and spread his thighs wide. His dick, as it normally responded whenever Ciara was near, bulged, creating a hump under his zipper.

"Solomon," Ciara rubbed the nape of her neck, "We need to talk." Her eyes drifted toward his hard-on then back to his disintegrating smile as she pressed the power button on the universal remote, turning off the CD player. Nervously Ciara plucked her lashes, causing her lids to detach from her eyeballs. "I love you. But—"

"But what, Ciara? Damn. Here we go again. I coulda swore we had this same conversation last night." Solomon leaned forward then scooted to the edge of the sofa. "But, you can't continue seeing me. Right? You need to make up your damn mind. One week you want me and the next week you don't. I can't continue like this, Ciara. You know how I feel about you. And I believe you feel the same about me. But if you don't want a brother around, just tell me to leave and I'm out."

Ciara focused on Solomon's dick then exhaled. Why did she have to choose brothas who had more drama than her? Ciara crossed her legs, burying her pussy into the cushion. "Solomon, it's just that . . ."

Solomon placed his glass on a black hand-carved coaster on the antique chestnut end table and remained quiet.

"Baby, I want more," *dick* was what she thought but said, "I want to be your wife. I want us to be together. Grow together. I'm ready to," *ride that big black dick,* "have kids. Yeah, um, our kids."

"Oh, I see. This is about you. Forget about what Solomon wants?"

"Solomon, baby, what do you want?"

"I want a woman who supports me. A woman who's not going to stress me out. But baby, if you can't wait until I sort things out, then I'm out."

"Oh, I see. You want a woman who's going to support you. Whatever that means. And you want your woman not to stress you out. And you—"

"Ciara, don't play on my words. You know what I mean."

"No, Solomon. I don't. It's not all about you anymore. What about me? I've waited two years for you to start your own business. You've been separated since we met. And. Well. You still haven't filed for a divorce." Neither had Ciara but since Solomon assumed she was single, Ciara hadn't lied. Her husband, Allen, kept his dual citizenship and moved back to France. Allen was the finest African-American Frenchman with the sexiest make-a-woman-wanna-take-her-panties-off French accent that Ciara had met. Ciara wasn't sure if she married Allen because of the way he asked her to marry him, because Allen had no boundaries in the bedroom, or because of the lucrative financial proposition.

"Why should I pay for the damn divorce when she's the one who left me?"

"Solomon, don't you see? She's never going to file. And why should she? If you die before her, she's entitled to everything you own because you don't have a will or a living trust. Nothing. She has control over all of your funeral arrangements. And from what you've told me, she'll gladly cremate you and literally flush your black ass down the toilet. Solomon I told you, I'll pay for the damn divorce." Ciara seldom cursed but the more she cursed, the madder she'd become. Solomon had agitated Ciara so she rolled her eyes toward the back of her head. "Shit!" Ciara blinked several times. Touching her eye, she searched for the irritating lash stuck to her clear contact lenses. Tears streamed down her cheeks.

"Let me handle my soon-to-be ex-wife. And I've told you. I don't ask for you to do anything for me, Ciara. I got a job. Remember? I work for Brinks."

Work for. Not *own.* Yeah, then why in hell was Solomon always suggesting she buy him something like the shirt, shoes, and socks he wore? Maybe he didn't love shopping like Ciara.

"Don't look at me like that. I know what you're thinking. You're the one always buying us stuff online. I could've bought all this myself, including the boxer-briefs. Ciara, this is small stuff compared to what I'm going to do for you when I'm your man. Come here, baby. You know how Solomon feels about you." Solomon slapped his knee.

No he did not say *when he's her man.* The phone rang, commanding Ciara's attention. Ciara shook her head, knowing it was Monica.

"Monica," Ciara answered in the kitchen, watching

Solomon slide his slacks over his beautiful thick cucumber-shaped, portabello mushroom–headed, beautiful black circumcised dick.

Solomon walked up to Ciara, hung up the phone, and spun Ciara facing the kitchen sink. He leaned her over, placed one leg on the step stool, and her warm thigh on top of the cool tile counter, then spanked his head against her clit. "Stop trying to take my pussy away from me, woman." Solomon circled his head over her moist vagina, meshing their juices until she became slippery wet. In. Out. In. Out. His head probed hard against her G-spot.

"Baby, please," Ciara moaned, "Let's finish talking."

"Ssshh. I am talking. Don't you hear me baby?" Solomon deliberately penetrated at a snail's pace as deep as he could. Ciara's hips rocked, cradling Solomon's dick into her deepest spot. Solomon embraced her breasts then kissed her earlobe. His tongue traced the outer part of her ear, slipping the tip inside.

Grinding her hips downward, Ciara moaned. "Aw, baby. Aw, yes. You know that makes me . . . aw, she's cumming daddy."

Solomon pushed deeper, jerked his dick out, then carried Ciara a short distance. He whispered in her ear, "Bend over the island so I can fuck you like you like it." His dick grew harder. Longer. Rapidly pounding inside, generating pleasure. Pain. Pleasure. Each time Ciara's titties clapped, the island rolled an inch farther. Refusing to lose contact with the pussy, Solomon stepped closer.

Ciara shook her leg. "Ow, wait, baby. You're pressing against that nerve."

Solomon kept stroking so Ciara reversed her hip rotation. By the time Solomon stopped fucking Ciara, the island was in the living room and so was Monica.

"Damn, girl, don't you knock?" Solomon said, covering his partially erect dick.

"Let's see. Do I want to go to Barbados, Portugal, Okinawa, or Puerto Rico?" Monica said, eyeing the semen streaming down Ciara's legs.

"Monica," Ciara sang, pointing toward the door. "Please."

"That's what you two get for hanging up on me. I'm leaving," Monica said as she turned the knob. "But you my sister owe me a trip. Good night."

"Good night, Monica." Ciara closed the door. This time she didn't bother locking the top.

"When you gon' change your locks? When we do get married, she can't come walkin' up in my house whenever she feels like it."

That statement wasn't worthy of a reply. Since both of them lived alone, Ciara's parents, who'd retired in Los Angeles then moved to Florida, had told them in case of an emergency they were never to place a lock on the door that neither of them had keys to, which meant Monica would forever have twenty-four-hour access.

What? When we do get married, Ciara repeated in her mind. She was beginning to question not only why she was still with Solomon but why in the hell did she want to marry him? She could do a lot better. He was inconsiderate, at times. Unfaithful, sometimes. Demanding, all the time. Didn't do anything special for her on her birthday or holidays but was quick to not only remind her of his birthday but to specify what he wanted. Christmas was a joke. New Year's too. Whatever country she visited, he wanted to go, of course at her expense. Maybe delaying his divorce was Solomon's protection from fully committing and a good thing for Ciara.

"You know nobody else can make love to you like I do," Solomon said, holding his dick in one hand and rolling the island back to its rightful place with the other, "So stop trippin'. Everything's gonna be all right. Trust me."

Solomon must have thought that his dick was some sort of magic wand casting spells upon her pussy. He was right. But one day Ciara was really going to let Solomon go. Pompous man believing he was the only brotha who could sex her to tears and cheers at the same time. Ciara went to her master bathroom then showered without saying another word to Solomon.

Damn, why couldn't she leave his ass alone? Ciara knew Solomon wasn't the one. Was she so blind that she couldn't see she was settling? But all of her men were just alike. Liars. Cheaters. Maybe Monica was right. Maybe Ciara didn't need a man. The only thing a man could do for her, Solomon was excellently providing. Maybe she'd quit procrastinating, make that trip to the pleasure store, and buy herself one of those big mechanical dicks with the rabbit ears. "Ooh." Ciara shook her head. What if she became like Monica and started fucking herself on the regular so that she'd become content being manless? Or worse, what if she'd become asexual? Anal sex was an option Ciara occasionally fantasized about. One day she'd try it but not with Solomon's jumbo dick.

While Solomon washed her back, Ciara reflected on her failed marriages. Her first husband had just lost interest in her for an undisclosed reason. Packed his clothes. Left her and everything else in the house. Never returned. Never called. And the second one claimed she worked so much she didn't need him. Maybe the first husband felt the same. Unneeded. Unappreciated. Unwanted.

As Solomon repeatedly washed his trophy dick, more than any other part of his body, Ciara slid the glass door ajar enough to get out without wetting the pink marble floor.

Ciara toweled herself dry, parted the sheer canapé veneer cover surrounding her bed, pushed twelve decorative pillows of various sizes to the floor, and snuggled under her red flannel sheet.

Solomon cuddled behind Ciara and hugged her waist.

Curious, Ciara asked, "Solomon, do I make you feel unneeded?"

Solomon sighed heavily. "You dah man. Why do you think I let you pay for everything? Yes, you do. But what's new. You set the alarm?"

Was Ciara any better than Solomon? While she'd admit Solomon was her best lover, he wasn't her only lover. Discreetly she still fucked Allen whenever she went to Paris. Rome, in D.C., was a certified freak disguised in a business suit. Roosevelt in London, and Donavon minutes away in Long Beach. Donavon. Damn, her pussy was overdue for Donavon's cunnilingus special.

"Of course, I set the alarm." Ciara closed her eyes. "It's always set. Two o'clock. Solomon's standard time to get up so he can hit the gym before going to work."

Ciara's mind drifted. Who was she kidding? The one time, one week, she'd ended her relationship with Solomon, she was unbelievably miserable. Couldn't eat. Couldn't sleep. Didn't want to hang out with Monica. Didn't enjoy fucking Donavon. Sexing Donavon was only fun if Solomon was her man. Ciara, the control supreme queen, had unintentionally fallen in love, again.

CHAPTER 7

To no avail, Darius spent the better part of the previous evening trying to convince Candice to award him the contract. Candice maintained her loyalty to Ciara. "Sorry, Darius. My decision is final." Hell, no. No way. *No* wasn't an option. Darius vowed to make Candice say yes. Angel tapped on the square windowpane, interrupting his thoughts.

Darius motioned for Angel to enter his office. "How long have you been standing there?"

"Not long," Angel replied, closing the cherry wood door. "It's seven-thirty. You ready to go over today's schedule?"

"Sure. Come on over. Have a seat."

Angel sat at Darius's desk and crossed her legs. Angel was model material. Flawless honey-colored skin. Nineteen-year-old long legs that could wrap around his waist. Twice. Slanted eyes. Thick lips. Today she wore a tan blouse that clung to her C-cup breasts. The navy miniskirt with tan pinstripes covered half her thighs standing. Whenever Angel smiled at him, his dick double pumped with joy. And to hear her answer the phone, "Somebody's Gotta Be on Top," was orgasmic. All of his male clients loved Angel. The women dealt with Angel as little as possible. Ciara would probably become the same.

Each workday began the same. Comparing his palm pilot schedule to hers, Angel said, "Eight-thirty, your new employee arrives. Nine-thirty, review financial reports with the director and sign checks. Eleven, call Ciara. Noon to one, lunch with Crystal. One-thirty to two, return phone calls. Two-thirty, meeting with Tony at Parapictures. Three-thirty, staff meeting with all departmental heads. Six o'clock, client meeting. And seven-thirty, dinner with Kimberly." Angel smiled. "Any changes?"

"One-thirty to two, set up a meeting in my office with HR. I'll return calls between appointments."

"Certainly, Mr. Jones." A few taps on Darius's screen then hers, and Angel placed his palm pilot in his hand.

Angel left and reappeared moments later. "Mr. Jones, your new employee arrived early and Ms. Monroe is on the phone."

Darius nodded. Ah, yeah. The lady had called sooner than expected. "Good first-day impression for my new employee. Introduce her to the staff, show her to her office, then call me when she's at her desk."

"Certainly, Mr. Jones."

When Angel turned to walk away, Darius eyed Angel's thighs and ass. He cleared his throat, picked up the phone, and added bass to his voice. "Darius Jones speaking."

"Good morning, Mr. Jones. This is Ciara Monroe. I

need to make immediate arrangements to retrieve my pen."

Ow. Darius purposely exhaled into the receiver. Ciara's voice was sexier than he'd remembered. Or was he turned on from watching Angel? "Sure, how's Friday night?" Darius replied, admiring Ashlee in the photo on his desk. Man, oh, man. Darius shook his head. So many fine women in the world. Pussy should come in assorted six-packs. "I'll pick you up around seven." Wellington had given Darius great tips on how to romance a woman.

"Friday? Pick me up? No, thanks. I don't need to be picked up, Mr. Jones. I just want my pen. Today. That's all."

Was she serious? She wanted something but that ninety-nine-cent pen was not it. Darius opened his desk drawer. Darius had said Friday and that's what he meant. He had whatever Ciara had wanted, which meant he was in control. "So, you're turning me down?"

Ciara's voice escalated. "How old are you, Mr. Jones?"

"Legal. Single. Now, if you're feeling too old and not up to the challenge, I do understand. We can make other arrangements."

"What? Old? If there's one thing I welcome it's a challenge. You, of all persons, should know that. Too much testosterone perhaps."

Darius noted her wit. Wealthy women were clever whores. Closet freaks. "So I take that as a yes."

"Mr. Jones. Holding my pen hostage is an undermining way to get a date. If you'd like to stroke my mind, invite me out."

Who's undermining whom? In his sexiest voice

Darius said, "May I have the pleasure of taking you out?"

Ciara casually responded, "Why not. Friday it is. Seven. I'll meet you in the lobby of the Mirage hotel."

"Whoa, not so fast. Pack an overnight bag."

"Now, you're going too far. There's no way I'm checking into a hotel with a stranger. I don't know you."

"Loosen up. I don't know you either. But I would like to get to know you."

"How do you know Solomon isn't my husband?"

"I don't. Nor do I care. But if he is, you're not happily married. Not enough testosterone, perhaps."

"So, you're not only young but you're also a smart-ass."

"I don't apologize for my observations. I have a business meeting in Oakland Saturday afternoon. You can stay with me at my place. And we'll be back in LA early Sunday morning. I look forward to seeing you Friday night. And I will have your pen. Good-bye Ms. Monroe." Darius victoriously hung up the phone.

Angel cracked the door. This time she stood in the doorway and straddled the door like a stripper teasing a dance pole. Her leg rested against the door. "Mr. Jones, Kevin Williams is on the phone and your employee is waiting to meet with you." Angel could have buzzed Darius on the intercom but had said before she was hired that she had too much energy to sit behind a desk all day.

"Tell her I'll be there in a few minutes and tell Kevin I'll call him back." His half-brother, Kevin, could wait. Conversations with Kevin gave Darius insight to his other side of the family's happenings.

Darius exited the back stairway en route to greet his

new employee. Thankfully she wasn't playing solitaire. "Welcome aboard." Darius extended his hand. "Now, get settled. And get to work. I want you to start off with profiling my clients. Angel will e-mail you the confidential list. You need to learn the clients' likes. Dislikes. Favorite restaurants, spa, sports teams. Their kids' birthdays. And of course the wife's birthday and their anniversary. Be creative. Don't interview my male clients. Men hate being asked a lot of personal questions. The wives are generally the opposite. Report to me tomorrow morning at ten."

She frowned, blinked. "But I was hired to write and review screenplays."

What, a joke? "Correction. You were hired to work. Ten o'clock. Tomorrow. My office. Don't be late."

Darius went to his office and returned Kevin's call. "Hey, Kevin. Man what's up?"

"Just livin' man. Look, I called to invite you to the family reunion on the fourth of July."

What? Since when did Darius need a fuckin' invitation to his own family's reunion? Kevin had just confirmed that Darius was better off not having a relationship with Darryl. "Man, that's my dad's birthday barbecue. I can't make it to your dad's reunion."

"I heard that. Well, the reunion is to be in Oakland too. You can do both. Don't forget your real dad is my dad. He loves you too. I know how you must feel. Anyway man, it'd be nice if you met the folks. Then we can hang at your crib."

To hell with that empathy bullshit. Kevin had no idea how Darius felt. The only men who understood the depth of pain a biological father's rejection created were men who shared Darius's position. Yeah, Darius agreed he should meet his cousins so he wouldn't end up screwing one of them if he hadn't already. But Kevin's real motivation was wanting to stay at Darius's house.

"Man, you don't know nothing about me. I don't need Darryl and his fucked-up way of showing love. I'll let you know if I can make an appearance." If Darryl called and extended the invitation, Darius would without reservation attend the reunion. "So what else is going on?"

"Nothing much. Might be out your way in Los Angeles soon. I need a break from New York. Just to chill out. Meet some new honeys. I'm tryin' to live large like you mein." Kevin pronounced "man" like he was ordering Chow Mein noodles.

"Well, you're welcome to break at my cribs in Oakland and LA. Look, man. I gotta handle my business. Peace." Darius hated talking on the phone all the time—business, personal, annoying females calling with nothing to say, just breathing in his ear waiting for him to say something—so Darius kept his personal conversations brief.

Darius hung up and dialed his mother's office number. There was no answer so he called his dad's office.

"Wellington Jones and Associates. How may I help you acquire wealth today?"

"Hey, this is Darius."

"Oh, yes. Hello, Mr. Jones. May I place you on hold?"

"Sure." Darius drew tiny circles on a sticky.

"Hey, Son."

"Hi, Dad." Darius welcomed hearing Wellington's voice. "You and mom headed to Oakland this weekend?"

"Yeah. We're leaving on the nine-o'clock flight tonight."

Ah, man. Darius didn't want to introduce Ciara to his parents as a casual date. His travel agent would re-book their flight to depart tomorrow. "Well, have a good flight. I'll be in Oakland in the morning."

"If Ashlee's meeting you in Oakland, ask her to call me. I need to see if she's interested in selling a few of her stock shares to a very interested buyer."

Ashlee had called once since she'd left. She'd said, "I made it home safely. I'll talk to you later." No bye or good-bye. Maybe having his driver take Ashlee to the airport at the same time Darius had left his house to pick up Crystal, hurt Ashlee's feelings. If Ashlee didn't like where he went, she shouldn't have asked. Women. Too sensitive.

"No, Ashlee won't be there but I'll talk with her later and let her know. Bye, Dad."

"I love you, Son."

"I love you too, Dad. Bye."

Before shutting down his computer to meet Crystal again, this time for lunch, Darius e-mailed Angel to send Ashlee a dozen long-stemmed white roses.

The Mirage must have been the new meeting spot. The last three women he'd met for nooners, or lunchtime sexcapades had made the same request. Darius arrived early, rented a room hoping Crystal would agree to a quickie, then sat at the bar facing the door so he could see his new fuck buddy walk in. Crystal had brought her own toys to his house last night. She'd forgotten her battery-operated remote-controlled butterfly clit mas-sager so Darius packaged the pink strap-on Crystal wore when he serviced her doggy-style, and placed it in his top inside pocket.

The bartender laid a white napkin on the bar in front of Darius. "Sir, what would you like?"

Crystal. Straight up sucking his dick at the bar. "Rémy Martin Louis XIII."

"We only serve Louis XIII by the bottle for one hundred seventy-five dollars."

Normally Darius would've responded rudely but thoughts of Crystal licking his balls made him smile. Darius removed his Platinum American Express from his black leather wallet and placed it on the bar.

"Will that be all?" she asked, delighted.

"Yes," Darius firmly replied without giving her a second look. She wasn't worthy of his attention. Her daytime job was bartending. Her clear nail polish was chipped. Her eyes locked on his wallet before and after he removed his credit card. Why did women think men overlooked the small stuff? Darius had several laws and "never date a woman who had nothing to lose" was in the top ten.

Rule number one, Ma Dear had instilled: Pray. God answers prayers.

Number two: Self-preservation. Take care of Darius first. Mentally. Physically.

Three: Always use a condom.

Four: Self-actualization. Make success happen.

Five: Never date a woman who has nothing to lose.

Six: Women do as I say, not as I do.

Seven: Never apologize.

Number eight: Never cry.

Nine: Work out every day.

Ten: Tithe ten percent faithfully.

Crystal strutted in on a pair of clear high heels wearing a black miniskirt business suit. Stockings. Garter. Darius mumbled, "It's on."

Crystal hugged Darius then kissed his cheek. "Hi. Good seeing you again, boo."

This woman was too comfortable too soon. Darius lowered Crystal's arms and noticed Candice entering the lobby. Darius frowned as Candice headed toward the bar. Why was Candice at the Mirage? Darius waited to see if Candice was meeting a man. When he saw Ciara trailing a short distance behind Candice, Darius pushed Crystal aside and said, "Excuse me a moment. I'll be right back."

Quickly Darius disappeared into the men's restroom. Was this a setup? What if Crystal was now engaged in conversation with Candice and Ciara? Hopefully she wouldn't say she was waiting for him. Darius washed his hands. He could lie his way out of leaving Crystal at the bar but if he returned to the bar, Ciara would know the truth and right now he couldn't jeopardize his plan to take over Ciara's contract. Slipping out the side exit, Darius retrieved his car from the valet and left. Like the other women Darius stood up, Crystal would eventually forgive him too.

CHAPTER 8

"Well Mr. Jones, I sure hope this weekend in Oakland is going to prove worthy of my time," Ciara said studying the lunch menu at Jordan's restaurant in the Claremont Hills.

Darius reached into his pocket and said, "Here's your family's fake jewel pen." Lying the pen on the white tablecloth, Darius looked at Ciara.

At the airport, on the plane, after they landed in Oakland, she was so turned on by Darius's gentlemanly qualities she'd forgotten to mention the pen. Rotating the silver ball on the roof of her mouth, Ciara replied, "Well, in that case keep it. Consider it a gift in remembrance of our first meeting together."

Good, the waiter arrived. Darius ordered the salad Ciara wanted and a steak for himself. When the waiter left, he said, "Nothing in my home or my office or my life is fake. You keep it. But the pen did give us a reason to communicate. I'm not gon' lie. I really like you. I was attracted to you the moment I saw you. I don't meet many real women. You're definitely all woman. Intelligent. Sexy. I want to take my time getting to know you."

Was Darius serious? Perhaps. In time every man revealed his true intentions. Darius hadn't kissed Ciara on the plane, or touched her inappropriately. Ciara wanted to sex Darius.

Between bites from her salad, Ciara asked, "What do you think about partnering with me on this contract? If you were able to get a commitment from Morris, obviously you have the contacts. And I definitely have knowledge of this industry. But there's certain barriers women haven't broken yet." If Darius agreed, Ciara would help him build his company's reputation.

"I'm definitely interested. But right now, this weekend, is all about me getting to know you. For starters, I've scheduled a two o'clock massage for you at Claremont Spa with Robin. If you come here again, I guarantee you you'll request Robin."

"Are you serious? A massage? That's wonderful." Ciara had promised herself a massage for over a month but never found time to schedule an appointment.

Darius paid the bill then escorted Ciara downstairs to the spa. "My driver will pick you up outside at three-thirty."

Ciara hugged Darius. "Thank you."

"No, thank you. I'll see you when you get to the house."

The attendant inside the spa handed Ciara a pair of brown slip-on shower shoes and said, "You can enjoy the Jacuzzi, steam sauna and help yourself to fresh-squeezed orange juice, tea, or water. Here's a key to your locker. Your robe is in the locker and Robin will meet you in the waiting area at ten minutes to two."

Ciara sat in the Jacuzzi. The view from the top of the hill was serene. Ciara must have dozed off and awakened to Robin calling her name. She answered, "I'm Ciara Monroe," then followed Robin to the massage room. Lying on the table, the last words Ciara remembered hearing Robin say was, "Turn over onto your back and scoot down."

Ciara was awakened by Robin tapping her shoulder. "After you get dressed, I'll be waiting outside the door to escort you back to the waiting room."

Ciara dressed. Her body floated on air to the Town Car. She slept until the driver said, "Miss, you're here."

Staring out the window, Ciara thought, the mansion before her wasn't Darius's. Where was she? Where was Darius? The driver opened the door and escorted her to the door.

He tipped his hat and said, "Do have a good evening."

Darius opened the door wearing a black smoking jacket and pajama pants. "I don't have to ask how was the massage."

Ciara followed Darius upstairs. "I didn't realize I was so tired."

"I come to Oakland at least twice a month just to get away from the hectic day-to-day in LA."

Ciara stretched across Darius's rotating round bed that floated in midair. Leaning over the side, Ciara waved her hand under the mattress and bumped a clear frame that started adjusting to a height so high the only way for her to escape the bed was to jump. "What the hell! Get me down from here!"

"You're in good hands. Relax. You never have to

wait for sunset to see the stars," Darius said. As he re-
motely dimmed the lights, his ceiling filled with simu-
lated stars and constellations. Ciara fell asleep
dreaming of Darius's masculine hands roaming. Their
sweat meshing, sliding. This time when Ciara awakened, she was in the guest bedroom. He could have at
least brushed against a sistah's titty.

Ciara approached Darius's bedroom and peeped inside.

"You don't have to peep. Come in. I had some things
to do and I didn't want to disturb you so I put you in the
other bed."

Ciara glanced at the furniture in Darius's bedroom.
"I'm just curious. Do you have a living room inside
your bedrooms in LA and D.C. too?" Ciara asked.

"As much as I love sex, I don't get busy on furniture
where my parents and other guests sit. My bedrooms
contain everything I desire to host a pleasurable evening.
Door number one." Darius pressed a button on his remote. A wall retracted, revealing a large transparent
Jacuzzi elevated on a black platform. "Door number
two." Behind the wall was a stripper stage, with a dance
pole, a cage, and one spectator reclining chair. Or was
the chair designed for sex? Ciara fantasized being on
stage hanging upside down on the pole.

"Damn, so what's behind door number three?" Ciara
asked, pointing.

"You're not ready for that. Next time you visit, you'll
see." Darius pressed several buttons and the two walls
closed.

"Those murals weren't there. Where's the tropical
scenery?" Ciara blinked several times. Shit, the youngster might teach her a few new tricks. Darius hadn't

acted cocky since the meeting. He was surprisingly cool, not arrogant. Ciara liked arrogant men.

"I'm sorry. I have to know what's behind there."

"If you insist." Darius pressed another button.

Ciara frowned. "That's a weird-looking swing."

"It's not just a swing. It's a vibrating sex swing." Darius hit another button on the remote. Stars formed a galaxy under the dimly lit room. The swing began to gyrate to the tune of Prince singing *Do Me Baby* in the background. Darius touched another button. The music stopped. Swing froze. Door closed.

"Whoa, I see you take sex seriously."

"I take everything I do seriously. Like you, my queen." Darius patted the empty space on the sofa beside him. "Come here. Sit with me."

"Aren't we supposed to be someplace in an hour?"

"It's not far. We have time. Come. Sit."

The way he said *come* made Ciara want to cum. This man was smooth in so many ways. Darius had changed into a pair of black slacks and socks. His muscular upper body was shiny but not oily. Ciara desperately wanted to touch his bare chest. Glide her juicy tongue all over his muscular body. His neatly groomed locks pointed down to his dark brown tasty nipples. His washboard stomach sunk into his slender cobra-shaped waistline. Shoulders wide and strong. Slowly Ciara pranced toward Darius, enacting her best stripper walk that she'd learned in Cardio Strip class, crossing one foot in front of the other. Ciara sat beside Darius, positioning her legs slightly to reveal her thighs.

"Nice." Darius nodded. "Real nice. Please don't do that again. I'm trying hard to control him. Lay your head in my lap."

"Maybe we should—"

"Don't. And don't take off your boots. I love my woman in boots. And don't touch Slugger so you can size him up." Darius patted his thigh.

Slugger? Ciara would judge for herself. Ciara exhaled and moaned, laying the back of her head on Darius's thighs and avoiding contact with his dick. Any man that fine, with a bedroom like Darius's had to be compensating for something.

"Okay, what's next?"

"Relax," Darius said, stroking her hair. Slowly his fingertips traced her hairline along her face. Starting at the forehead he glided along the temples, past her jawbones down to the entrance of her ear. Ciara's breathing quickened. Massaging her earlobes, Darius whispered, "Relax."

Darius placed his palm against her abdomen. "Slowly take a deep breath into your nostrils. Okay, hold it. Now slowly exhale through your mouth." He paused then said, "Again. Again."

Shit! Ciara's pussy pulsated. Thighs squeezed. Ciara felt her entire body become heavy and relaxed. When was the last time she lay long enough to listen to her body. Her eyes closed.

Darius asked softly, "Tell me about your childhood."

Ciara exhaled. She looked up at Darius who was looking down on her like they were best friends.

"Tell me," he said.

"My parents—"

"No, I want to know about you. Ciara Monroe. Your middle name. Favorite colors. Birthday. Movies. Where you were born. Restaurants. Food. Hobbies. I'm listening."

"Okay." Ciara smiled. "I grew up near a hundred

and fifth and Crenshaw. So although I didn't like being tough, I had to kick a few asses to make the kids leave me alone. I love my parents and my sister Monica with all my heart. I always wanted to have my own business so I majored in Business Administration at UCLA. Graduated with honors."

"When you were a little girl, what were your favorite colors? Movies? Hobbies? What were your dreams?" Darius's fingers found their way to her scalp. He gently massaged, tangling her Afro.

Ciara no longer cared about her hair; she was beginning to care about this young, good-looking, inquisitive man. Ciara smiled. "We were poor, but my childhood was great. My favorite color was yellow because it reminded me of the sunshine. My mother used to tell me and Monica that 'the sun shines every day even when we don't see it.' So whenever I see the color yellow, no matter what time of day, I know the sun is shining somewhere and that makes me smile on the inside. My favorite movie was *Coffee* because Pam Grier was so beautiful but she didn't take no shit off no man and somehow she still managed to be a lady. When my mother showed us that movie, I became just like Coffee."

The tension growing behind Darius's forehead drew his eyelids closer. What the hell did that mean? He'd have to rent the movie and find out. Hopefully Ciara wasn't some psychopath pistol-carrying woman waiting to audition for a leading role in a Western. Just because Ciara was older didn't mean she was more mature. Darius had encountered his fair share of lunatics.

"... and dreams ... I want the kind of love my mother and father had ... have ... they struggled together and prospered together but they always stayed together. They slept in the same bed every night. When I was *nine* my dad bought us the house I now live in. Monica and I were so happy we had our own rooms. . . ." Tears rolled down Ciara's cheeks into her ears. "What about you? How was your childhood?"

"We'll discuss me another day. It's almost time. Go freshen up. We need to leave."

Darius braced Ciara's back until she stood erect. "Thanks for sharing," Darius said, kissing her lips. "I'll meet you downstairs."

Was this the real Darius Jones? Ciara thought, closing the guest bedroom door. Ciara stood in front of the ceiling-to-floor bathroom mirror. Regardless, he was refreshingly different. Ciara told her reflection, "Don't start off being judgmental. Give Darius a chance to prove himself worthy of loving you."

Pulling a tissue from the gold box on the counter, Ciara wrapped her fingers. Gently she pressed the bottom corner of the mirrored medicine cabinet. What if everything fell out like on that Southwest Airlines commercial? She'd lie and say she was freshening up her makeup and accidentally hit the glass. Ciara scanned the empty rows, closed the mirror then opened each drawer beneath the black vanity. Each drawer was empty. What was she searching for anyway? Lifestyle clues. Was this Darius's house? Did another person live with him?

Ciara tossed the tissue into the empty wastebasket. If she stayed in the bathroom any longer, Darius was sure to come and get her. Hurrying downstairs, Ciara smiled. "I'm ready. But you never told me. Where are we going?"

"To dinner."

"Where?"

"You'll see. Get in."

The chauffeur held the door. Darius held Ciara's hand until she was comfortably seated then sat beside her. The driver cruised along Highway 101 and exited into Half Moon Bay until they arrived at another beautiful home.

"Who lives here?"

"Be patient. You'll see," Darius said, escorting Ciara to the front door. His keys jingled loosely in the air. Then he unlocked the door. "Mom! Dad! We're here!"

Ciara's eyes bucked. She whispered, "This is your parents' home?"

Darius smiled. "Yeah, one of them. They invited us to dinner."

"Darius, why didn't you tell me?"

"Because you probably wouldn't have come."

Ciara smiled as Wellington and Jada approached the foyer. Wellington's brown linen suit complemented Jada's tan linen jumpsuit.

"Hey, Son," Wellington said, hugging Darius.

"Hi, honey." Jada extended her arms and rocked Darius side to side.

"Mom. Dad. This is my guest, Ciara Denise Monroe. Los Angeles native."

"Is that so? Pleased to meet you again, Ciara. I'm Jada Diamond Tanner, Darius's mother. And this is my husband, Wellington Jones."

Maybe their introduction was a formality because Ciara had read the screenplay about their lives three times.

"Dinner is ready," Jada said, leading them into the dining room.

A gold table runner accented the table. Each placemat was a different color: blue, green, red, and purple.

Wellington said grace, and then asked, "Ciara, how did you meet Candice?"

Ciara expected one of Darius's parents to ask about her business but not her relationship with Candice. "Candice and I met through Terrell."

"Really," Jada said. "So are you Terrell's agent?"

Okay, where were they going with this conversation? "Well, I am a casting director."

"So who do you think will play our roles? And can you change our names?"

"Terrell will play Wellington or whatever the final character's name will be."

Darius covered his mouth and coughed. His lips parted as his hand lowered but then Darius changed his mind about commenting. He nodded and tightened his mouth.

"And I'm undecided about an actress for Jada's role. Kendra Moore is perfect. She's dark-complexioned. Shaped like you, Jada." Jada smiled as Ciara continued, "But Gabrielle Union is a bigger name. What do you think?"

"Honestly, I think Candice shouldn't have optioned the rights to our life story. Just so you'll know if this movie comes out, I anticipate many of my clients will terminate their contracts with Black Diamonds," Jada said to Ciara.

Now Ciara's lips were tight. Ciara observed and listened throughout the remainder of the meal and dessert. The less she said the better. When dessert was over, Wellington helped Jada clear the table.

"You ready?" Darius asked. "You've been extremely quiet. You look tired."

"Just have a lot on my mind with the contract, comments, and all. Honestly I'm having second thoughts about us partnering."

"Don't," Darius said, holding the back of Ciara's chair as Ciara eased from under the dining table. Darius yelled from the dining room to his parents in the kitchen. "Ma! Dad! We're leaving! Thanks for dinner!

"I wanted you to meet my parents so you'd know what we're dealing with. They're well respected in their respective professions and understandably sensitive to being exploited. Let's get my partner and future lady home," Darius said, escorting Ciara back to the limousine.

Ciara leaned her head against the leather seat and closed her eyes. The dinner conversation hadn't been bad. Now, at least she knew to inform her attorney which obstacles might occur.

Darius nudged her. "Wake up. We're here."

Ciara wasn't asleep. She opened her eyes and glanced out the open car door. "Wow, I guess I am tired." Darius had ruined his chances of making love to her tonight or any other night.

Darius escorted Ciara upstairs to the guest bedroom. He kissed her lips and whispered, "Good night. Sweet dreams, sunshine."

Darius turned on the light then closed the door. The room was decorated with countless bouquets of yellow roses. One rose lay atop the pillow. Ciara smiled. How could she not have interest in Darius? That man was undeniably unbelievable. A keeper. What about Solomon? *What about him,* Ciara thought. For the first time in years, another man made Ciara forget about Solomon. Perhaps the time had come for Ciara to stop thinking about letting Solomon go and just let him go.

Daddy used to say, "Keep what you got 'til you find what you need." Ciara refused to second guess her instincts this time. Darius's family wouldn't protest if Ciara were their daughter-in-law. Against Monica's advice to slow down, for business purposes, Darius Jones was Ciara's next husband.

CHAPTER 9

A woman's work was never done. Back from Oakland. Back to reality. Back to business. Back in Los Angeles, Jada Diamond Tanner had to make time to resolve her own issues. Dealing with Darius's erratic behavior. One day he practically ignored her, now he was trying to convince her to back off and stop calling Ciara about the screenplay. Jada felt partially responsible for Darius's mood swings. How could she forgive herself for lying to Darius? How could she help heal her son's wounds without pushing him away again? Her husband, Wellington, was truly God sent. Loving. Honest. Forgiving. But, if Wellington were to discover the truth, would he forgive her, again? How did Jada, the woman who had it all together, or so it seemed, end up with skeletons in her closet? There weren't many. But the few she had were potentially detrimental to her relationships. Especially her marriage.

"Living life," Jada whispered.

Jada knew Wellington, with his take-it-to-the-grave

attitude, had secrets too but he was better at evading confessions. And then there was her back-stabbing girlfriend, Candice. Fed up with Candice's ruthlessness, Jada gathered her purse and keys. Passing the study, Jada noticed Wellington was engrossed in reading the Bible.

Jada peeped inside then tapped on the door. "Honey, I'll be back. I have to have a face-to-face with Candice. I can't take any more of her trifling ways."

Wellington's finger rested center page. "Are you sure this is what you want to do? Jada, I know you're upset but if you confront Candice she may not accept Darius as Ciara's partner. And right now we just need to let Ciara and Darius handle Candice. Why don't I take you out to brunch so we can come to a reasonable resolution. Then you can talk to Candice."

"My mind is made up. I've decided the only way to stop Candice is to sue Candice."

Closing the large white desktop King James Bible with gold-trimmed pages, Wellington scratched his head and said, "Bah, no. That doesn't make any sense. You can't sue your best friend. Just ask her to change the names. You must admit," Wellington smiled, "the things we did were exciting. We could add to the list right now." Wellington's eyebrows fluttered.

"Not as exciting as what's to come. And I will take you up on that offer. Later." The tip of Jada's tongue extended beyond her lips then flickered in the air.

"Whoa, keep that up and I'm gonna have to—"

Retracting her tongue Jada sternly said, "No, not now. Later."

"Seriously, baby. You should be patient. You're really overreacting. But I know you. I'll be here when you get back."

Jada blew Wellington a kiss. "Bye, honey."

Wellington's car blocked hers. The keys were in his ignition so Jada eased into Wellington's platinum Jaguar and sped out of the driveway. What the hell was Candice thinking about? Maybe if Candice had asked permission, Jada would've understood. Arriving at Candice's home in less than twenty minutes, Jada parked in the driveway behind Candice's car.

Jada sighed then rang Candice's doorbell.

"Just a minute!" Moments later, Candice stood in the doorway wearing a blue sweatsuit. Candice's hair was tied with a pink scarf that hung lower than her ponytail. "Well, isn't this a pleasant surprise. I thought I'd lost my best friend." Candice swung the door wide and smiled. "Girl, come on in. Give me a hug."

Jada remained stoic. No smile. No frown. No hug. "I wish I could be as friendly but you know why I'm here. We need to talk." Jada stepped a few feet inside the doorway and stood.

"Well, since you showed up unannounced at my front door, and you're not dressed for Sunday morning service, maybe I need to listen. Let's sit in the living room and catch up on old times. Can I get you something to drink?"

Jada didn't move. "No, thanks. I won't be long." Jada's thumbs rested tightly in her beige low-rise corduroy pockets. "Candice, why in the hell did you write a damn screenplay about my life?"

"I thought we were over that. Girl, all the drama in your life, I just beat someone else to the punch. You must admit you have to be somewhat excited. You'll be a quasi-celebrity once we start filming. And of course I'll invite you and Wellington to the premiere."

"Premiere my ass, Candice. What about Darius?

Why didn't you give him the contract? That's the least you could've done."

"Oh, now I see what this conversation is really about. Jada, everyone in California knows your son's reputation of being a womanizer and trust me I'm putting it mildly. Why would I invite him into a circle of stars and allow him to sabotage my business like he almost did yours? Darius slept with not one, not two, but all four of your top-level executives. And his poor ex-fiancée Maxine, Darius is responsible for that poor girl contracting HIV. If he'd kept his 'chocolate dipstick, Slugger' as you say he calls it, under control, Maxine would've never cheated."

Jada instantly wondered why she'd told Candice all of Darius's business too. If Candice were to write a screenplay about Darius, Darius would never forgive her. "That was then. Darius is mature now."

"What? Are you serious? I saw him at the Mirage hotel with Crystal last week. Stood Crystal up when he saw me but thought I hadn't seen him. Besides, Ciara was the only one smart enough to make my Terrell the leading actor. Everybody else was trying to impress me by selecting big box-office actors. To tell the truth, that's the main reason I gave Ciara the exclusive."

"That was dumb. Stupid in fact. You're not even sure if she's qualified to handle the contract. I'm through with you—"

"Again."

"Whatever. And Terrell's old washed up behind could never play the role of my Wellington. Just so you won't be surprised. I came here to tell you I'm going to sue you."

Candice gasped as her bottom lip fell toward her chin. "You can't. I have every right to my script."

"Then you don't have anything to worry about. Do you?" Jada dug her thumbs deeper into her pockets then shifted her weight from her right leg to her left." By law you cannot plagiarize the life of anyone, except celebrities, and even with them you'd better be careful. You weren't even smart enough to change the damn names."

"That's because I thought you were my friend."

Terrell walked through the open door. "Hey, Jada. What brings you here? Darryl told me to tell you hello."

Now, Terrell was telling Jada about Darius's selfish father. Thanks to Candice who told her husband everything, Terrell relayed to Darryl what was happening in Jada's life.

"Terrell, since you talk so much, you need to talk some sense into your wife. She cannot go forward with this movie."

Terrell stood between Candice and Jada. "Oh, she can and she will. Y'all not the only ones who deserve to be rich. Shit, my goal was to be a multi-millionaire by the time I turned forty. I'm three years behind but thanks to my baby, we're one step away from signing a contract that's going to make our bank accounts fat! Jada, get off your damn high horse and be happy for someone else for a change. As long as Candice was beneath you, she was good enough to be your friend. Now, you're trying to block her blessings."

"What! Block her blessings? Beneath me?" Jada tugged on her pockets, narrowed her eyes at Candice, and said, "You actually said that nonsense to him?" Candice hadn't said a word since Terrell walked into the house. "Oh, I see whose idea this was now. Candice, look at me." Narrowing her eyes, Candice looked at

Jada. "Tell me this screenplay was your idea and not Terrell's."

"Baby, you don't have to tell her a damn thing." Terrell pointed toward the front door and said, "Jada, see yourself out."

"Fine, I'm gone. But I wouldn't break out the champagne. If I were the two of you, I'd get the best damn attorney in town. I'll see you in court!" Jada slammed the door and got in her car. Jada started to head home but figured she'd get no compassion there so she went to Darius's house instead.

Jada rang Darius's doorbell several times.

Darius opened the door holding his robe closed. "Mom?"

"Hi, honey. I need to talk with you."

Tying the belt in a knot, Darius asked, "Mom, why didn't you call first?" The last time Jada heard those words was when she first started dating Wellington and showed up at his house unannounced. Maybe if she had called first, the ménage à trois she had with Wellington and Melanie would've never occurred.

"If you're too busy for your mother Darius, I can come back or call you later."

Darius sighed, "Naw, Ma. It's okay. Come on in."

Jada walked through the foyer, into the kitchen, poured a glass of fresh-squeezed orange juice, then joined Darius in the living room.

"My company is still asleep, Ma, so keep it down. What's so important that you had to talk at," Darius looked at the time, "eight o'clock?"

Jada sipped the juice. "I've decided to sue Candice."

Leaping from his seat, Darius yelled, "Are you crazy?! You can't do that, Ma. The industry needs that film."

"Watch your words. The industry can live without my life story being broadcast on the big screen all over the world." Sex on the beach, slow screws in her office, in garages, on the planes, Candice's bathroom, anywhere Wellington wanted to have sex, Jada had agreed.

"Oh, I see. This isn't about Candice or Ciara or me being successful. This is about you and your highly respected reputation."

"Of course it is. If I'm associated with this production, I could lose my business. Why is everyone trying to make me the culprit when I'm the victim?"

Darius bit his bottom lip then shook his head. "Ma, you're always the victim. Nothing is ever your damn fault."

"Darius Jones, I just told you: don't you use that word nor that tone with me!" Tears formed in Jada's eyes.

A sigh of disgust escaped Darius's nostrils. "Ma, please don't shed those fake tears. If you sue Candice, you'll ruin my chances of making it big. I'm closer than ever to becoming Ciara's partner." Darius nodded toward his closed bedroom door.

Ciara walked into the room wearing one of Darius's robes. "Excuse me. Did I overhear you say you're suing Candice? Jada, you can't be serious."

Jada looked at Ciara, then squinted at Darius, and then looked back at Ciara. Jada dried her tears then shook her head. Clearly the robe was all that Ciara was wearing. "I've got to go, honey. I'll call you later. And call your father. He needs to speak with you."

Darius looked at his mom. "Which one?"

"He wants to lease you an office next to ours in the building in downtown San Francisco. He thinks it'll be a good expansion for your business. So, now I think you know which one. Mister smartass."

Jada walked out of Darius's front door and slammed it. Why was everyone so damn upset with her about her life story? *Which one?* Jada was starting not to care if Darius would ever forgive her for lying to him.

CHAPTER 10

Darius listened to Ciara console Candice. Ciara had quietly moved from his bed to his sofa as though she didn't want Candice to discover he was in the background. "Um-hmm. I see. I can't believe you stayed awake all night. Don't worry. Get some rest. I'll have Mr. Brentwood and my lawyer research the legalities. Good-bye."

Darius questioned Ciara. "So, what's up? Must be important for Candice to call at six in the morning." Refusing to disclose the details of her conversation with Candice, Ciara said, "I'll handle this," then slid under his sheets. Darius already knew Ciara's conflict. Yesterday his mother's attorney had Candice served with a lawsuit for specific performance not to produce the movie.

At first Darius was mad at his mother but thanks to his mother's lawsuit, Darius's romantic involvement with Ciara had progressed to a more intimate level for him and a more emotional level for Ciara. Ciara realized, but didn't acknowledge, that without his help, her lucrative contract would terminate. Women.

Darius reached under his black-and-gold comforter and uncovered Ciara's head, which was buried a few inches deep. Darius was amazed she hadn't suffocated under the heavy wool cover.

"Good morning," Darius said. His lips pressed in the crevice above Ciara's collarbone.

"Good morning to you." Ciara pranced to the bathroom and returned. "Ah, now that's better. Give me a real kiss."

Slowly, Darius's tongue parted Ciara's lips. He gently sucked her tongue, then her lips. "You are so beautiful in the morning," he lied. Ciara's afro was flat on both sides. Without makeup Ciara easily appeared too old for him. As he tossed back the cover, his dick sprouted long and firm. Darius watched Ciara's juicy lips smother his head. Seductively she glided his head in and out of her mouth. Saliva trickled down his shaft as Ciara massaged the wetness into the base and his balls.

Darius whispered, "Damn, that feels good," pushing Ciara's head lower. "Suck that dick, girl."

Ciara's hands floated down to his thighs as she whispered, "Turn over and brace yourself on your knees."

"Aw, shit." Darius followed her instructions. Ciara knelt behind him and positioned her head between his knees, then pulled his dick backward slipping the head into her mouth.

"Ah, yeah." Darius moaned, arching his back to give Ciara more space to take in more of his erection.

Ciara's hand felt so good, stroking long and firm. Gripping his balls with the opposite hand, she sucked each testicle.

"Damn, woman. What are you doing down there?"

Ciara licked back and forth alternating between his nuts. Then her tongue traced from his balls to his perineal muscle below his balls, to his rectum. Darius closed then opened his eyes. Lifting onto his elbows, Darius watched Ciara until she began French kissing between his rectum and balls.

"Whooaaa. Mm. Oh. Mm," Darius moaned.

The tip of her tongue circled the exterior of his anus. Her thick lips planted kisses on his opening while she stroked his dick and squeezed his balls.

"Mmmm. Oh, yeah. That feels real good. Do that again," Darius requested.

Slipping his dick deep into her mouth, Ciara massaged his balls. Slowly she inserted the tip of her middle finger into his rectum. In. Out. Each time penetrating a little deeper, simultaneously stroking his shaft while sucking his dick.

Darius rotated his ass onto her finger. She'd better not tell Monica how much he loved the stimulation of her penetration. Ciara's advanced bedroom skills satisfied Darius's sexual appetite. She applied the right amount of pressure. Stroked him at the perfect pace. Darius hated when women pushed their finger in and didn't pull out. No rhythm. No gradual movement. Those were the ones he'd stop. Not Ciara. Darius repeatedly squeezed his sphincter muscles around Ciara's twirling finger. She pressed a little deeper into his anal canal, applying orgasmic pressure to his prostate gland. Ecstasy. Sheer ecstasy. Ciara definitely hit the jackpot by stimulating his G-spot!

Darius groaned. Grunted. "Fuck. Yes." Darius was ready to fire off the most powerful orgasm when suddenly he heard Ciara say, "Turn over. I wanna get on top."

"Whooaaa." Darius's energy level deflated. "Don't," he exhaled then said, "do that again. I was so ready to cum." Darius exhaled again. "I know, baby but mama wants to get there with you." It took a few minutes to push the pillows out of the way, retrieve a condom from his top drawer, then roll the rubber to the base of his penis.

Darius watched Ciara straddle him, then she rocked her amazingly hot pussy onto his dick. Balancing herself on her feet instead of her knees, Ciara guided his hard-on on the inside like she was giving him a tour. Controlling the depth of his entry, Ciara probed three inches into her vagina then pressed his head against her G-spot. "Aw, yes. Right there daddy. That's my spot."

Darius coached her on. "Get your dick, girl. Ride that shit." He had to feel his head hit the bottom of her pussy so Darius held Ciara's hip into his.

Ciara's ass swayed back and forth like she was practicing for the swing back at his home in Oakland. "I want you to cum with me, daddy." She raked her clit along his pubic hairs. "Aw, baby. Give me my dick. I can feel the head pressing against my belly button. I love this big, strong, chocolate dick inside me, baby. Oh, Darius. Here she cums. Mama's cumming. Cum with me, daddy." Ciara rode faster.

What the fuck?! Ciara squeezed Darius's nipples harder and harder and harder. "Hell, yeah!" she screamed. Ciara was deep in the zone.

Darius held Ciara's hands. "Get that dick, girl. Get it. It's yours. You earned this cum, woman. You ready? You ready?"

"Oh, my, God. Oh, my, God." Ciara kept repeating the same three words.

"Here it comes. Catch it." Darius thrust harder. To

his surprise Ciara kept pace. Her hips bucked so fast he held them. For an older woman, Ciara had great stamina.

Opening her mouth wide, Ciara shouted, "Yes! Yes!" as loud as she could. Her breaths—quick, short—raced long after she'd lay beside him.

"You're incredible," Darius said. "But it must almost be that time of the month woman because you were doing the damn thing," Darius slapped Ciara's ass as she collapsed face down onto the sweaty sheet.

"Yeah, kind of." Ciara inhaled deeper.

Darius commanded, "Lay on your back. Bend your knees and spread 'em."

Ciara smiled.

Darius inserted the tip of his middle finger. "Squeeze my finger," he said, wiggling the tip. "Harder. Squeeze tighter."

"That's as tight as she gets, okay. What are you doing?"

"I thought so. It's okay. Relax. I'm going to teach you what you need to do to please me more. And trust me, you'll get more pleasure than me."

Ciara closed her thighs. "You didn't complain a few minutes ago."

"Don't go gettin' an attitude. You know you got skills. I truly enjoyed you." Regardless, if Ciara was going to keep him satisfied, Ciara had to learn how to work her vaginal muscles like Kimberly. Parting Ciara's legs, Darius inserted his finger deeper.

"Squeeze. No. Just this middle muscle." Darius's long finger pushed deep inside Ciara. "Now, isolate and tighten this top muscle."

"The other ones keep moving too."

"That's okay. Just squeeze as hard as you can from

the bottom to the top. Okay. Push my finger out."
Darius pushed against Ciara's movement. "Push harder."

Pulling his finger out, Darius lay beside Ciara. "When
you're sitting at your desk or in a meeting, squeeze my
pussy. I want you to isolate each muscle as tight as you
can for ten seconds. Do that at least one hundred times
a day, every day. Bottom. One hundred times. Middle
and lower the same."

"Is that all, Mr. Kegel cardio instructor?"

"No. It's not. Then, I want you to squeeze as fast as
you can as many times as you can within twenty seconds. Then, I want you to roll my pussy all the way up.
Push her all the way down. One hundred times. Every
day. Next time we're together, you don't have to move
your waist, I want you to handle this dick with this."
Darius slid his finger inside Ciara then kissed her lips.
"I'm gonna dig in that ass too. So I want you to start
sticking your finger in your ass like you do mine."

"I already do, thank you very much."

"Well, then you should know when you shower use
soap to make that opening slippery and clean yourself
out. You do that. And I'll handle the rest."

"You are crazy if you think I'm letting you put that,"
Ciara pointed to his dick, "in my ass."

"I'll be gentle. And I promise you. It won't hurt as
long as you learn to relax your muscles. I know how to
take it slow around the rectal curves. I'mma prepare
you proper with a day of pampering at the finest spa."
Darius smiled. "Wait and see, you gon' beg me to do
you again. Cause you ain't never had an orgasm like to
one you're going to have when I'm tapping inside that
ass hitting that G-spot from the back. Trust me."

Ciara sighed heavily then said, "So can you convince your mother to drop the lawsuit or not?"

"Talking about business after sex must be like smoking a cigarette to you, woman."

"I've never smoked but I know talking about business any time is better than poisoning my lungs."

"Well, I'm confident I can convince my mom to drop the lawsuit but only if I have a vested interest. Meaning, if you want this deal, be true to your word and make me more than your bed partner. And my mom will have no choice."

"I don't know. At first it sounded like a good idea but your mom can ruin this deal. Let's explore other options to forming a partnership. Like subcontracting."

"Fair exchange is no robbery. I can provide what you need. But if you refuse to partner, then I guess we'll all lose out. I thought you were brighter than that to throw away a multi-million deal. I see I was wrong."

Ciara exhaled. "I'm bright enough to know I should follow my instincts. And my instincts say no partnership. I never should've mentioned it in the first place."

Darius refused to give up. "If it'll make you feel better, your attorney can draw up the contract. My lawyer can review, respond, and finalize. Your company will partner with my company. I control fifty-one percent. You control forty-nine. We both end up rich."

Ciara laughed hysterically. "Okay, that's a deal but only if I control everything. One-hundred percent."

Darius wanted to hear Ciara laugh at his next statement. "Well, let's see. I already know I can convince my mother to drop the lawsuit. If you don't agree fifty-one forty-nine then I can convince desperate-ass Terrell to persuade Candice to give me the entire contract or he'll never be a millionaire. I need your experience and you need my contacts. But realistically you need me more than I need you."

Shifting her eyes to the corners away from Darius, Ciara said, "Let me think about this."

"What's there to think about? Either we have a deal or we don't."

Ciara twirled Darius's lock and said, "Okay, deal. I'm going to trust you on this one."

Like she had a choice. Darius handed Ciara the phone. "I don't like wasting time or money. Call your attorney. Then I'll call my mother. Come next Friday, we gon' sign the contract and to celebrate I'mma tap in that asshole." Darius looked down at Slugger and smiled. "Everybody's gonna be happy."

CHAPTER 11

"**S**o what's up with you spending nights out lately?" Solomon asked Ciara. "You're never home. When I call you at work, you're unavailable."

"I told you, I'm busy working on this contract. Why? Is that a problem? I'm stressed enough, baby. All I need right now is your love and support." Ciara wiped her side of Solomon's double vanity and proceeded to brush her teeth.

"I've got plenty of backed-up love for you," Solomon said standing behind her. His strong naked body pressed against her back and butt. Solomon wrapped his arms around Ciara's waist.

Staring at Solomon through the bathroom mirror, Ciara continued brushing her teeth. Either Solomon looked better or her working until midnight in her office and working Darius overtime in the bedroom was wearing on her appearance. The puffy bags underneath her hazel eyes were beginning to darken. Not that

Solomon or anyone else could notice, but Ciara's hair had recently started shedding.

Ciara removed Solomon's hands from her waist and went into the bedroom. "I need a few more minutes of sleep." She crawled onto Solomon's bed and pulled the cover up to her neck.

"What you need is a few more strokes of this," Solomon said, standing at the side of his bed and holding his dick in Ciara's face.

"Solomon, please. Not now. I'm tired."

Solomon protested. "Too tired to take care of me? Well, don't blame me if I have to find another woman to handle your business."

Ciara tossed the cover aside and said, "It won't be your first time. I can't sleep with you constantly talking. I might as well get dressed and go to work." Ciara selected her coral blue two-piece pantsuit, cream lace crew-neck blouse and caramel-colored low-cut boots from her side of Solomon's closet.

"Maybe we should take a break from each other for a while. You're busy. And I'm tired of trying to make time for you."

Ciara looked up at Solomon. Tired? One week of her not being available and he's tired? "Okay, Solomon. Whatever you want. Call first before you come by my house."

"If that's the way you want it, take all of your things with you." Solomon snatched a handful of Ciara's clothes that were on hangers and flung them onto his bed.

How had their conversation gotten to this point? All Ciara wanted was a few minutes of rest and now Solomon was losing his damn mind. Whatever was bothering Solomon wasn't related to her not wanting to have sex—but Solomon, as usual, acted out instead of talking out his problems. Several of her designer suits slid from the comforter to the floor.

Ciara clenched her tan purse under her armpit and calmly said, "I'll send a mover to box my things and deliver them to my house." As long as Solomon was controlling the relationship, he was happy. Fortunately for Solomon, Ciara didn't have the energy to debate or match his energy level. Normally Ciara's temperature would've exploded. Her words or her actions could easily dehumanize a strong man like Solomon by significantly deflating his self-esteem.

"Don't bother. I'm off today. I'll drop your stuff off tonight."

Tonight? Ciara had plans for Darius to stay the night. "Solomon, I'll call you later. Bye."

Ciara exited the hallway into Solomon's garage and drove away in her SUV. Placing her headset over her ear, Ciara voice dialed her office.

"CMCA," Megan answered on the first ring.

"Hey, Megan. How's everything going?"

Megan, her best office assistant and an aspiring actress, was incredibly efficient. Megan understood the business. She was competitive but not cutthroat like some of Ciara's former staff who'd do underhanded things to get parts—like lie and claim that certain parts were turned down by actors who'd never seen the script.

"Quiet. I was just reading the screenplay for *Soul Mates Dissipate* and I'd like to audition for Candice's role."

"We can discuss that when I get into the office. Has Darius called?"

"Once. To see if he can get on your calendar for a late lunch at two."

"Confirm him at two."

"But you have a one o'clock with First Call, Inc. to renegotiate salaries for Kimberly Stokes and K'Nine beverage commercials."

"See if we can move that meeting up a half hour," Ciara said, exiting off I-5. "If we can, then confirm Darius at two. If not, see if Darius can reschedule for two-thirty. I'm pulling into the garage so the call will probably drop. I'll be up in a minute. Bye."

Ciara parked in one of her five reserved spaces marked CMCA. One space was for Megan and the other three were for her clients and visitors.

Ciara flattened her key card against the security box and entered the office.

Megan looked up. "Everything worked out. Your meeting with First Call is confirmed for twelve-thirty and Mr. Jones is confirmed for two. He said he'll pick you up. And Candice just called."

"Megan, girl you're fast. How are you this morning?"

"Fine. Can you believe my husband called already because the baby was out of diapers? Men. I told him to pack the kids in the car, go to the store and buy some diapers."

Megan was barely twenty-one with a husband and two kids, a baby girl and two-year-old toddler boy who smiled all the time. Megan had asked Ciara to be their godmother but Ciara declined because she wanted her own children and feared she'd become too attached to Megan's kids. And if there were ever any personnel-related issues with Megan, Ciara didn't want to have an emotional commitment that would hinder her from conducting business. But holidays and birthdays, Ciara spoiled Megan's kids with clothes and gift certificates.

Ciara said, "Well, you guys have been together since the ninth grade, seven plus years. So I know you weren't surprised."

"No, you're right." Megan laughed. "Here's your revised schedule."

"Thanks," Ciara said glancing at the card. Holding a different key card against the box outside her office, Ciara unlocked the door. The confidentiality of her files required protection from Megan, janitors, clients, and other staff members. Ciara conducted all meetings in the conference room. Ciara learned from experience that aspiring actors were desperate and would steal clients' files, filmographies, press releases, and especially her contact information.

Ciara closed the door and dialed Candice's number.

"Hey, Ciara. I was waiting by the phone for your call. What's this I hear, you're considering partnering with Darius?"

Okay. Ciara exhaled. The only person that would've told Candice is Mr. Brentwood. "Candice, I have the knowledge we need to make this deal successful and Darius has the contacts."

"Says who? Darius hasn't been in this business four months yet. How can he possibly have the contacts? The only person backing him is Tony."

"That's right. And everyone knows Tony Briscotti is the go-to man for Parapictures and the hottest newest producer in Hollywood. Every film he's produced has grossed at least thirty million the opening weekend."

"Yeah, but every film Tony has produced cost at least twenty million to make and that doesn't include paying top actors like Morris Chestnut and Gabrielle Union."

Okay. Now Mr. Brentwood's loyalty was obviously

to Candice. Ciara had thrown out big-screen names and numbers to get the attorneys thinking about all the possibilities. Based on Ciara's prior conversations with Candice, Candice's knowledge about the industry was limited to watching, not producing, movies.

"I have not signed a partnership agreement with Darius. I'm considering contracting versus partnering with Somebody's Gotta Be on Top. But either way, we need Darius on board to keep Jada in check. She hasn't withdrawn her lawsuit yet."

"She can't sue me."

"Candice, reality check. Your best friend has sued you. I'm collaborating with the attorneys to prepare and present our best defense. But depending on what judge we get, Jada might win this case." Ciara looked at her flashing intercom light and said, "Look, I'm having lunch with Darius. I'll call you back this evening."

"Just don't end up sleeping with the enemy. Darius is not to be trusted. Bye."

"Bye." Ciara hung up and buzzed Megan. "Yes, Megan."

"Your mom called. Monica called. And Mr. Brentwood called."

"Thanks." Ciara dialed her mother's number. The line was busy. Her parents refused to get call waiting. Knowing her mother, she was probably on the phone with Monica. Ciara would get the update on her parents from Monica later. Returning Mr. Brentwood's call could wait until after lunch. If it were important he'd call her back.

Ciara unlocked her file cabinet and retrieved Kimberly's and K'Nine's files. Kimberly was beautiful and could easily earn lots of money modeling if she were taller. Kimberly was five-seven with shoulder-length hair she kept neatly wrapped under wigs, unless she was auditioning. The checks Ciara received for Kimberly clearly weren't enough for Kimberly to drive a new BMW, own a three-bedroom house in Beverly Hills, and not work a nine-to-five job like most aspiring actors. Having K'Nine as a client was like money in the bank because K'Nine never had to audition. Companies pleaded and offered top dollars for K'Nine's endorsement.

Megan buzzed, interrupting Ciara's thoughts. "It's twelve o'clock."

"Thanks. I'm on my way out."

Grabbing her purse and files, Ciara closed her door and hurried to the garage. First Call's office was a short distance but lunchtime traffic left Ciara minutes to spare after parking at a meter halfway down the block. Her short legs moved swiftly, gathering her pants legs into her crotch. Racing inside the elevator, Ciara took a deep breath and straightened her clothes.

The receptionist greeted Ciara as she entered the office, "Hi, Ms. Monroe. Let me escort you to the conference room."

"Thanks, I know where it is. I'll be fine." Ciara entered the meeting exactly at twelve-thirty. "Hello, all." Ciara sat at the round table with three of First Call's staff members. After small talk, they got down to business. "What's your position on our counter-offer for Kimberly?"

"Two thousand additional dollars. That's the maximum we can do for this project."

"K'Nine?"

"The counter offer of five hundred thousand is accepted."

"Okay, increase Kimberly's offer another three thousand and this project is a deal."

"Two thousand five hundred. Final offer."

"Deal." Ciara wasn't going to argue over five hundred dollars when six thousand dollars was the maximum she'd ever negotiated for Kimberly. Ciara glanced at her watch. One-thirty. "Send me the paperwork via messenger today and Kimberly and K'Nine can review their respective contracts tomorrow. Thanks."

Ciara left as quickly as she'd arrived. Rushing through traffic, switching lanes, Ciara saw Darius standing next to his Bentley speaking with . . . was that Kimberly? Parking in the garage, Ciara hurried to the lobby and exited the building. Darius was deeply engaged in conversation with Kimberly.

Ciara politely interrupted their conversation. "Hi, Kimberly. I have some good news for you. Call me tomorrow." Ciara smiled from Kimberly to Darius. "Hi, baby. You ready?"

Kimberly's eyes shifted to Darius.

Darius said, "I'll tell my mom you said hello." Before Darius started the ignition he asked, "So Kimberly is one of your clients?"

"Yes, but she doesn't get many parts. Why? You know her?"

"Not really. Her mom is one of my mom's clients."

"That's strange. I thought Kimberly's mother passed away last year."

"Well, she used to be a client. Anyway I didn't pick you up to discuss Kimberly. You hungry?"

"Yes. And tired."

"Then we'll have a light lunch and I'll order out for dinner tonight. How's that?"

What was Darius's affiliation with Kimberly? "Sounds good," Ciara answered absently. Thoughts of how well

Kimberly and Darius knew one another troubled Ciara's mind.

"You really look tired. Maybe you should get some rest tonight and we can get together this weekend. You got the partnership docs?"

"Actually, I do. Now you know we're already getting resistance from Candice but I believe I can convince Candice that the partnership is best. And I'll take you up on that raincheck."

"That's my girl," Darius said reaching for the package. "I'm going to Oakland this weekend. You wanna go?" His lips stretched into a wider smile. "We can have a private celebration."

"No, thanks. I'd love to go but I need to stay local. I have some unfinished business."

Darius nodded. "With Solomon?"

"Yeah, him too."

CHAPTER 12

Everything went according to plan, so Darius was in a great mood. Ciara was officially his partner. His mother dropped the lawsuit. Wellington reserved Darius's new corner office with a partially obscured view of the Oakland/San Francisco Bay Bridge. And after Ciara declined to travel with him to Oakland, Ashlee flew into Oakland on a last-minute request to accompany Darius to Byron's fundraiser in San Francisco. Suddenly the world wasn't so fucked up to live in after all.

Darius was officially forty-nine-percent owner with Ciara. Ciara's attorney was savvy enough to form a new joint partnership, keeping Ciara Monroe Casting and all of her holdings separate from the new partnership, Monroe, Jones, and Company. That was all right. In time, things would change to his advantage and he'd drop the Monroe—renaming his business, Jones and Company, a subsidiary of Somebody's Gotta Be on Top.

"Ashlee, you look absolutely beautiful." Darius admired the knee-length strapless dress with streams of material flowing around Ashlee's calves. Seeing Ashlee in the foyer of his Oakland Hills home made Darius realize he'd missed her terribly. More than he'd admit.

"Thank you. You look good yourself in your white linen suit." Ashlee fastened one of Darius's buttons, completely covering his chest. "Now, that's better."

"So, when you gon' accept my job offer and take over my finance department? Now that I've expanded, I really need you." Needed. Wanted. Lusted for. All of the above. Darius held Ashlee's fur-collared sweater as she eased her arms into the sleeves. San Francisco, no matter what time of the year, was cold at night so Darius slipped on his cashmere cardigan then tied the belt around his waist.

"Yeah, I've been thinking about that. And I decided if you asked me again, I wouldn't say no."

Ashlee must've missed him the same. "So, is that a yes?" Darius lowered his face to Ashlee's and stared into her eyes.

Ashlee nodded. "Against my dad's advice, that's a yes. But I have to give my job two weeks' notice. I'm ready for a change. To live someplace else. I like Dallas but since my dad moved back, he's always interrogating my dates. Space to grow up and become a real adult would be nice."

Darius picked Ashlee up from her waist, swung her around, and kissed her lips. "I love you! You can live with me. Wow. This is incredible news. Everything is going according to plan."

Ashlee placed her hands on Darius's chest. Gently pushing she said, "Only until I find a place of my own, which will be soon. I love you, too."

Darius escorted Ashlee to the limo, waited for

Ashlee to slide over, then sat beside her. Darius held Ashlee's hand. The drive from Oakland to San Francisco was beautiful. The stars brighter. The moon fuller. Darius was super hyped. And closer to making Ashlee Mrs. Jones. No hyphenated last names for his wife.

"Ashlee, I have something to tell you."

"Why the sudden change in your voice? You sound so serious."

Darius nodded. His mouth curved to the right. "I've partnered with Ciara Monroe."

"Darius, that's wonderful news. Why didn't you tell me sooner?"

"We hadn't really talked since you met dude. You took long enough to fire that Loser. It's June. A lot has happened. It's like I'm getting ready to blow up. Inside I'm jumping up and down on a trampoline doing flips and shit. It's scary. I didn't know if I could pull off being an agent. It's not like I know the business. I'm still learning as I go. But finally, my hard work is paying off and I won't have to live in my parents' shadow. I'll have my own reputation. And I did it by myself."

Ashlee's forehead wrinkled. "By yourself? No, Darius. You're where you are because of your mother and father who loaned you a lot of money which you know they don't expect you to repay. Don't forget they paid for your LA commercial building and they're paying for your San Francisco office."

"That's what parents are supposed to do. But I created my business and insisted they let me run it. Of course you're always by my side and that's why I want you to . . ." Darius became silent.

Ashlee looked at Darius. "Want me to what?"

Darius hesitated. "Share in my success. I'm just

glad you're going to be my money person. I know I can trust you with my bank accounts."

"Yeah, we do make a good team." Ashlee's eyes sparkled when she smiled.

The driver parked in the hotel driveway and opened the door. Proudly Darius extended his arm and waited for Ashlee to loop her arm inside his. Looking at the limo driver, Darius said, "I'll call you when I'm ready. And when I'm ready, I'm ready." Darius proudly escorted Ashlee inside the hotel.

Entering the banquet room, Ashlee nudged Darius's side. "Who's that?" she nodded toward the gentleman standing under the huge crystal chandelier, immaculately dressed in a black pin striped suit, tan shoes, and a tan collarless shirt. His shadow hair-cut complemented a sexy well-trimmed beard.

"Oh, him. That's just Byron."

Ashlee smiled. "He looks good. Is he single? Introduce us."

"My future wife can't date my associate. In fact, I don't want you dating anyone. You want to go out, I take you out."

"Darius, get real. You know how I feel about you. Have you heard anything I said? We've had this conversation. And you know I'm not comfortable with us being a couple. It's simply not right. Besides, I'm not the Miss Goody Two-shoes you think I am. When I'm with you I act more like a sister, not a girlfriend, and sisters don't tell their brothers about their sex life. It's like when it comes to talking with one another, we discuss everything except our intimate relationships. It's like I'm afraid if I tell you about my other lovers, you won't feel the same about me."

Darius partially heard what Ashlee had said. Damn, that woman across the room, whomever she was, was fine. She had a strut, a nice ass, sexy calves, silky thighs, a classic short black dress, shapely breasts. No doubt whoever she was, she definitely spent as much time as Darius working out. Not wanting to make Ashlee jealous, Darius walked by the woman as if he hadn't noticed. Her perfume clung to his senses.

"Hey, Byron man what's up?" Darius gripped hands and bumped shoulders with Byron.

Byron gestured toward the woman Darius had noticed. "No way man. That's you?"

Byron smiled. "Indubitably."

"I heard that." Byron had better watch out. If he messed up, Darius was seriously sampling that.

Darius strolled by Byron's woman to get a closer look. Byron was lying. Byron's women never looked that fine. Byron's females dressed more like Ashlee. Conservative and plain. Fine as hell. Hell, no way in hell was she Byron's lady.

"Hi, I'm Fancy Taylor." She extended her hand. "And you are?"

Darius flashed his sexiest smile. *She's not ready to get caught up,* Darius thought. *Could she handle the challenge?* Darius arrogantly replied, "If you don't know who I am, you'd better ask somebody." She definitely wouldn't forget him. If she did, she'd be the first.

Ashlee stepped between them and shook Fancy's hand, "Don't pay him any attention. He's always this way." Ashlee handed Fancy the check Darius had written earlier, for seventy-five thousand dollars.

While Ashlee became acquainted with Fancy, Darius

took the opportunity to scan the room until he felt a tap on his shoulder.

Ashlee said, "This is Darius Jones and my name is Ashlee Anderson."

Fancy looked at Darius. "Excuse me. Do you have a card?"

Looking down at Fancy, Darius pictured eating her pussy up. She definitely had *freak* written all over her. The way she moved her lips when she spoke. Slow. Deliberate. The way she arched her back and parted her legs when she stood. Shapely thighs. Calves. Perfectly toned biceps. Firm but very ladylike. Damn, one day he was going to sample that pussy. Ashlee frowned at Darius so he replied, "I'm highly visible but hardly accessible. I don't even carry I.D." Darius walked away. Ashlee trailed him.

How'd Byron luck up on a dime like that? Darius had known Byron for years and none of his females came close to Fancy Taylor. He probably bought her something expensive like a car or some shit. The only woman Darius would ever buy big-ticket items for was Ashlee.

"Well, man," Darius patted Byron on the shoulder, "See ya at your crib in a few."

Byron might as well kiss Fancy's pussy good-bye because once she met Slugger, like all the rest, she'd become a jockey, and leave Byron alone. Fancy was obviously a paper chaser. Who cared? Darius wasn't going to marry her. He just wanted to fuck her.

Ashlee interrupted his thoughts. "Let's go."

"Huh? What?" Darius shook his head in protest.

"I'm not feeling up to a party at Byron's. You go. The driver can take me home."

Did Ashlee believe he needed her permission? Relieved Ashlee decided to go back to his place, Darius lied, "I won't stay too late," knowing his words would make Ashlee feel better. At least at that moment.

CHAPTER 13

Darius's tall stature barely cleared the doorway to Ashlee's office. "So, how's it going? Are you settling in yet?" he asked. The start of Ashlee's second week made Darius proud. Ashlee's corner office was on the opposite end of the third floor down the hall from Darius and Angel, between the elevator and the exit door.

"Yeah, it's going well. I don't know how you managed without me. Your finance person spoke as though he knew the software program for your business but he really didn't. At best, all he was doing was inadequately babysitting accounts payable and receivable. No budget projections or spreadsheets. He hadn't even reviewed the employees' charges to the company's credit cards. The employee you fired last year had set up an online monthly recurring payment of twelve hundred dollars to her landlord. Because she returned the American Express card, he said he never canceled her card."

Angel tapped on Ashlee's door and peeped her head

inside. "Excuse me, Mr. Jones. There's a Kevin Williams in the lobby to see you and Ciara is on the phone."

Darius scanned Angel's short red dress that stopped midway at her thighs. "Did you say Kevin was in the lobby?"

"Yes, Sir. The receptionist phoned and said Mr. Williams is downstairs."

"Well, well. Have him come up to my office. Ashlee," Darius winked at her, "Lunch at two. Make us a reservation." Darius briefly considered telling Angel to give Ashlee access to his schedule but women were unpredictable. What if Ashlee invited herself to lunch? Or dinner? Bad idea. Besides, he'd heard Ashlee's confession at Byron's fundraiser about not being a Miss Goody Two-shoes and that was good but Darius would test her conservative limits later.

Darius sat at his desk and picked up the receiver. "Hey, lady. I was going to call you. We're still on for dinner tonight?"

"That's why I'm calling. Can we reschedule? I'm tired."

"Tired? From working in the office? Or from keeping late hours with Solomon? Because you sure haven't spent time with me lately."

"Darius, don't. You know I'm working late hours dealing with K'Nine's contract. And the producer is so pleased with Kimberly's performance that he's offered her a major role in two upcoming music videos."

Darius's lips tightened and curved to the right. "Is that so? Good for her." Why was Kimberly so secretive with him? Darius didn't know her mother had died, or that Kimberly had acting abilities. Maybe that's why she was great at role playing.

"Sounds like you have a vested interested in Ms. Stokes," Ciara remarked.

Darius began reading the mail Angel had placed in his in-box. What did Kevin want? Distant relatives didn't suddenly show up without a hidden agenda.

"Look, I gotta go. Don't forget our meeting tomorrow with Tony. Bye." Darius hung up the phone before Ciara could respond. What was taking Ciara so long to dump this Solomon dude?

"Excuse the interruption Mr. Jones, here are your phone messages." Angel extended her arm across his desk. "Call Tony. Your parents invited you and Ashlee over for dinner tonight. Call Morris. He says it's important. And Kevin is on his way—"

"No introduction necessary, pretty lady. Here I am." Kevin's cologne, which he must have purchased at a convenience store, invaded Darius's office moments before Kevin sat in the chair on the opposite side of the desk.

Darius shook Kevin's hand and patted him on the shoulder. "Hey, man. What's up? What brings you out here twice in one month? Make yourself comfortable." Darius reclined in his leather chair.

"I need to speak with you, brother. I'll get straight to the point. My company laid me off. I need a job. I'm at your mercy, mein."

What Kevin needed was a new wardrobe. Those ridiculously worn crooked sole imitation leather shoes, with his see-through white dress shirt, and flimsy black over-starched slacks with a double crease were pathetic.

"Yeah, man this economy is rough. But you sure you wanna work for me? You know after I hired Darryl, Jr. I had to fire him, man. I take my bizness seriously. And no one, not even family comes before my success. If you can handle that, you've got yourself a job. Provided that you promise to upgrade your wardrobe and work on probation."

Working in public relations, Jada had reared Darius image conscious. If Kevin didn't change his attire, in three days Kevin would find himself in search of another job. That lazy accountant. He was so busy coming in late and leaving early he hadn't done his job. One more bad hire and Darius would contract out for human resource services. He should've hired his Aunt Jazzmyne, Wellington's sister, to handle employee matters but Darius didn't want family having access to his business.

"Man, you ain't said nothing. I'm not Darryl. Our brother is full of get-rich-quick schemes. I know. I lived in the same house with him, remember? I wouldn't hire Darryl my damn self."

Yeah, Darius did remember and didn't want a reminder. Or a repeat.

Leaning back in his swivel chair, Darius clamped his hands across his waist. "So what's the real reason you want to work for me?"

"I just told you, mein. I was fired."

Shaking his head, Darius leaned forward. "Naw, my brother. You said you were laid off."

Kevin hunched his shoulders. "Laid off. Fired. What's the difference? When you're unemployed, it's all the same. But I was laid off."

Darius shook his head, making a mental note to have his human resource director follow up to verify Kevin's reason for termination. Being laid off had better be true or, brother or no brother, Kevin's ass would be unemployed.

Ashlee tapped on the door then cracked it. "Ready when you are. I'll be at my desk."

Darius looked at Kevin. "We're going to lunch. Care to join us?"

"I had another interview scheduled, but if I've got the job then sure 'cause afta flyin' cross country a brotha is hungry. Unless you travelin' first class, they don't feed ya, mein."

Darius leaned down to Kevin's face and stared into his eyes. "Man, I'mma tell you right now, I don't trust nobody." Especially short men with cocky attitudes. Kevin was five-seven.

"Straight up mein, I'm from Harlem. Neither do I."

Darius stood tall. "We'll see. How'd you get here? To my office. You on public or rental wheels?"

Kevin lifted his eyebrows. "I'm not that bad off. I parked out back in your lot next to the Bentley. Is that okay?"

Darius didn't bother answering Kevin's question. "Follow us in your car," Darius ordered, not wanting Kevin to get too comfortable thinking he could return to Darius's office and hang out all afternoon.

When Darius, Ashlee, and Kevin arrived at the restaurant, Darius zigzagged through the crowd holding Ashlee's hand.

"Jones for three," Ashlee said, turning to see if Kevin was close behind them.

The waitress seated them at a table inside with a view of the outdoor patio.

Kevin's eyes roamed the nearby tables, the door, the patio. "This is nice, brotha. I can hang with this lifestyle. So, Ashlee. Brief me on what to expect when I come to work for my big brother."

"I thought you were older than Darius."

"I am. Four years. But Darius is the mein. Running his own company at twenty-one and carrying on. Me, I'm just tryna make it to the top."

Ashlee's eyes shifted to the corners as she watched Darius bite his bottom lip. "HR will brief you thoroughly. Aren't you from Harlem?"

Kevin laughed. "You ask that question like a Harvard grad and shit."

Ashlee watched Darius as his teeth clenched a little harder onto his lip. "I graduated from Spellman."

Kevin continued, "Probably got some fancy titles behind your name too, huh?"

Darius released his lip. His eyes narrowed. "Man, if you're going to work for me you can't speak to my clients saying things like shit."

"Mein, I'm a chameleon. I know how to adapt to my environment." Kevin adjusted his collar.

"Good. For your sake, I hope so." Darius glanced at his Rolex. "I've got about thirty minutes to eat. So what kind of salary are you expecting, my brother?"

"Shit, I wanna have your salary. How much you rakin' in, mein?"

Darius braced his elbow on the table. His head rested on his hand. He bit his lip again.

"Aw'ight. I'm just frontin' mein, relax. I know how to conduct myself." Kevin looked at Ashlee. "How much he paying you?"

Ashlee smiled. "We negotiated a fair salary. Kevin, do you have any kids?"

"That's a lovely necklace. Did you get it from your husband?" Kevin asked Ashlee.

"I'm single. My mother gave this," Ashlee touched the amethyst choker, "to me."

"Nice mom. She look anything like you?"

Darius's voice escalated. "That's enough. Man, you've got to leave."

Kevin nodded, and rubbed his short crew-cut. "Yeah, Dad was right. I think I'll make that second interview. Just in case. You know. Plan B. A brotha don't want to end up homeless like Darryl, Jr. Not even for a day. You know."

"Bye, Kevin."

Laying his menu aside, Kevin said, "Bye Ash. Peace, D." He pushed his chair underneath the table.

Darius exhaled. "Call me tomorrow, man. We'll talk about your working for me."

Ashlee waited until they had eaten to bring up Kevin again. "Why are you being so hard on him? He was just being friendly. Trying to fit in."

"First impressions. I was thinking about the first time I met Kevin. He seemed cool. Maybe I was stunned to have two brothers. Maybe I offered Kevin that job too soon. But I really need a VP and you know New Yorkers can negotiate anything. Kevin could be good for business if I can polish him up." Darius stared at the people at the next table but didn't see them. "Ashlee?"

"Yes."

"Whatever you do, promise me you won't date my brother."

"What exactly do you mean by date?"

"Go out. Have a relationship. Sex. All of the above."

"With all your women, you think that's fair to ask of me?"

"Who cares. Life isn't fair. Don't disobey me. If you cross me, I'll never forgive you."

Ashlee stood, placed her napkin over her plate, and said, "Darius, I am not going to let you control me. Every woman is not going to be passive with you like your mother. I am not responsible for the pain she caused you. No woman is. If you don't trust me, your true friend, then fire me."

Darius refused to respond to Ashlee's statements. Darius placed a hundred-dollar bill on the table, then followed Ashlee out of the restaurant to his car. The drive back to the office was a long silent blur.

CHAPTER 14

Kevin Williams had managed a small commercial janitorial service in Harlem for ten months. Locked into the same dead-end position, he had to have a change before going insane. When would someone recognize and compensate him for his skills and abilities? Over the last seven years Kevin had had thirteen jobs. It wasn't his fault most of the bosses fired him during probation without cause.

Working paycheck-to-paycheck just to live in a modest one-bedroom brownstone apartment off Lenox Avenue was tiring. Fortunately he couldn't afford and didn't have a wife, a steady woman, or any kids, so there was no added baggage. After his father introduced him to Darius, Kevin realized he was going about becoming wealthy the wrong way. The first time Kevin met Darius, Darius was designer dressed from head to toe. The hands on Darius's Rolex watch, which wasn't the Rolex Darius wore when they went to lunch, had so many diamonds Kevin couldn't distinguish the hour from the minute. One thing Kevin did realize: A major lifestyle change was gonna come to Kevin Williams.

Kevin didn't waste money hiring a moving company to ship the used furniture he'd bought from the second-hand store. The loveseats had more holes than Swiss cheese. The wooden coffee table had three matching legs. And since Kevin was accustomed to sleeping on a mattress and box spring placed on the floor, he'd treat himself to new full-sized set for his apartment in Compton. Packing his clothes and a large box of personal items, Kevin sat on the stiff cardboard and dialed his best friend, Lamont.

"Lamont, mein this is it!"

"You out playa?!" Lamont yelled.

"I'm out, mein. This is the break I've been waiting for. Peace."

Lamont said, "Hit me up when you get to the land of milk of honeys. When a nigga gets settled, I'm comin' to visit, mein. Peace."

Kevin hung up and dialed his father. "Hey, old man! What's up!"

"Nothin' much. Just getting ready to drop your sister off at basketball practice," Darryl replied.

"Man, you gon' make one of us a professional baller before you die, huh?"

"What's this I hear Darryl Junior talkin' 'bout you quit your good job to go work for Darius? Is that true?"

"Yup. I'm headed out to LaGuardia airport in a minute."

"You know he fired your brother. What makes you think his pompous arrogant ass won't do the same shit to you?"

Kevin crunched a roach under his black sole then mumbled, "I hope these SOBs don't crawl in my box.

Got enough of them at the apartment in Compton." Raising his voice, Kevin replied, "Dad, you worry too much. I got this on lock. Trust me."

"Well, I'm tellin' you now. Do not call me like Darryl did lookin' for a place to lay your hard head when—not if, but *when* he fires you. Kevin, this is the dumbest thing you've ever done and you know you've done some dumb shit, boy."

"Dad, just chill. And whatever you do, promise me you won't tell anyone I quit my job."

"Why not? Wait a minute, Kevin. What the hell are you up to?"

"Dad, Ashlee is fine."

"Ashlee? Darius's stepsister? The one I met at Jada's mother's funeral two years ago?"

"Yup, that would be the one. That's the future Mrs. Kevin Williams."

"Boy, you sho' nuff learn the hard way. You know you goin' straight to hell when you die."

"You first." Kevin was a lot like his father. Basically a good man, but once Kevin set his mind to doing something—right or wrong—nothing else mattered.

"Daddy, you're going to make me late for practice again and Coach is going to make me do twenty-in-two." Kevin's sister Diamond pleaded in the background. "Daddy, please. Get off the phone."

"I told you the first ten laps up and down the court are mental. The last ten are physical. Stop whining. It'll make you a better athlete." Darryl returned his attention to Kevin. "If Darius weren't such a know-it-all like his rich-ass mama and her filthy rich-ass husband, I could've helped him make it into the NBA."

"Dad, when are you going to admit, being spoiled wasn't why you benched Darius. You benched him because every female at Georgetown and in D.C. wanted to give him a piece of ass. Have his baby. And become the first Mrs. Jones. And you should see him now! Twenty-one. Pushin' a brand new Bentley, running his own business, and sportin' diamond cuff links like it's no big deal—just part of the fit. That's why I'm going to work for him. So I can live the lifestyle of the rich and famous. You're getting old, Pops. It's our turn. We all turned out just like you. Ladies' men. And it's not Jada's fault you blew your bankroll when you were in the pros so now you have to work a nine-to-five like the rest of us."

"Daddy!" Diamond yelled.

"Okay, Diamond, wait a minute. Don't fool yourself, Kevin. You're nothing like Darius. He's tall. You're short. He's smart. You're not. He's rich. You're poor. We'll continue this conversation later."

Whateva, old man. "I'll call you when I get to LA."

"Where're you stayin' when you get there?"

"Same place I stayed the last two trips. My new apartment in Compton. Bye, old man."

Kevin speed dialed Ashlee's number. "Hey, Ash. It's me, Kev. My flight gets in at five. You think you can still pick me up from the airport and let a real man take you out to dinner tonight?" Kevin thumbed through and recounted his entire savings and last paycheck. Two thousand dollars. Kevin smiled. Very soon two Gs would be pocket change.

"Sorry, Kevin. I have to renege. Darius made plans for us tonight. But I'll see you in the office tomorrow morning. Bye."

Ashlee had done him a favor because Kevin didn't need to spend money on Ashlee so soon. Waiting a few weeks would pique Ashlee's interest in Kevin. What he needed was to find the best second-hand store in LA and buy a few suits and a pair of shoes. He'd heard about the garment district having nice suits at a cheap price. After he ended the call, Kevin didn't bother removing the furniture from the apartment, cleaning the place, returning the keys, or paying his court-ordered rent during his stay of eviction.

Since he looked enough like Darius, with the exception of being five-foot-seven instead of six-foot-seven, and minus Darius's dreadlocks, once he was settled into his position at Somebody's Gotta Be on Top, Kevin contemplated stealing Darius's identity. Never again would Kevin hear his dad call him short, dumb, and poor at the same time. Kevin Williams was on his way to the top of everything and everyone—and he was starting with Darius Jones and Little Miss Innocent Ashlee Anderson.

CHAPTER 15

Jada sat behind her desk at Black Diamonds wondering how to stop the film from going into production without jeopardizing her relationship with Darius. Either way, one of their companies would fold. She couldn't afford to invest more money into Darius's company. If her clients discovered she was a freak, they'd fire her. No client wanted representation from a public relations firm with a bad reputation.

Jada buzzed her executive vice president on the intercom. "Zen, have we received any inquiries to do PR for *Soul Mates Dissipate?*"

"Two. Just this morning. I can return the phone calls if you'd like."

"No. Forward the messages to my voicemail. And if you or anyone else receive any more inquiries, notify the staff that I'm the only person authorized to respond."

"I'll take care of that right now," Zen replied. "Is there anything else?"

"Not now. Thanks." Jada disconnected the intercom call.

Jada sat at her desk thinking about Wellington, the voice of reason who still sided with Candice. There was no use calling him again this morning. The one and only person to get the job done and leave her out of the picture was her private investigator, Theo, who'd just arrived on time for their appointment.

"Theo." Jada spread her arms wide and embraced him.

"What's up babydoll?" Theo hugged Jada before closing her office door. "You the finest over-fifty woman in America, you know that? Still drinking that wheatgrass, I betcha."

Jada laughed. "Yes, and lifting weights and working out every day. I work hard to maintain this figure." Jada spun around, then sat behind her desk. "You should join our gym. Go with me. I can add you to my corporate account and take you to my Cardio Strip class."

"No thanks ya, babydoll. I gets my exercise staying on the run for, not from, clients like you. Not to mention da LA minors. Those young thangs are gyrating all the time. Now Theo runs real fast away from them." Theo shook his head. "So what ails ya? You look stressed but not for long. Theo gon' handle whateva your problem is."

Jada exhaled. "Darius."

"I should've known. That boy—"

"No, it's not like that. I'm sure you've heard about this screenplay about my life floating around Hollywood."

Theo's left eyebrow raised high. "Yeaahhh." He shook his head. "Um, um, um."

Jada's eyes stretched wide. "Not you too, Theo. Come on."

"What can I say, babydoll? I'mma man."

"Well, anyway. I want the screenplay to go away. Disappear. And never resurface. Can you find a loophole, keep my name clean, and find Darius a new contract so he won't be pissed? I'm not concerned about Ciara. She's been in this business long enough to land another deal. Can you do that, Theo?" Jada pressed her hands flat and begged, "Theo, please make this screenplay vanish."

Theo sighed heavily. "You know how much money is behind this film? I mean big moneymakers. Wouldn't doubt if the real big boyz had a piece of the action. You know what you're asking?"

"It's my life!" Jada lowered her voice. "Don't I have some say-so in the matter?"

"Theo can't promise he'll deliver on this one, babydoll, but he'll scope out the scene and get back at cha."

"One more thing. I want you to trail Darius, Candice, Ciara, Terrell, and especially Darius's brother Kevin. Darius told me he hired Kevin but I don't care if Kevin was laid off from his job, I can't figure out why Kevin would relocate from Harlem to Los Angeles, over three thousand miles, to work for Darius. Besides, my motherly instincts don't trust that child. Kevin is too much like his father."

"Now, *that* Theo can do. I'll see you soon. And don't lose any sleep over this. Does Wellington know what I'm doing?"

Jada's head tilted upward, eyes widened, and eyebrows lifted.

"All I can say babydoll is be careful what you ask

for. I sure hope you've thought this through and know what you're doing. Peace."

What was the worst that could happen? Jada hadn't given that any thought at all. Jada walked into Zen's office. After Jada had fired Darius from Black Diamonds, and appointed Zen to Darius's position, Zen had increased the company's net proceeds by twenty percent over the last two years.

"Zen, how are the contributions for the multicultural festival coming along?"

Zen smiled. Her beautiful slanted eyes complemented her Asian features. "We've received all financial commitments except Somebody's Gotta Be on Top."

Jada quickly replied, "I'll take care of Darius." Like last year, Darius refused to submit a payment to Zen. Jada would submit his contribution and have Darius cut her a check later. This year he was definitely repaying her ten grand. Kids. Darius always selectively forgot to repay his debt to her.

When Jada returned to her office, Wellington was sitting in her chair.

Jada smiled. Her body tingled with excitement and then tensed with concern. "Honey, what are you doing here?"

"Taking my favorite lady to lunch." Wellington licked his lips and smiled.

Hearing Wellington's reason for showing up unannounced made Jada's heart dance. She smiled lovingly. Kissed his lips. "I love you." Jada grabbed her purse.

"I love you too, ba. Why was Theo leaving your office when I came in?"

Jada concealed her tension and lied, "Oh, he just dropped in to say hello. That's all."

CHAPTER 16

Rat-a-tat-tat. Darius tapped on Ashlee's door. Today was the launch party for his business, Monroe, Jones and Company. To keep the entertainment industry attendance at a minimum, Darius decided—despite Ciara's objection—to host the party at his mansion in the Oakland Hills.

Ashlee's curls dangled over her shoulders, surrounding her face.

"Wow," Darius said. "You always look so beautiful."

"And you, handsome. Now let's go downstairs before the guests arrive. Shouldn't Ciara be here by now?" Ashlee closed the bedroom door behind them.

"She's running a little late."

"Yeah, Kevin too. They must be on the same delayed flight out of LAX."

Darius ignored Ashlee's comment about Kevin. Ashlee was teetering on disobeying his explicit order for her not to date Kevin. If Ashlee should happen to slip up, Darius would fire them both.

Ding-dong.

"Oh, I guess the caterers are here." Ashlee danced down the spiral staircase with Darius. When Darius opened the door, six women dressed in high heels, fishnet stockings, garters, and white tuxedo vests with black pigeon tails said, "Hello" in unison. Smiled in unison.

Ashlee was taken aback. "Do you do everything together?"

Darius certainly hoped so. The night was young and he was horny. Darius's eyebrows lifted several times. "Well come on in, ladies. Ashlee, don't leave. I have something to ask of you. Let's go out back."

Ashlee followed Darius to the outdoor patio. Behind Darius's home was a thick forest of evergreen trees. "I need to have some of these trees removed before Mother Nature or some idiot starts a fire."

"Is that what you wanted to talk about?" Ashlee asked.

Darius smiled, then pinched Ashlee's cheek. "You're cute. You know me better than that. But since I've partnered with Ciara, and she's coming to the party with her mother, father, and sister . . ." Darius paused.

"Yes." Ashlee waited for Darius to continue.

"I need a favor."

"Okay," Ashlee agreed before hearing his request. "Just ask."

"I want you to befriend Ciara."

"What exactly are you asking? And why me?" Ashlee paused. "Darius, how well do you know Ciara?"

"Only through this business deal," Darius kinda lied but not really. "But I need you to meet her parents and her sister Monica too. Find out as much as you can about each of them." Concerned Ashlee might change her feelings toward him if she knew he was dating Ciara, Darius couldn't tell the truth.

"I don't know. This doesn't sound right. Darius, what are you up to?" Ashlee questioned.

"Nothing. It's just that I need to know who I've partnered with. That's all. You know I'm waiting on you to change your mind about marrying me." That was the truth. "I'll make the introductions and you handle it from there. Let's go. People are starting to arrive."

Darius positioned himself in view of the doorway until Ciara arrived an hour later along with her parents, sister, and Kevin. Kevin was laughing and joking as though he was part of the family.

Darius squinted, and his body tensed as he watched Kevin greet Ashlee with a kiss on the cheek.

Kevin smiled. "Ashlee, I want you to meet Mr. and Mrs. Monroe. Of course you've already met Ciara and this is Ciara's lovely sister Monica."

Kevin was overdressed in a rented tuxedo. Patent leather shoes. Had Kevin worn that on the plane? Why did Ashlee tell Kevin she'd met Ciara? When did Ashlee have that conversation with Kevin? What else had Ashlee discussed with Kevin? Darius watched as Ashlee escorted the Monroes to the secluded family room reserved for his VIP guests. Very good.

Darius headed toward one of the waitresses, then he noticed Byron entering the front door escorting the same pretty woman Darius saw at Byron's fundraiser. She was even sexier than before.

"Hey, Byron. Glad you could make it, man." Darius eyed Fancy. "All-star?" Darius looked at Byron and raised one eyebrow.

Byron nodded. "For sho. This is my lady, Fancy Taylor. Fancy, this is Darius Jones."

Darius remembered her name from the first time he'd met Fancy. Well, he really hadn't met her. This was a more formal introduction.

"Look, man," Darius patted Byron on the back, "enjoy yourselves." Darius smiled, winked at Byron, and kissed two of the model waitresses as they passed.

"Um, um, um," Darius murmured, watching Fancy walk away. He peeped into the family room where Ashlee was laughing with Ciara and her family. Darius scanned the family room for Kevin but was relieved to find Kevin wasn't there.

Darius socialized for an hour, then returned to the family room and announced, "Okay, it's time for the toast. I need everyone and my partner in the living room," hoping Ashlee had had sufficient time to obtain pertinent information. Where was Kevin? Darius hadn't seen Kevin since Kevin had introduced Ashlee to the Monroes. Darius decided to wait to introduce his parents to the Monroes after the toast.

Ashlee was the first one out the door. Darius grabbed Ashlee's arm and pulled her aside. "How'd it go?"

Before Ashlee could answer, Ciara walked over and asked Darius, "You don't mind if I spend the night with you tonight, do you?"

Darius stared at Ciara in disbelief. What the hell was Ciara trying to do? Broadcast to her parents, Monica, Kevin—who had mysteriously reappeared—and everyone else in hearing range that they were more than partners? Darius shook his head and replied, "No."

"Thanks, darling." Ciara walked away with her family.

Ashlee frowned. "Darius, you lied to me."

"What? No, I didn't. I told her no. I don't know her like that."

"No, you didn't mind? Or no, she couldn't stay?"

"No, means no. Now let's go."

Women.

CHAPTER 17

Darius refused to allow Ciara and Candice control the most important aspect of his contract. Angel had just handed him the revised contract. After carefully reviewing the entire document, Darius closed his office door and dialed the main number to Parapictures.

"Yes, this is Darius Jones. Owner of Monroe, Jones and Company. I want to set up a meeting with the president of Para-pictures to finalize the details—"

The receptionist interrupted, "Hold, please."

The next voice Darius heard was Tony Briscotti. "Hey, Jones. You were beginning to make me nervous."

Obviously Tony was anxious to get moving on this deal too. "I told you not to worry. Everything is taken care of. The other company is out, and you're in. I had to have my lawyer alter the contract so I need you to execute the revised documents today."

"*Execute.* Jones, you're a powerful man. You use powerful words. And you're a man of your word. I like that. Meet me at Lucy's Spa on Rodeo Drive in one hour."

"I have a meeting scheduled with Ciara and her lawyer this afternoon to make sure the other contract is delayed until tomorrow. By then it'll be too late for them. But I'mma send my Executive VP, Kevin Williams. He can meet you at Lucy's in an hour."

"Yeah, Kevin. I like him. He's good people. Jones, your people are my people. Kevin takes care of business."

Darius's back arched and forehead buckled. "When did you meet Kevin?"

"Yesterday. He said you sent him over to make my acquaintance. And Anderson. She's cute. My brother could use a good woman. She married?"

Tony had seen Ashlee New Year's Eve, and although Ashlee stood by Darius's side the entire time he spoke with Tony, Darius intentionally omitted Ashlee from their conversation. Kevin had overstepped his authority.

Darius replied, "Yes. I mean no, but she's seriously dating someone."

"Too bad. Tell my man Williams I'll see him at three o'clock sharp and don't be late. Bye."

Darius hung up the phone and sat at his desk staring at the family photo. Darius dialed one-two, and said, "Kevin, I need to see you in my office."

Kevin strolled into Darius's office minutes later, smiling. "Hey, brother. What's up?"

"Have a seat. You tell me. When did you meet Tony?" Darius braced his chin in the arch of his hand.

Kevin leaned back in the chair. "Yesterday. Why?"

"We didn't discuss you meeting Tony."

"Mein, I hope a VP don't need permission to meet the clients. I've met all of our clients."

"In less than a month?"

"Hey, the name of your company says it all. If I'm going to work with your partners, I need to put faces with names, man. That's all."

"Well, you need to meet Tony. At Lucy's. At three. Take this contract. Make sure he signs and dates it by each tab."

"Mein, I know how to conduct business. All you have to say is handle this and it's done. We'll be back by five, me and Ashlee."

"Hold up. Not so fast. Don't do that. Unless Ashlee is with me, Ashlee stays here in the office."

"You can't be serious. Ashlee's your money person. She needs to know these jokers . . . I mean clients. In order to cover your ass and your back, you need everybody in the field, D."

"Don't take Ashlee out of this office or any place else again. Ever. Call me D again and you're fired."

"You da boss. I'll be back, playa." Kevin hurriedly disappeared beyond the glass door. Darius was beginning to feel uncomfortable. There was only enough room in his company for one aggressive personality. And Kevin's aggressiveness was borderline ignorance. If he didn't need Kevin to get the contract signed, Darius would've fired him ten minutes ago.

CHAPTER 18

Ciara marched by Angel without speaking, pushing Darius's office door so hard the wooden frame sprang back, almost hitting her. Ciara pushed the door out of her way. Ciara slammed the door just as hard as she'd opened it. The walls rattled. "Darius Jones! What in the hell have you done?"

Darius leaped from his seat, swiftly hanging up the phone. "Are you crazy? Don't you ever bust into my office slamming my door! What the hell is wrong with you?"

"Just answer the damn question! What in the hell have you done?" Ciara placed one hand—filled with folded documents—on her hip, and the other hand on Darius's desk.

"What? What are you talking about?"

"How in the world did this contract," Ciara waved the stack of legal-size pages in front of Darius, "end up on my desk? First thing this morning! This is not what we agreed to do in the meeting yesterday!" Loose white pages flew around Darius, landing on the floor behind him.

"Calm down. Yes, we did agree. Remember when we were in bed and you said that's a good idea?" Hunching his shoulders, Darius softened his voice. "Baby, I took that as a yes."

Lying ass. Ciara knew what she'd said and Darius knew what she meant, but he'd plotted against her. "You know damn well I was talking about ending my relationship with Solomon and us taking our relationship to the next level."

"No, we always discuss business after sex. Remember?" Darius nodded. "But, now that I'm thinking back to our conversation," Darius said, scratching his jaw, "I can see how you confused the two."

Ciara heaved. "Confused my ass! Darius Jones, don't you play games with me! This is serious business! This is *my* business! And you need to explain how in the hell Parapictures got this contract."

"Are you listening? I just told you. Anyway, look. The contract is signed. It's a done deal. If we back out now, Tony will sue us."

"He can't. We have seventy-two hours to rescind."

"No, actually we don't. The way the contract reads, Parapictures has seventy-two hours. But they won't rescind so let's move forward." Darius smiled. "You're working too many hours. You need a vacation. We still on for Vegas next month? I have a surprise for you." Darius walked over to Ciara and hugged her.

Ciara sighed heavily. "Honestly, I had considered changing the contract offer to Parapictures but I wouldn't have made that decision without first consulting you. Parapictures has better industry connections with directors, editors, and writers. Candice did a decent job writing the script but we have to scrap her version. With the revisions, we are definitely changing the names. I believe we can make your mother happy."

"Woman, you're speaking in circles." Darius held on to Ciara's waist. Tilting Ciara's head back, Darius looked into her eyes. "Why are you fighting me on this? If you knew I was right, you should thank your partner for making the best decision instead of almost breaking my door off the hinges."

Ciara whispered, "Sure. We can go to Vegas, if you'd like. I've got a surprise for you too." Surprise? Ciara didn't have one, but it sounded good because she was pissed. How was she going to make Darius respect her position? "But I have to warn you. Don't play games with me when it comes to my business. I'm a fair person. I don't like getting angry. But don't you ever piss me off again. Consider yourself warned."

Ashlee walked in the office. "Oh, I'm sorry. Didn't mean to interrupt."

Darius stepped back, pushing Ciara away. "No. It's okay. What is it?"

Avoiding eye contact with Darius and Ciara, Ashlee flashed a forced smile. "Is everything okay? So are you guys . . . Never mind. Don't answer that."

Ciara said, "Ashlee, how are you? Girl, take it from me, get those few pounds off before they join forces against you. You look good, though." Ciara frowned at Darius. "I have a meeting to go to but we will continue this conversation. Tonight. And don't make any more decisions without my permission. Trust me, you've been forewarned." Ciara walked out of the office, leaving the door open.

Walking to her car, Ciara thought, *young. Impulsive.* Darius needed a woman to slow him down. Make him think before making radical decisions. Ciara knew exactly how to change him.

Cruising in her convertible, Ciara hurried to the restaurant at the Mirage to meet Solomon. Solomon had claimed he was accepting of her ending their relationship, but Ciara didn't trust herself enough to invite Solomon to her house. She'd changed the locks and given Monica a new set of keys. When Ciara entered the hotel, Solomon was waiting in the lobby, dressed in a stylish pewter designer suit she hadn't bought.

"Hey, baby. You looking good," Solomon said, kissing her cheek. "I thought you weren't going to make it."

Ciara was provocatively dressed in a two-piece low V-neck pale yellow pantsuit. The neckline was parted to expose lots of cleavage so Solomon could say goodbye to his twin playmates. "Have you ever known me to stand you up? I was delayed. My business partner."

"What business partner?"

"Darius Jones. We established a new company. Monroe, Jones and Company. To handle my new movie contract."

"So you trust him that well."

Ciara smiled. "Actually, I do." Ciara eyed Solomon's suit from head to toe. "You look good your damn self."

Solomon shook his head toward her breasts and exhaled. "I made reservations."

Trying to take her mind off of Solomon's big black dick, Ciara changed her tone. "That's nice, Solomon," she said, walking toward the restaurant.

"Wrong way. This way," Solomon said.

Ciara stopped and turned to Solomon. "Which way?"

"Room 3206. Penthouse suite."

"You shouldn't have. I told you, Solomon, our relationship is over." Ciara wanted Darius and Solomon. Maybe at the same time.

"Baby, please. I just want to talk with you in private. I don't want everyone in the restaurant listening to our conversation. Please, Ciara. I deserve that much."

"Okay, Solomon. You have exactly one hour. I have some unfinished business to attend to."

"Me too." Solomon pressed thirty-two on the elevator.

When the doors opened, Ciara followed Solomon to the room. She glanced to the right, left, and behind her.

"Are you expecting someone?" Solomon laughed while opening the door.

"Suspecting is more like it," Ciara said, glancing at Solomon's dick.

"I see you haven't lost your sense of humor. He's happy to see you but don't worry. He's under control." Solomon locked the door and kissed Ciara.

Ciara pulled away. "Look, if this is why you invited me here, I've got to go."

"No, look. I'm sorry. I apologize. It's just that I didn't realize how much I love you until you were gone. Took my keys. Stop returning my calls. I miss you, baby."

"Well, Solomon, you should've done better. I was tired of telling you what I wanted. You didn't listen. Or perhaps you didn't hear me. But either way, it's too late."

Ciara wanted to kiss Solomon. She wanted him to hold her in his arms again. She turned away from the bed. Her pussy pulsated for Solomon's mushroom-head to thrust deep inside her. Ciara wanted to unzip Solomon's pants and suck his dick until his cum exploded all over her throbbing titties. Attempting to redirect her focus, Ciara shook her head.

"I ordered lunch for us. Have a seat." Solomon patted the empty space on the loveseat.

"I'll sit over here in the chair," Ciara said, tossing her purse on the bed.

Knock knock. "Room service."

Solomon opened the door. The waiter rolled the cart in. "You can just leave it. Thanks." Solomon scribbled on the bill, handed it back to the waiter, then locked the door.

"Smells good. But I can't have any champagne. It's too early. What else did you order?"

Solomon set Ciara's plate in front her, spread her napkin in her lap, and kissed her lips. Ciara placed the back of her hand against Solomon's forehead and asked, "Are you running a fever?"

Solomon pressed his moist lips against her hand like it was her pussy.

Pulling her hand away, Ciara asked, "Solomon, why couldn't you be more like this when we were together?"

"Stupid, I guess. Thinking you'd never leave me." Solomon set up his plate. He uncovered Ciara's tossed green salad with grilled chicken in peanut sauce and his slab of baby back ribs.

"So, you can't be serious about this guy. You just met him."

"Who said I was seeing anyone? Solomon, I waited three years for you. For what? Nothing. And I'm afraid even if I stay with you, you'll revert to your old ways."

"Give me a chance to prove you wrong. I filed for my divorce."

Ciara whispered, "What?"

"She didn't contest it. Said I beat her to it. Soon I'll be a legally single man."

Ciara whispered again, "What?"

"Baby, losing you woke me up. I want you back in my life. I miss you."

Ciara focused on the meaty rib entering Solomon's mouth. A clean bone slid out. Ciara picked at her baby green lettuce. Why was this happening? Darius was so wonderful. But, she loved Solomon not Darius. Even if Darius had so much more to offer. He was a better business partner. They could talk business for hours and not grow tired. But she loved Solomon. Ciara quietly began to cry.

Knock knock. "Room service."

Ciara looked at Solomon and sniffled. "Not again."

Solomon opened the door. He scribbled on the paper, handed it back to the same waiter, then moved the champagne to the nightstand. Solomon rolled the old tray toward the waiter and the new table in front of Ciara. Solomon's look was warm. Sincere.

"I know how much you love dessert." He smiled.

Solomon uncovered his plate. A large slice of Ciara's favorite chocolate layered doberge cake. Solomon fed Ciara the first piece, then tasted a bite. The only place Ciara knew made doberge cake was Gambino's in New Orleans. She'd mail order for holidays and special occasions. What other things had Solomon realized she liked?

"Um, this cake tastes almost as good as you," Solomon said, helping himself to a second bite.

Then Solomon uncovered Ciara's plate. Ciara frowned. "What's this?"

"Open it."

Ciara unwrapped the envelope and screamed. "Oh, my, gosh! Two open round-trip tickets to anywhere in the world! Oh my gosh! Solomon!"

Ciara kissed Solomon. "Hopefully we can use those. But you don't have to take me. You can take Monica."

Monica? What if Ciara wanted to take Darius? Or Donavon. Solomon couldn't dictate, if she weren't his woman, how she should use his gift.

Knock knock. "Room service."

Solomon opened the door, rolled the old tray toward the waiter and the new table in front of Ciara.

"Solomon, you have truly outdone yourself. What this time?" Ciara asked.

Solomon uncovered his plate. Three huge chocolate-covered strawberries.

"Didn't we just have dessert?" Ciara said.

"Ssshhh." Solomon fed Ciara again. Ciara placed her hand against his forehead as she licked then bit the juicy red-ripe fruit.

Solomon poured two glasses of champagne, then uncovered Ciara's plate. A sparkling marquis-cut diamond solitaire set in platinum mounted the center of the brightest yellow butter cream rose. "Baby, I know I've acted a fool. Foolish. But I never meant to lose you. Ciara Denise Monroe, will you marry me?"

Solomon treated her better in one hour than he had all the years they were together. The first year was fun. New. Solomon took her to plays, concerts, dancing, dinner. The second year, he'd changed. Always busy. Not enough time for many things outside of sex. As their relationship continued, they argued more. Even when they weren't fussing, Ciara was constantly debating in her mind. Leave? Stay? Or keep him until she found someone better?

CHAPTER 19

Darius glanced around his conference table, pleased his organization was finally fully staffed. His nine o'clock meeting began with Angel outlining the morning agenda topics: delegation of responsibility, revised calendar for staff meetings, required attendees for Monroe and Jones meetings, attendees for industry meetings, attendees for celebrity-hosted or -sponsored parties, and office coverage. Observing the professionally dressed LA people hurrying to their destinations, Darius wondered why Ciara hadn't noticed or didn't care that his nightly visits to her house had become weekly.

Angel placed a set of documents before each attendee. "The first agenda item for today's meeting is to discuss delegation of responsibility. Now that Somebody's Gotta Be on Top is fully staffed, Mr. Jones is relinquishing some of his responsibility. Let me reiterate: I said *some* of his responsibility. But *none* of his authority."

"Thank you, Angel." Darius noticed that Kevin followed Angel's tailored black pantsuit, layered underneath with a sheer white blouse, around the room until she sat.

"Finance. Ashlee, I'm increasing your signature limit. Kevin, you'll attend designated meetings in my absence and act in my capacity whenever I'm out of the office; however, you will not sign any legal documents on my behalf. HR will give the remainder of you a memorandum of understanding and revised job descriptions. Your cooperation will facilitate growth by freeing my time to solicit new business, make lucrative deals, and simply to assume the true role of President. If anyone has questions, follow the chain of command. Don't speak to me unless you've discussed your concerns with your department head, HR, and my VP, Kevin. Any questions?" Darius glanced around the table. The room was quiet. "Good."

Angel stopped Darius by the exit door after the meeting was adjourned. "Mr. Jones, you have a call from Darryl."

"Darryl? Which one?"

"Senior."

Concealing his excitement, Darius swiftly entered his office, closed the door, and answered. "What's up?" The last person Darius expected to hear from was Darryl.

"Actually, I called to speak with Kevin. I can't reach him on his phone."

Darius bit his bottom lip. "Man, this is my office. The least you could do is say 'Hello, Son' or something."

"You sure are one ignorant arrogant immature dude. But hey, you can't help it. You got it honestly," Darryl said.

"Man, if that's how you're going to talk to me, don't call my place of business."

"If it's a place of business, why come no one's answering the damn phones. This is serious. Otherwise, you know I wouldn't call you. Is my son Kevin there? Or not?"

"You talk with Kevin every day. And you can't have a decent five-minute conversation with me."

"Even if I am your father, I don't owe you anything. But I will say it was mighty big of you to offer Kevin a top-level position."

"If you can't trust family, who can you trust? He is my brother, right?"

Darryl yelled, "You questioning me, boy! Don't think I didn't catch that."

"If you want to talk to Kevin, you're going to have to call him on his phone."

"I don't have to do—"

Darius hung up the phone, dialed Angel and said, "Decline all calls from Darryl Williams. Junior and senior," then headed into Ashlee's office. Kevin and Ashlee were laughing but stopped when they noticed him enter.

Kevin immediately walked toward the door. "Ashlee, I'll speak with you later. Mr. Jones, you won't be disappointed. I'm going to bring in lots of new clients. The kind you like. Wealthy."

"That's what I like to hear." Kevin had become extremely formal. Too polite. Darius wanted to say, "Relax, brother." Not knowing how drastically Kevin would revert to his old way of speaking, Darius accepted and liked the new Kevin, who was more professional with everyone except Ashlee.

Darius didn't care how serious Darryl's call was, he

refused to give Kevin the message. Darius closed Ashlee's door. "I just got off the phone with Darryl."

"Your dad or your brother?"

Darius's lip curved on one side.

"Oh, okay. Your dad."

"I can't believe he talks to me like I don't fuckin' exist. That shit burns me up. Then he has the audacity to call on my phone. My phone! And ask to speak with Kevin. Can you believe that shit?"

"I'm sure he's hurting too."

Darius's eyebrows drew closer together. "Who's hurting? I'm not hurting behind his deadbeat sorry ass. I'm pissed."

Ashlee calmly said, "I know. So what are you going to do?"

"Fuck him! I told Angel to reject all of his calls. If he wants to call Kevin, he can call Kevin on his cell. Then I hung up in his face." Darius kicked the wall and walked out."

CHAPTER 20

Ashlee accompanied Darius to San Francisco to select furniture for his new office. Any reason to have Ashlee to himself and get her away from Kevin was good. Kevin quickly proved himself valuable to Somebody's Gotta Be on Top, so Darius felt comfortable leaving Kevin in charge of the Los Angeles office for a day.

"I've noticed you're spending more nights away from home or coming in very early in the morning. Are you seeing someone?" Ashlee asked.

"No, just hanging out with the fellas. Trying to sprinkle some fun between working so hard."

Late nights at Kimberly's satisfied Darius's sexual appetite. Since Ciara had recently booked Kimberly for more videos and commercials, Kimberly's day schedule was full. Ciara had gone overboard when she recommended having Kimberly audition for a part in *Soul Mates Dissipate*. If Kimberly started earning six figures from acting, she might get crazy and cut him off from the pussy. Luckily Darius convinced Ciara that having Kimberly audition was a bad idea.

"Oh, I see," Ashlee said.

"Why? You care?"

"Of course, I care. About you. I want to know you're safe. I worry when you don't come home or call before midnight."

So Ashlee wanted him to act like a husband, but she didn't want to get married. "I'll try to call when I'm staying out late," Darius lied to appease Ashlee.

Recently, when Darius wasn't at Kimberly's, Darius had been spending a few more nights at Ciara's house. Eventually Ciara would begin questioning why, after her first month of spending nights and mornings at his house, he was suddenly visiting her. Until Darius's plan to completely take over Ciara's company was implemented, Darius didn't want Ciara to become familiar with his habits or the fact that Ashlee lived with him.

Darius stood alone in front of the skyscraper in downtown San Francisco trying to locate his seventeenth-floor corner office when he felt a light touch to his shoulder.

"Darius, is that you?" a woman asked.

Darius froze. His eyes widened in amazement. She was still beautiful. Ladylike. Dressed well. He wanted to hug her but resisted, knowing her condition. Instead he said, "Hey, Maxine. It's good to see you. You look good."

Maxine's chocolate cheeks rose high when she smiled. "I feel good. Most of the times." She nodded. "I'm married and have two kids."

Darius frowned. "Two kids. Really? That was fast."

Two years hadn't passed since he'd ended their engagement.

"Yes, twins. We adopted."

"Oh, I see. You know, I think about you all the time. Wish I could've changed my ways before ruining your life."

"My life isn't ruined. People live with HIV and other diseases every day. Some are terminal, some not. But life isn't over until you take your last breath. Remember that. I'm fine." Maxine smiled. "Tell your parents I said hello. And take care of yourself."

Darius watched Maxine until her body disappeared into the Montgomery Street crowd. Although Darius had debated changing his promiscuous ways, he really hadn't. But Maxine had taught him something more important than fidelity. She had taught him how to love. She was the first woman he'd loved. She was the only woman he felt vulnerable to. When Maxine slept with Rodney, Darius realized he wouldn't have forgiven her even if she hadn't contracted HIV. His woman had to be faithful regardless of his interactions. It wasn't his fault men were born protectors, providers, and predators, while women were given the innate ability to nurture, serve, and submit. Maxine. Married? With two kids? The brother had to be infected too because what sensible man would marry a woman with a sexually contagious virus?

"Darius, you okay?" Ashlee asked, returning with two caramel-flavored coffees.

Sipping from the tall paper cup, Darius answered, "Yeah, I'm fine. Let's go check out our new office space."

Darius was quiet on the elevator. Seeing Maxine

brought back memories of when they were teenagers walking on the sand past their beachfront homes. Maxine was different from Ashlee. Maxine had that quiet confidence and somehow, even when Maxine didn't speak much, people respected Maxine and valued her opinion. Not that Ashlee wasn't respected, but Ashlee was a little too passive. Darius's staff respected Ashlee because of her position in his company. If they made Ashlee upset, their company reimbursement checks might sit on her desk an extra week or two.

"Darius," Ashlee said, waving her hand in front of his face, "We're here."

When Darius and Ashlee arrived inside the newly renovated office, Jada and Wellington were surveying the space.

"Well, Son, this is it. Our new offices right here in the Financial District."

Darius smiled. "Dad, as always, you done good."

Jada said, "We done good."

Ashlee walked around the empty space. She faced Darius and held his hands. "We can fit about four desks and one private office in this space."

"Two private offices and two desks," Darius replied, releasing Ashlee's hands.

Darius noticed his mother frowned, then cut her eyes toward Wellington, who was also frowning.

"Son, let me speak with you in private for a moment."

"Ashlee, you come with me," Jada said.

Dammit, Ashlee. Of all the times she could've looked at Darius with love, lust, whateva the hell was in her eyes, why now?

Wellington pulled him aside and said, "Son, now I know that look. But I know you're not having sex with your sister? Let me take that back. With you I don't know."

"No, Dad. I'm not." *At least not yet,* Darius thought.

"Then why did Ashlee have that look in her eyes? And you too."

"Not me." Darius hunched his shoulders. "Her. You know how women are. I already answered your question. Besides my mind was someplace else," Darius lied. "I saw Maxine a few minutes ago."

"Oh, okay. That's nice. But I see you don't want to talk about this. But there's something you're not telling me. And as usual, whatever it is will come out eventually."

"Since Ashlee's started working for me, she's like my best friend and confidante. She's become protective of me. That's all."

Wellington patted Darius on the back. "If you say so, Son. If you say so."

CHAPTER 21

This time Ciara didn't wait for Darius to get to his office. Dressed for work, Ciara sped out of her driveway, glad Monica's lights were off, and for the first time in months Ciara drove to Darius's home.

Traffic at seven-thirty in the morning was ridiculously slow. Ciara crept along until I-5 became a parking lot. Ciara tuned her radio to the AM traffic station. "Folks if you can have an alternate route to work, avoid Interstate Five. There's been a major collision involving two trucks. Reportedly there are two casualties. Three survivors are being rushed to the hospital."

Ciara glanced at her ringing cell phone. Megan. The clock on Ciara's dash displayed 8:05. Thirty-five minutes and Ciara had barely moved one mile. Ciara answered, "Yes, Megan."

"Ms. Monroe. Good morning. I called to tell you there's a terrible accident on I-Five. If you haven't left already you may want to take an alternate route."

"Too late for that. It's one big parking lot out here."

"Well, the good news is Kimberly would like to reschedule her nine o'clock appointment for two this afternoon."

"That's fine because with this traffic jam, I was going to have to reschedule her anyway. Thanks, Megan. Bye."

Ciara refused to lose her momentum. Driving in the right emergency lane, Ciara exited off the freeway and drove until she parked in Darius's driveway. Leaving the keys in the ignition, Ciara stood at Darius's door with a raised fist.

Bam! Bam! Bam! There was no answer. Since Darius had delegated his responsibilities, his office hours had decreased significantly. Ciara sensed Darius hadn't left for work. Ciara glanced at her watch. Nine o'clock. Fortunately Kimberly had canceled her morning appointment.

Bam! Bam! Bam!

"Forget this." Ciara turned away took three steps when she heard a squeaking sound.

"Ciara? Is that you? Why are you knocking on our door so hard?" Ashlee stood in the doorway wearing a long lavender silk nightgown and matching robe.

Ciara bypassed Ashlee and entered the house. "Why are you here?"

"I live here. Well, at least until I find a place. But Darius isn't here. I don't know where he is."

The traffic jam was airing on the morning breaking news on Darius's flat wide-screen television. Moving closer to the living area, Ciara mumbled, "That's worse than I thought." Looking back at Ashlee, Ciara said, "Don't lie to me." Ciara stormed into Darius's bedroom and froze.

"Ow, baby mama's cumming," a woman's voice muffled from underneath a pillowcase. The woman's hands pulled Darius's face closer to her pussy, then she rotated her hips. As Ciara watched in disbelief, Darius's face rose from between two chocolate thighs. His mouth looked like he'd been lapping in a bowl of milk.

Wiping his mouth with the sheet, Darius said, "What the hell are you doing coming to my house?"

The woman sighed, "Uhhh," then disappeared into the bathroom.

"That's right. Get your shit and get out." The woman's body was tight. Shapely. Perfect. Ciara rolled her eyes at Darius. Ciara wanted to punch Darius as hard and for as long as she could until her arms felt numb like her heart. How could she have fallen for Darius? Just like with Solomon. The dick. In that moment, Ciara was glad she hadn't ended her relationship with Solomon.

Why did she keep choosing the wrong man? Lord, please! Was there a right man? Anywhere? Most men weren't faithful. Especially rich, young, black, arrogant men like Darius who had women throwing pussy at him all the time.

Darius retrieved his robe from the foot of the bed. "Ciara. You care to tell me what this is all about?"

Ciara was so mad she'd almost forgotten the real reason she was there. Ciara's eyebrows drew closer. No she did not hear the shower running. She looked toward the bathroom, then back at Darius who was now stretched across his solid black cum-stained comforter.

"She'll leave as soon as she gets dressed." Darius propped several pillows behind his head. "I'm waiting."

Darius was luckier than Solomon. Ciara recalled the night she'd seen Solomon out with another woman. Solomon stood on the curb and pretended not to see her sitting at the red light in her Benz. Hell, the top was down and she intentionally blasted the music; how could Solomon have not noticed? Maybe because he was laughing with and hugging the other woman so hard Ciara could hardly breathe. Solomon's mistake was crossing the street in front of Ciara's car. Ciara didn't want to hit them but she definitely scared the shit out of Solomon when she zoomed by so close they fell to the ground. Ciara screamed out, "Laugh at the mutherfucka!" She made Solomon beg for a month before letting him back into her life.

Ciara rolled her eyes again at Darius and sighed. Her personal relationship with Darius was over but she needed clarification on his business decision. "Why did you remove Terrell Morgan from our casting list?"

"It's simple. I had to."

"You had to? Without consulting me! You had to?"

"Ciara, you know nobody in the movie industry thinks highly of Terrell Morgan. Everybody knows and loves Morris. If Terrell had gotten the part, I would've lost money. Besides, my financial backers won't support the film if Terrell has the leading role."

"Your financial backers. This is my damn company! Monroe, Jones and Company! Not Jones, Monroe and Company!"

"Just like before, when you stop yelling, you'll see it my way."

Ciara already knew Darius was right. But she'd given Candice her word that Terrell would have the lead. Ciara was more frustrated because Darius hadn't consulted her on the decision. But if he had, she wouldn't have agreed.

Ciara pointed toward the bathroom. "Who's the bitch in there taking a Hollywood shower?"

"Kimberly Stokes. There. Satisfied?" Darius walked over to embrace Ciara and whispered, "She's auditioning for the lead. That's all."

"Liar! Don't touch me! You bastard! Don't you ever touch me again!"

Darius fell backward. His dick flapped as his body bounced on the bed. "Look, I'll call you from the office. Let's do lunch."

"Unless it's business, don't bother calling me again. Ever! And why is that bitch out there lying for you. Saying you weren't home when she knew you were."

"Ashlee wasn't lying. She didn't know. I came in late. And don't call my sister a bitch."

"Sister? Yeah, right. You're one mentally ill individual." Ciara grabbed the doorknob.

"Ciara, don't slam it," Darius said, hurrying out of bed.

The weight of her anger slammed his bedroom door and created a miniature earthquake throughout his house.

Ciara marched into the living room and stood in front of Ashlee. "Are you—"

The breaking news interrupted Ciara's thoughts. "The two confirmed casualties in this morning's accident were Melvin Stunner of Santa Anna and Solomon Davis of Long Beach."

"What?" Ciara stared at Solomon's picture displayed on the television. "Noooo!" Ciara yelled from the pit of her stomach.

Darius rushed into the living room with Kimberly trailing a short distance behind. Ciara's body collapsed onto Ashlee's lap, then fell to the floor.

CHAPTER 22

Darius had to escape Ciara's depression and was pleased Ashlee had accompanied him on another trip to San Francisco. Ciara had been breaking up with Solomon, so why was she acting like she'd lost the love of her life when Darius was trying to fill her life with love? Or something like that. The new office furniture had arrived earlier than scheduled, giving him a reason to celebrate his upcoming grand opening.

Darius nudged Ashlee. "Let's go hang out in the city."

"No, thanks. I'm tired. I think I'm just going to stay here and relax. Go ahead without me."

Darius sensed Ashlee's feelings for him were dwindling. Maybe having her live with him wasn't a good idea. The late nights. Ciara catching Kimberly in his bed. Fortunately Ciara had blanked out and, with the exception of Solomon's death, didn't remember any of the events, including Terrell losing the leading part. Ashlee had witnessed his other women. She wasn't supposed to experience those situations until after they were married. Darius dabbed on his most expensive cologne and drove to the city.

Darius parked on a hilltop overlooking the Pacific Ocean and walked inside his favorite private club in San Francisco. The hallways were dimly lit, with muscular men in dark suits and sunglasses standing at each of the three doors.

Darius flashed a small gold key and the man in the suit stepped aside. When the door opened, another one opened, then a third double-automatic sliding glass door parted.

"It's on," Darius said, heading straight for the platinum room. When the entrance doors parted, Darius was in paradise. He walked over to the bar and greeted the finest woman in the room. Hopefully she had more going for her than her honeydew-melon breasts, a flat stomach, and an apple-bottom ass. There was no need to offer her a drink because all drinks were included with membership.

Standing in her three feet of space, Darius said, "Hi, I'm Darius Jones."

Sucking on an ice cube, she seductively replied, "I know exactly who you are."

"Well, I'm at a disadvantage."

She exhaled cool air in his ear then whispered, "Call me Desire."

Damn. She had that right. "Are you from this area?"

"Me and my girls," she nodded toward the opposite end of the bar, "we're from London."

With her accent, he'd guessed some part of England. "I'd love to show you the town," Darius offered.

"I don't travel without my girls. They're down for whatever I do." Then she repeated, *"Whatever* I do."

"Cool. Then let me show you and your girls my town."

"Give us a moment to talk it over. Come back in about thirty minutes."

"Peace." Darius decided to see who was in the main lounge. The first person he'd noticed was Fancy. Darius spotted Byron, walked up behind him, and said, "What's up? Where you been?"

"Man, where've you been?" Byron replied.

"Brazil. Okinawa. Amsterdam. Paris. Spain. Trinidad. London," Darius lied to impress Fancy. Darius was looking to get with a new woman. The truth was Darius had grown tired of visiting Ciara. Monica was family. That was her job. And Ciara's parents' responsibility. Darius had two-plus companies to run.

"Speaking of London, man, did you see that?" Darius shook his head then continued, "That all-star, all-pro, first-round draft honey from England in the platinum lounge?"

All the men nodded as Byron shook his head. Fancy frowned then smiled when she noticed Darius watching her.

Darius said, "She's freaky, man. Her girlfriends look okay, but they're willing to tag. I could use some help on this one." Darius's eyebrows shifted upward. As he smiled, all but two of the men left the room.

"Give me a minute," Byron said. "Don't go anywhere. Let me take this call."

"Hurry up, man," Darius said, winking at Fancy while Byron wasn't looking.

"Hello." Byron paused. He nodded and said, "Yeah, okay. I'm on my way."

Byron kissed Fancy and said, "Sorry, baby. I've gotta go." Then he asked Darius, "How long you in town?"

"Until tomorrow. But I'll be here for a minute."

Byron nodded upward which let Darius know not to leave with the ladies until he returned from dropping off Fancy.

Darius re-entered the platinum room to find the fellas smothering the women at the bar. He took a seat and had the waitress send a message to Desire. Darius watched Desire ease from her chair then seductively stroll over to him. She sat so close she was almost in his lap.

Desire whispered, "We're ready."

"I need a few more minutes. One of my boyz had to leave but he'll be back in a minute."

She whispered in his ear, "Desire loses her desire when she has to wait."

Darius stood. Desire winked at her friends. They all rose in unison and followed Darius and Desire to the parking lot. Darius's first choice was to take them to his mansion but damn, Ashlee was there.

Darius made a phone call to K'Nine. Thankfully he was out of town and agreed to let Darius use his place. Lucky Byron had pulled up just as they were driving off so Darius had signaled for Byron to follow him. Darius drove across the Golden Gate Bridge, as the entourage caravanned into Sausalito.

Darius motioned for everyone to enter the huge wrought-iron gate and park in the cobblestone circular driveway. Once inside Darius turned on K'Nine's surround sound to KKSF smooth jazz, then headed upstairs to the master bedroom with Desire.

Desire washed every part of his body, then asked him to watch her masturbate. Desire made love to herself in the shower. Slugger stood straight out when Desire motioned for Darius to join her. Desire gave him the best brain-sucking his dick had had since his first oral orgasm. Then she led him to the bedroom, dripping wet, and licked him dry.

Desire was patient. She took her time. Her tongue traveled from his feet, caressing his toes, to his lips.

"Turn over." Desire's fingernails lightly traveled along his back and onto his cheeks. "Desire wants you to get on your knees."

Darius hoisted his butt in the air.

"Right there, baby. Desire wants you to stay right there. Don't move."

Darius felt Desire's tongue circling the perimeter of his rectum. Then her luscious lips kissed him square on his asshole. Desire circled. Then kissed. Circled. Kissed. Her tongue slowly traveled downward and French kissed the spot between his balls and rectum. While kissing him, Desire stroked his dick. Then she eased his balls—both balls—into her mouth at the same time. She continued stroking. Darius felt his head slip into her mouth. Desire stroked his shaft. Sucked his head. Then the tip of her finger penetrated his ass.

Damn, this freak was a keeper.

Just when Darius was about to cum, Desire stopped and said, "Turn over. Desire wants to ride this big dick, daddy."

When Darius rolled over, Desire squatted, then bounced her booty on top of his dick. Where was the video? Because Ciara had followed the same script.

"Desire wants you to cum, baby. But not until my pussy tells you."

Desire gave him the best dick massage he'd ever had. Her pussy squeezed harder. Then softer. Tighter. Darius opened his eyes. Desire rubbed her clit. "It's showtime daddy. You ready to cum for mama?"

Darius nodded at her beautiful breasts.

Desire's lower vaginal muscles suctioned the cum from his balls. Her middle muscles moved his cum up higher and her upper muscles sucked the cum right out of his dick. She repeated the motion until Darius's balls were drained and his dick was limp.

Desire whispered, "Next round Desire wants you to get on top."

Those were the last words Darius heard before dozing off. When Darius awoke, the next morning, everyone was gone. Including Desire. Had he used a condom? Darius ripped the sheets off of K'Nine's bed. No prophylactic. Darius checked the bedside for an empty wrapper. None. He searched the trash can in the bathroom.

"Fuck!"

CHAPTER 23

Darius wasn't as impressive as Kevin had initially thought. Darius, the spoiled rich kid, didn't know what it was like to fight for anything. His life. His rights. His beliefs. To keep his lunch money in his pocket. Girls. His reputation. Darius's assault on Ashlee's dad had been a punk way to deal with his emotions. From what Ashlee told Kevin, Lawrence could've hit Darius one time and killed Darius instantly. Darius's concept of survival was spelled *m-a-m-a may I have a million dollars to replace the million I just fucked up,* and most of the time Darius didn't respect his mom or any other woman—not even Ashlee, whom he claimed to care for. Kevin wondered about the root of Darius's problems. Darius underappreciated Wellington. And Kevin's conclusive opinion was formed when Darius abandoned Ciara after promising to accompany her to Solomon's funeral. Kevin despised watching Darius prey on Ciara's mental incapacitation and vowed to avenge all of Darius's victims.

What goes around comes around, Kevin thought as he sat in his small office on the second floor. Darius deserved to have someone mutilate his perfect world. With the majority of the staff on the second floor, outside of casual greetings, Kevin restricted his socializing to Darius, Ashlee, and occasionally Angel. Darius had denied Kevin's request to trade offices with Angel. Why did a secretary need a plush private office? Darius was probably fucking Angel. Ashlee wasn't one of Darius's sex objects because she was Darius's stepsister. Otherwise, Kevin was certain Darius would've done Ashlee. Kevin trotted up the staircase through the third-floor fire exit, walked into Ashlee's office, and closed the door.

"So when are you moving out of his house?"

Ashlee stopped reviewing the bills and stared at Kevin. "Why are you questioning me about something like that this early? I told you. When the time is right."

"Well, I guess you'll tell him we're dating," Kevin mimicked Ashlee, "when the time is right."

"Dating? No, we went out on a date. You refused to take me to your place afterward. You said you'd like to date me more. I didn't agree but I didn't disagree."

Kevin sat on the corner of Ashlee's desk and crossed his ankles. "So what? Now you're changing your mind about us. If I didn't know better, I'd say you were fucking him."

Ashlee stood and opened the door. "I have work to do. I don't have time for this conversation right now. Let's discuss this some other time."

"Dinner. Tonight. I'll pick you up from the office at seven."

"I'm working past seven and I'll be tired when I leave here. Let's just wait until the weekend, okay?"

Ashlee poked Kevin's hip. "Move. Please. You're wrinkling my statements."

"Okay. Friday at seven." Kevin walked out.

Darius wasn't slick, putting Ashlee's office on his floor and everyone else's on the first and second floors. Kevin returned to his desk, closed his door, and dialed his dad's number.

"What's up, old man?"

"Livin'. How's the job working out?"

"You ask me that same question every day. It's all good. But the great news is . . . I've started my own company. NyVek."

"Nivac?"

"No." Kevin spelled the name of his company.

"So, what exactly are you doing?" Darryl asked.

"Nothing, yet. Just created the fictitious business name. Opened the bank account. I'm going to wait to register with the state. Don't want these honeys tracking me online you know and seeing my name attached to a business."

"Did Darius help you start this business?"

"Hell, no."

"Does he know you've started this NyVek business?"

"That's not his business. All I need to do for Darius is what he pays me to do. Dad, you need to call him and apologize. Your rejection is killing him." Kevin didn't care if Darryl called Darius. In order to gain control of Somebody's Gotta Be on Top, Kevin needed to have Darius's trust. And helping Darius get to know Darryl was a good way to gain Darius's trust.

Darryl objected. "It'll be a cold day in hell before I do that. I don't apologize to no one for nothing."

"Whateva, old man. I gotta go. I'm getting ready to present this proposal to Darius. I'll call you tomorrow."

Kevin hung up the phone, grabbed two copies of his proposal, and trotted up the back stairway leading into Darius's office. Since Darryl's attitude toward calling Darius was negative, Kevin would attempt to have Darryl call Darius again tomorrow.

Darius pivoted, facing Kevin. "Man, make this your last time coming through my back door."

Right. Kevin had copied a set of keys to Darius's office and around midnight, every night Kevin crept into Darius's office and reviewed his computerized documents and read every piece of correspondence on Darius's desk. Snooping was how Kevin had discovered Darius had started drafting a proposal to take over Ciara's companies.

Kevin sat at Darius's conference table. "Man, join me over here."

Kevin never liked sitting at Darius's desk while Darius was seated behind it. Sitting at the conference table, Kevin felt he was Darius's equal.

"I've been thinking, mein. Since you have all the power, this is the time to strong arm Ciara and gain that extra controlling interest you need. You know. While she's dependent upon you. Here's a draft proposal. It's rough but I'll clean it up by Friday."

"Let me see that." Darius thumbed through the pages. Nodding, Darius said, "You slick dawg. I like this. Yeah, tighten this up. I'm taking Ciara to Las Vegas this weekend. So your timing is perfect."

"You going to be around later today?" Kevin retained both copies. For liability purposes, Kevin's name would not appear on the final contract. Kevin had no interest in Ciara's company.

"Naw, I'm on my way to a meeting with Ciara's attorney, Mr. Brentwood, and Candice. I'll be back in tomorrow." Darius studied Kevin "Don't bother Ashlee. Whatever comes up, see me in the morning."

"Cool. You the boss." Kevin exited through the front door. Kevin paused on the stairway by the door and listened until he heard Darius's heavy footsteps enter the elevator. The old warehouse-style three-story walk-up building Darius had converted into an office was conveniently located near downtown. Kevin stepped into Ashlee's office.

"We have an important meeting today. I need you to cut a check for one hundred thousand dollars payable to NyVek and give it to me by noon."

"It's eleven-thirty. Where's Darius?"

"He just left. I know what time it is. I have to hand deliver the payment. I'll give it to Darius for signature at the meeting."

Ashlee shook her head. "I haven't heard of NyVek."

"They're one of our newest partners. Here's the proposal." Kevin waved the package in front of Ashlee.

"Let me see that," Ashlee said, grasping for the package.

Kevin pulled the nine-by-twelve brown envelope away. "NyVek is on board through the end of production. I have to take this copy with me. I'll make sure you get your copy." *Yeah, of something else,* Kevin thought. "Friday. At seven. Don't forget."

Kevin returned to his office. By the time he'd finish depleting Darius's bank account, Darius would have to file Chapter Eleven. Kevin stopped by Ashlee's desk on the way out, picked up his check, and walked downtown to his bank.

CHAPTER 24

Flight 1279 to Las Vegas was filling up. Darius lounged in his first-class seat next to Ciara. The more time he'd spent listening to Ciara reminisce about Solomon, the less Darius liked her. When Solomon was alive, Ciara had countless reasons for ending their relationship, including her expressed love for Darius. Now that Solomon was dead, Ciara acted as though she had never wanted her relationship with Solomon to end. Women.

Darius reluctantly tolerated Ciara's emotional breakdowns and moments of depression; some were worse than others. Ciara was extremely vulnerable, and Darius had every intention of taking advantage of her weakness. Business, women, and weakness didn't mix, which further supported his belief that a woman would never become President of the United States.

Darius leaned Ciara's head on his shoulder and asked, "You comfortable, baby?"

Wrapping herself in the gray blanket, Ciara trembled. "I am cold. It's not cold on the plane but I'm freezing."

Darius twisted the air vent above Ciara's seat, then tapped the stewardess. "I need another blanket."

"Sure, give me a moment." The flight attendant reached into the overhead compartment and handed a plastic wrapped blanket to Darius.

Darius lifted the armrest, wrapped their bodies together under both blankets, and kissed the nape of Ciara's neck. His hand gripped Ciara's breast. "Feel better?"

"You are so crazy," Ciara chuckled. "Yes, I do feel a little better. Better because you care. Thanks."

"Baby, I know you're still grieving over Solomon but I need to know how you feel about our relationship."

"Oh, no you won't. You're not going to set me up again. Talk personal. Then business. Then act as if I'm the one who misunderstood."

"No, I'm not trying to set you up. I'm trying to see if you love me enough to marry me. This is strictly a pleasure trip. To help you relax. No business. And I am serious about taking our relationship to a higher level. Seeing how Solomon was here one day and gone the next made me realize I didn't want to take you for granted," Darius lied then hugged Ciara tighter.

"Marriage? I think we're growing in the right direction. Lately you've proven that. Like most relationships, we started off pretty rough. Business and personal. But if we can't survive the hardest times, we'll never make it to the best times."

Darius pinched Ciara's nipple. "Speaking of hard. I'll admit, the first time I met you, I was somewhat intimidated. When you stepped into that conference room, you commanded everyone's attention."

"Yeah, everyone except yours."

"Not true. Especially mine." Darius massaged Ciara's neck and shoulders. In order to draw Ciara emotionally close, his hands had to maintain contact with specific parts of her body. Neck and shoulders for relaxation. Breasts and hips for sexual stimulation.

Ciara exhaled. "But you acted as though you didn't notice me."

"Why do you think I borrowed your pen? I knew that cheap-ass pen was fake but I also knew I had to have a way of seeing you again." *To steal away the contract,* Darius thought. And if Ciara continued falling for his bullshit lines, she'd soon lose her business.

"Really? You put that much thought into seeing me again?"

"Really." Darius kissed Ciara's forehead but continued massaging her breasts.

The flight attendant closed the curtain separating first class from coach, nodded then winked at Darius.

"Excuse me," Darius said, leaning Ciara forward. He deepened his voice and spoke to the first-class passengers. "There's a very special woman on this plane. One that I love. Respect. One that makes me happy. Keeps me focused. One that I want to spend the rest of my life with."

Ciara sat up. She turned to take in the view Darius saw. Everyone was quietly watching Darius. Darius knelt. He retrieved a small black box from his pocket. When he opened it, everyone in first class gasped. Darius held the box in front of Ciara. He'd buy Ashlee another ring.

"Darius," Ciara whispered, shaking her head. "No."

"Yes. It's time. Ciara Monroe." Darius forced water to his eyes. "Will you accept the honor of becoming my wife?"

Ciara was silent.

The flight attendant said, "If you don't, I will. Accept the ring and think about it later darling."

"Yes. Yes, I will," Ciara said.

Between the applause, Darius kissed and held Ciara. The attendant gave a glass of champagne to each person, coach and first class, over twenty-one.

"Darius, you are so unpredictable. I had no idea. This ring is beautiful."

As soon as the plane landed, Darius hurried Ciara to the stretch Hummer limo, and instructed the driver to take them to a chapel. "Let's not wait," Darius insisted, "Let's get married today."

Ciara's eyes widened. "You are crazy. I was kidding when I said yes. There's no way I'm getting married on a whim. I'm still grieving over Solomon. Baby, I didn't want to embarrass you."

Darius refused to give in. Rule number four: self-actualization. Make success happen. "Now, baby. Come on. You're the one who said we're good for one another."

"Yeah, but you're too unpredictable. Spontaneous. You act first and think later. I don't like that."

"Precisely. That's why I need you. To help balance me out."

Getting out of the car, Ciara said, "You're serious."

"Yes. I am. I need you in my life. As my business partner. And my wife."

"Okay, I'm going to see if you're serious. I've been married before. Hell, if it doesn't work, we'll get a divorce and I'll get half of everything you own. Have you at least thought about that?"

"Of course. I'm not worried about money dividing us." In her dreams she'd get half.

Darius escorted Ciara inside. "We'd like to get married."

"Sorry, Sir. The minister is performing his last wedding for today. We can schedule you for tomorrow."

"We'll wait. I'll see if he can accommodate us." Darius gestured to Ciara to have a seat.

When the minister entered the lobby, Darius greeted him with five hundred-dollar bills in hand. "We'd like to get married now."

The minister shoved the money in his pocket and said, "Praise God. Well, of course young man. Right this way."

Darius looked at Ciara and extended his hand. "Ready?"

"If you are," Ciara said, walking up to the small altar.

"Since it's just the three of us, my receptionist will be your witness," the minister said, opening his Bible.

Darius and Ciara had no wedding vows to exchange. After a brief ceremony, the minister pronounced them husband and wife. Marrying Ciara was a brilliant idea. If everything went according to plan, Darius would divorce Ciara well before the New Year and long before celebrating their first anniversary.

Ciara asked, "So, where are we going to live?"

"You have enough things to worry about. We can discuss that later. Until we find a home, we'll continue living as we do," Darius said. They returned to the car.

Ciara smiled and sat closer to Darius inside the limousine. "I have an idea. Now that we're husband and wife. So I'm not alone, why don't I move into your house?"

Darius shook his head. "That won't work. Ashlee has to move out, then you can move in." Darius had no intention of letting Ashlee move out and every intention of keeping his marriage to Ciara a secret.

Thinking of secrets . . . Darius had no way of contacting Desire.

"So what now?" Ciara asked, getting out of the limo in front of the Bellagio Hotel and Casino.

"Don't tell anyone in your family about our marriage yet. I want your parents to take part in our formal ceremony. First, we'll announce to your parents and mine our plans to get married. Then we'll have a big wedding. Let's wait until January. That's only a few months away."

Ciara shook her head. "That won't work because you know I tell Monica everything."

"No, especially don't tell Monica. I'm your husband and confidant. Don't betray me."

Ciara rubbed the nape of her neck, silently staring at Darius.

"Stop looking so serious," Darius said, escorting Ciara into the lobby. "Wait right here. I'll be right back. I have to use the restroom."

Darius stood inside the men's restroom and dialed Kevin from his cell phone. As soon as Kevin answered, Darius said, "Go ahead and expedite the takeover papers. Have them ready for the attorney to review Monday morning."

Kevin said, "Solid. You the mein. I gotta run to a meeting with Tony. Call me later."

Darius frowned. "On Saturday? What's the meeting about?"

"Nothing you need to worry about. Enjoy your weekend. I'll talk to you on Monday."

Darius said, "Nothing I—"

Kevin hung up.

Kevin was tripping hard. Darius almost hit the redial button when he heard, "Hi, this is Kimberly. I didn't hear the phone ring. I hope I'm not disturbing you."

Darius signed heavily. "I'm really busy, can I call you—"

Kimberly interrupted, "I just called to ask if you've heard from Ciara because I haven't."

"I don't know Ciara like that. Try calling her on her cell."

"Darius, stop lying. The woman passed out in your house. I know you know her."

"I don't have time for this. Look, I gotta go." Darius hung up on Kimberly, returned to the lobby, and made a mental note to follow up with Tony first thing Monday morning.

CHAPTER 25

Ciara was back at home and thinking about her history with men. The first two marriages were for love. The last two, money. Ciara believed in love. But when love died, the things money could buy, kept Ciara happy. Solomon was gone but there was nothing she could do to bring him back. Dead. Wow. Marrying Darius was her smartest investment. Emotionally. Sexually. Without a prenuptial agreement, Ciara dialed her family law attorney who'd handled her previous divorces. Starting over financially after marriage was foreign to Ciara. With each husband Ciara was smart enough to secretly maintain a separate bank account.

If Darius ever asked for a divorce, he'd pay handsomely. Handsome. Solomon. Ciara still had Solomon's ring. She'd never worn it so Ciara locked the ring in her home safe along with her other rings.

"Yes, this is Ciara Monroe," Ciara said, plugging her headset into her cordless phone. Ciara opened the oven and removed the baked salmon steaks stuffed with dungeness crabmeat and placed the ceramic dish on a cooling rack to avoid overcooking the fish.

"Hi, Ciara. Surprised to hear from you this soon. You're not divorcing Darius already, are you?"

"Don't be funny." Ciara laughed. "I just got married. But I do want to protect my interest. So what did you find out?"

"Well, congratulations. Wish more women would do background research on the guys they marry. At least a credit check. You won't believe how many divorces I handle over bad credit. He didn't know she had a gazillion credit cards all over the limits whose creditors are garnishing her wages. She wished he would've told her about the back child support, alimony, and tax liens. I like you, Ciara. You're smart. Darius is a good catch."

Ciara gasped into the headset. "Oh, no. I hear a *but* coming."

"But, he's not the sole owner of his company. His parents hold sixty-six and two-thirds interest. Darius owns the rest. He does have a living trust worth . . . are you sitting down?"

"Oh, no. Don't keep me in suspense. Tell me."

"Okay, his living trust is worth over sixty million dollars. And that's his portion. His brother Wellington's account is separate."

"Yes!" Ciara tossed a roll in the air then snatched it with one hand. "What I need to know next is how long do I have to stay married to this man before I'm legally entitled to half of his assets. And I'd like a reference to the best private investigator you know so I can track my husband's every move. You know, just in case we go to court, I plan to stay one step ahead of Mr. Jones. I know he didn't marry me for love. Sooner or later he'll reveal his true motive and when he does, I'll have him by the balls. I hate men who undermine me."

Ciara heard the kitchen door open, so she knew Monica was listening.

"Who's undermining my baby sister?" Monica asked, entering and picking a black olive from the opened can.

Ciara's lawyer said, "Wow, you get more savvy with each marriage. Aren't you glad I suggested divorcing Allen to regain your marital status but waiting to resolve division of assets?"

Ciara smiled. "Yes, and thank you."

"Well, if you want a generous portion of Darius's assets, you should have his child, and stay married to him for at least five years to establish grounds for maintaining your lifestyle. And enroll your child in the best preschool and school in town. If he establishes any new businesses, let me know. And I have the best private investigator money can buy. You got a pen?"

"One second," Ciara said, gesturing to Monica. "Take the vegetables off the burner . . . Okay, I'm ready. Go ahead."

"His name is Theo. And his pager number is five-one . . . Theo will never give a new client any other number so don't ask."

Ding-dong.

"I got it," Monica yelled from the living room.

"Thanks. I have to go rescue my guest from Monica. Bye."

Ciara removed her apron and mitten. Tossing them on the counter, she said, "Monica, is that Darius?"

A male voice replied, "No, it's not Darius."

Donavon? Ciara's eyes widened. She hadn't seen

Donavon since he'd gotten married. The sleek black suit, the same designer suit Darius had on earlier, looked real nice against Donavon's light complexion but nicer on Darius's body. "Monica it's okay, you can let him in."

"I don't know why," Monica protested, "when you have company coming any minute."

Donavon bypassed Monica. "It smells good up in here. Looks like my timing is impeccable. I almost forgot how well you cook."

"Your timing is off. I do have someone coming over. You should've called me." Ciara's pussy pulsated. Her body jerked for Donavon's cunnilingus special.

Monica shook her head. "I'm leaving because I do not want to be here when you-know-who arrives."

"Aw, that's no way to treat Donavon. I knew if I called, you'd say no."

"And I'm still saying no, no, and please leave." Ciara wanted Donavon to stay. What was she thinking? Darius was her husband! Things were all wrong. Did she really love Darius if she wanted Donavon to stay?

Donavon hugged Ciara, then grabbed two hands full of ass. "You know you want me."

Darius stood in the doorway frowning. "Um, umm."

Pushing Donavon away, Ciara said, "Donavon, please, leave. Darius, I can explain. It's not what it seems."

"I'm not leaving. I was here first." Donavon sat on the sofa, picked up the remote, and changed to ESPN.

Darius stood near the doorway shaking his head at Ciara. "Either he goes, or I'm leaving. And if I leave, I'm not coming back."

"Donavon, get out!" Ciara yelled, pointing toward the door. *Men.* Now if she'd shown up at Donavon's house unannounced and sat on his sofa ignoring his wife, Donavon would have a fit. What in the hell was wrong with Donavon?

Darius turned off the television and said, "I have to take a piss. Brother, you best be gone when I return."

Ciara waited until she heard Darius close the bathroom door, then said, "Solomon, please. Just go. I'll call you tomorrow."

"Solomon? Did you just call me Solomon?" Donavon questioned.

Ciara shoved Donavon outside and locked the door.

Darius re-entered the living room. He smiled. "Smells good. What did you cook? I'm hungry."

If Darius didn't mention the name *Donavon*, Ciara wouldn't break down again over Solomon. Ciara tried faking her happiness. "How was work?"

"Fine. But I can't stay."

"Again?"

Darius said, "You think you can have some nigga up in here, then have me up in here? You must be crazy."

Ciara stood and said, "Is that what you're thinking? I fucked him?"

"Feeling guilty? Don't. I'm a busy man. I don't have time to babysit my wife. I need you to sign these documents. And I better not see that nigga up in my house ever again or I will burn this place to the ground with you and him in it." Darius ate in silence. He wiped his lips, handed Ciara a pen, turned to the signature page, and said, "Sign here."

"I need to read this first. Leave them and I'll drop them off tomorrow."

"Don't make me waste my time. Just because I'm quiet doesn't mean you don't have some explaining to do. I'm running late. Sign here and I'll have a messenger deliver copies to your office tomorrow."

Ciara hesitated.

Darius yelled, "Sign the damn papers, Ciara!"

Ciara watched Darius as she scribbled her signature. She could hear her father say, *don't sign nothing without reading it at least three times.* Since everything bad came in threes, Ciara figured with Darius being husband number four, he couldn't be too bad. But Ciara hadn't witnessed that part of Darius's personality before. Darius had just better pray Ciara didn't flash on his ass.

CHAPTER 26

The closing on Kevin's first home, a four-bedroom house in Long Beach, was scheduled for eleven o'clock. Kevin had spent almost five thousand dollars on clothes the past weekend. Sean John, Steve Harvey, and Kenneth Cole suits. Shoes, shirts, and coordinating accessories. Soon he'd dress as exquisitely as Darius. Before showering in his one-bedroom Compton apartment, Kevin left the bathroom door open then turned on the hot and cold water. Dark orange water flowed into the tub. Kevin turned on the water in the vanity. The same discolored water flowed from the faucet.

"No use in wasting five minutes waiting for the water to clear," Kevin said, returning to his bedroom. A gray suit, matching shoes, black shirt, and designer tie lay on his queen-sized Yankees comforter, which covered his full-sized bed. Socks and underwear were stuffed into a large cardboard box next to an overstuffed box of T-shirts. The walls were bare. No paintings. No pictures. Roaches scattered as he rumbled for his favorite boxers. Kevin was anxious to move out of the hood. If Darryl hadn't spent his NBA paychecks impressing women, and paid for Kevin's college education, like Jada had done for Darius, maybe Kevin wouldn't have to steal Darius's money.

Kevin's hair had grown long enough for twists. In about six months to a year his hair would completely lock. Kevin had swindled over six hundred thousand dollars from Darius's business account. Initially one million was all Kevin wanted. When advance checks from Parapictures started arriving for Candice, Kevin withheld signing off on payments to Candice and increased payments to NyVek.

Ashlee was smart. But Kevin was smarter. Ashlee secured the blank checks for Somebody's Gotta Be on Top in the safe and locked her door when she left the office, which was always late. Eight, nine, sometimes ten o'clock at night. Lately, any excuse seemed better than Ashlee going to Darius's empty home. By the time Kevin would convince Ashlee to live with him, he'd have a job working elsewhere. The easiest way for Kevin to control his cash flow was to slip into Ashlee's office while she chaired one of her departmental meetings. Kevin photocopied a blank check from Darius's business checkbook, and ordered duplicates—with a higher series of numbers—from one of those advertisements for check orders in his neighbor's Sunday paper.

Kevin stepped into the white chipped porcelain tub and closed the soiled shower curtain. Happily he sang, "I thought I told that we won't stop . . ." until the warm water ran scolding hot. "Shit! I hate this apartment!" Kevin jumped from underneath the shower head and yelled, "How many times have I told you not to flush while I'm taking a shower!" to his neighbor above who'd just flushed her toilet. Kevin knew she heard him through the thin walls. Just like he'd heard her moaning while fucking herself every night with a noisy vibrator. Drying off the remaining suds, Kevin slid the shower curtain aside.

"Seven! It can't be seven already." Kevin raced to the bedroom, dressed, and drove to work, praying his car wouldn't break down on the freeway again. Tomorrow Kevin was picking up his customized Escalade. When Kevin turned on his radio, an author by the name of Gloria Mallette was talking about her book *The Honey Well*. Kevin shook his head. While living in Harlem, he'd witnessed how some mothers sold their daughters' virginity then forced their little girls into prostitution.

"Damn, that screenplay would knock. Shit, I've seen so much, I can co-direct the movie." Kevin stuck his earbud headset into his ear and dialed the number to the studio.

"Caller, you're on."

"Yeah, I have question for Ms. Mallette."

"Go ahead man, she's listening."

"Are you live in the studio?"

"Yes," Gloria casually answered.

"Are you available for dinner? I'd like to discuss a movie option for *The Honey Well*."

The host interrupted, "Man, if you're talkin' real dollars, hold on. Otherwise hang up."

Kevin visualized having his own movie production company. Kevin dreamt of the possibilities of becoming one of Darius's competitors.

"This is Gloria."

"Yeah, Gloria. Thanks for taking my call. I'm serious about the option." Kevin could've pissed in his new suit when she agreed to meet him for dinner. "Okay, I'll meet you at seven."

Parking next to Darius's Bentley, Kevin smiled. Darius was young and dumb to have allowed Kevin to gain control of the San Francisco office too. Kevin arrived in the office two hours before his closing.

Kevin smiled than tapped on Darius's glass window.

"Hey, man. Come in and close the door." Darius motioned for Kevin to sit. "That little plan for Donavon to show up at Ciara's front door worked. She signed the papers."

Kevin knew women weren't complicated. Create chaos. Blame her. While she's feeling guilty, get what you want immediately. Then split still leaving her feeling guilty.

"Good. I told you you can trust me. I'm leaving at ten o'clock. Got a few meetings to attend," Kevin said, straightening his jacket.

Darius frowned. "With who?"

"A possible new client. And an insurance company. With all the new changes, we need more coverage."

Darius nodded. "Good looking out. In fact, I'll join you."

"Naw, mein. That won't be necessary."

"I'm not asking to join you," Darius said, easing on his jacket.

"You da boss. Okay, give me a few minutes. I'll be right back."

Kevin raced to his office. He dialed Darryl's number.

"Hey, old man. I need a favor. Call Darius in three minutes. I need for you to get him away from me so I won't miss my appointment."

"What appointment?"

Kevin ran his hand over his twists. "I'll tell you later, old man. You'll be proud of me."

"You know Angel won't forward my calls to Darius."

"Make her."

"And tell Darius what?"

"I don't know. Make up something. Say you have a friend interested in auditioning for a lead role. Then ask him to hook you up." Kevin hung up when Darius entered the room.

"You ready?" Darius asked.

"Yeah, just a second."

Angel appeared at Kevin's office. "Mr. Jones, you have a call from Darryl."

"I told him . . . send his call through to Kevin."

"I asked if he wanted me to do that. He said no. He needed to speak with you."

Darius looked at Kevin. "I'll be ready in a minute, man."

"Okay, " Kevin said, thumbing through the papers in his in-basket.

As soon as Darius exited the stairway, Kevin raced to the elevator, then to his car. With an hour and thirty minutes to spare, Kevin went to Lucy's spa and relaxed in the sauna, thinking about ways to avoid going to prison for fraud or embezzlement. Maybe buying the house would attract attention from undesirables. The Feds. The IRS. Maybe he should find a nicer apartment and chill until his plan was fully implemented. The thought of living in that apartment one more day, convinced Kevin to take his chances and buy the house.

CHAPTER 27

MONROE, JONES AND COMPANY. The gold-plated sign was prominently displayed outside the solid oak double doors below the inscription CIARA MONROE CASTING AGENCY. Darius swiped his electronic security key card and entered.

"Hello, Mr. Jones," Megan said cheerfully. "Ms. Monroe is waiting for you."

Darius imagined Megan playing Candice in the movie. Megan would do okay. Lisa Raye would be better. "You takin' care of those kids?"

Megan emphatically replied, "No, sir. That's why I have a stay-at-home husband."

Darius nodded upward. Sucker. A real man, even if he were unemployed, wouldn't stay at home babysitting his kids. That was a woman's job.

Ciara hurried to Darius with open arms. "Hi, baby. I missed you."

Good. Maybe Ciara had learned her lesson and stopped cheating on Darius with Donavon. Donavon, after promising he wouldn't, told Ciara that he was paid to show up at her front door unannounced. Darius lied, convincing Ciara that Donavon was bitter and jealous. Regardless, the documents were already signed.

Darius kissed Ciara and lied, "I missed you too." This morning's lovemaking session with Ciara was worth seconds. Short. Sweet. Unforgettable.

"I'm so excited," Ciara said, motioning for Darius to sit. "I finally figured how to keep production moving."

"Really? How?" Darius sat on the edge of Ciara's desk.

"Well, I don't think we should put the movie on hold like you'd mentioned—"

"Correction, the hold idea was my mother's. She doesn't like your changes to the screenplay."

"Keeping it real. Your mother doesn't want to be labeled a woman gone wild, freakazoid, porn star. You name it. But baby. Since we're married, what do you think about us, Ciara Monroe Casting Agency and Somebody's Gotta Be on Top financing the five million–dollar shortfall. That way we won't have to seek out another investor."

That was a possible solution but five million, even two point five, meant Darius had to appeal to his mother for support. That was the best idea Ciara had originated since Darius had partnered with her. But Darius doubted his mother would loan him that much money on short notice. Darius replied, "No, I don't think that's a good idea. Let's see what else we can propose at the meeting."

"We don't have time. We're not prepared to present anything else. Plus, everyone is in the conference room waiting on us."

"Then let's go." Darius straightened his slacks, shirt, and jacket.

Ciara locked her purse inside her safe. "I'm ready. But do you have a better suggestion?"

"Just let me take the lead in the meeting," Darius said, walking ahead of Ciara. Darius sat at the head of the table, Ciara to his right and Tony to his left. Ashlee, Kevin, and Ciara's secretary were present.

"Good, I see everyone is here," Darius acknowledged, scanning the agenda.

"Jones, you're late," Tony said, raising his sleeve and looking at his watch. "I have another meeting to attend. All I need to know is have you figured out a way to make my investment good?"

Darius eyed Ciara, then looked at Tony. "Tony, it's not our fault you exceeded the budget and don't have enough money to continue filming."

"Correction, Jones. I do have the money. I simply refuse to pay for the added cost of making your changes to the screenplay. Since your mother requested the changes, your mother should pay the five million." Tony pointed at his watch. "Time is money, Jones. What are you going to do?"

"Let's meet again in three days. We'll find another investor." Tony was right. His mom should pay. But convincing his mother would take time.

"Jones, do you realize how much money," Tony rubbed his fingers together, "I'm losing daily? I don't have three days to give you. Either you find five mil today, or I tell my crew to break down the sets."

Kevin cleared his throat. "I have a suggestion. I've drafted a proposal along with a phase-in budget on page nine that will allow everyone to prosper." Kevin retrieved the packages from his briefcase and passed five copies to his left for everyone at the table. "If Ciara Monroe Casting Agency contributes two million dollars and Somebody's Gotta Be on Top invests three million dollars we won't require an additional investor. CMCA can phase in five hundred thousand every eight weeks and Somebody's can phase in seven hundred fifty thousand dollars every eight weeks, and we can resume production as early as tomorrow morning. Since production for *The Honey Well* doesn't start for another three months, Somebody's can leverage its portion of the advance against *Soul Mates Dissipate.*"

"Mmmm." Tony kissed his fingertips, smiled, then nodded. "Jones, I like Williams. Whatever you do Jones, keep Williams on your team. That's the smartest idea I've heard yet. You agree?"

Darius felt Ciara staring at him. Darius looked at Tony. "Yeah, in fact, I just discussed a similar proposal with Ciara moments ago but I wanted to explore all options before liquidating any of my corporate assets."

"It takes money to make money, Jones. You're a smart man. I've put my ass on the line for this project. Make it happen. I gotta go. Williams, call me." Grabbing Kevin's package, Tony exited the meeting so fast he practically ran out the door.

Ciara glanced around the table. "Meeting adjourned. Kevin, I'll call you later. Darius, I need to speak with you. In my office."

Who in hell did Ciara think she was talking down to him? Darius followed Ciara into her office and slammed the door. "Don't you ever embarrass me in a meeting! You hear me?"

Ciara opened and closed her hand mimicking a puppet, then muffled, "Just let me take the lead in the meeting." Speaking normally, Ciara continued, "Why didn't you listen to me? You're making me look bad in front of our partners. Partners who don't even know we're married."

Yeah, that's right. They were married. Darius frowned. "Look, it's just that you hadn't thought out the idea. You just came up with the idea a minute ago. I can handle this."

"What you need to handle is Kevin. He's running your damn company and our company. Darius, he had a budget. A budget with projections of our money! A proposal we knew nothing about!"

"Baby, calm down. Listen to me. You're working too hard and I know you're still grieving over Solomon. It's time for you to take a vacation. Let me take care of Kevin."

"Vacation my ass! If you don't handle Kevin, trust me, I will. And you will see the sapphire in Ciara like you've never seen before. I've worked too hard to build my reputation in this industry and I'll be damned if you—" Ciara pointed at Darius. "Kevin—" Ciara pointed toward the conference room. "Or any," her hand whirled in a circle, "or any damn body else will destroy what I've built! Now get the hell out of my office and close my door on your way out!"

Darius walked out of Ciara's office, left the door open, and drove to her home. Fortunately Monica's car was gone. Darius used his key, entered, and went straight to Ciara's private room where she kept her unlocked fireproof safe. What was the point in having a safe and not locking it? Darius searched through her files. Darius discovered Ciara owned joint stock with someone named Allen worth over ten million dollars. T-bills for six million. Real estate worth nine million.

Darius frowned. Restaurants. Casinos. Gas stations. Darius choked. Marriage certificates. One was theirs. The other was foreign. From France? Allen Domengeaux? Was Ciara a bigamist? Darius neatly replaced each paper. When he closed the vault, Monica was standing in front of his face.

"What the hell are you doing going through Ciara's safe?"

Without saying a word, Darius brushed past Monica and left. *Women.* Darius swore they were more trouble than they were worth.

CHAPTER 28

Jada lay awake with her back to Wellington, silently thanking God for her blessings. She thought about her mother. Tears stained her silk pillowcase. *Lord, why did you have to take her from me?* The words to Luther Vandross's *Dance with My Father* played in Jada's mind, bringing forth more tears. Motherless. Fatherless. No aunts, uncles, or first cousins. The only persons Jada really had to love unconditionally were Wellington and no matter how out of control, Darius. Jada quietly prayed. *Mama if you're listening, and I know you are, please speak to Darius. I worry so much about him, Mama. He's so stubborn. Just like Darryl. But Mama he always listened to you and only you.* Jada buried her face in the pillow. The wetness stained the burgundy cloth.

"You okay, ba?" Wellington asked, rubbing her back.

"I'm fine. I was just thinking I'm so lucky to have you as my husband. I love you. I appreciate you," Jada said, rolling over to gaze into Wellington's eyes.

"I love you too, ba. With all my heart. Always." Wellington kissed her moist eyelids.

Jada braced herself on her elbow. "Wellington, do you think Darius and Ashlee are having sex?"

"It's hard to tell. But even if they're not, they're thinking about it. And that's not good."

"So should we confront Darius?"

"No, he's grown and so is Ashlee."

"But you just said it wasn't right."

"Ba, it's not."

"I disagree." Jada exhaled. "I think we should talk to both of them. Together."

"Let's not do any more talking. Leave them alone." Wellington kissed Jada on her breasts.

"See, now you're being bad. Simone said she was dropping little Wellington off in an hour, remember?"

Jada had been relieved when Wellington dropped his lawsuit for full custody of his four-year-old-son. When Jada married Wellington, Simone stopped allowing Wellington to see his son. Each time Wellington filed for custody, Simone would generously grant Wellington visitation. Every weekend. Chasing a kid around the house, planning her weekends, every weekend, around a child's schedule was a major inconvenience for Jada.

Wellington would play with his son for a couple of hours, then return home before dinner. Jada didn't mind that he was gone. She had a problem with catering to little Wellington for hours, and listening to the child repeat Wellington's last words before Wellington walked out the door. "Daddy be back." Jada was happier now that they only had Wellington's son every other weekend.

"You know how much strokin' I can do in an hour," Wellington said, spreading Jada's thighs.

Jada closed her legs in protest. "We don't have time."

"You know you want it. Don't act like you don't. You gon' mess around and miss out on your foreplay 'cause I'm gon' get mine."

Jada opened her legs wide. Wellington kissed her clit. His tongue danced in circles. "That's feels nice. Stay right there for a moment," Jada said, holding his head. Her juices trickled. Jada inhaled deeply and held her breath for five seconds, then exhaled through her mouth. Again. Again. Each time she exhaled more juices flowed.

Wellington braced himself on his knees, pushed Jada's knees to her shoulders, and slipped the head of his penis inside. Then the shaft. Lightly he stroked while massaging Jada's moist clit in circular motions with his fingers. The Ruler penetrated, generating small orgasms inside and outside Jada's pussy. He stroked softly almost all the way in but not quite. His other hand squeezed her nipple. Harder. Harder. All three rhythms were in motion.

Jada screamed with pleasure. "Let me get on top."

"You know you don't know how to get off of this dick once you're on top."

"I promise baby. Please. Just a few minutes. That's all."

"A few minutes?"

"Yes, I promise. Wellington, lay down for me."

Wellington smiled then stretched on his back. Jada mounted him.

"Don't hurt me, ba."

Jada positioned Wellington's dick at her opening and eased down. Up and down. Her hips rotated in a circular motion. Slowly Jada teased her deep spot and ground her pelvis deeper into Wellington's each time her hips rolled forward.

"Ms. Good Pussy. Could you squeeze a little harder please?" Wellington said, holding Jada's hips.

"Like that?"

Wellington shivered. "Aw, yes."

"How about that?" Jada tightened her muscles again.

"Yes, yes," Wellington moaned. "Ms. Good Pussy. Could you make your booty clap for daddy? And squeeze just a wee bit harder."

Jada bounced and tightened her vaginal muscles at the same time.

"Oh, shit. Ba, I'm about to cum."

"Well, cum on. Don't keep mama waitin'." Jada rolled her pelvis forward then folded her waist backward. Again. Again.

"Aw yes. Yes," Wellington moaned.

"See, I told you I'd only be a few minutes." Jada eased off of Wellington and lay beside him.

"Ms. Good Pussy, your pussy sure is good. You can ride this dick anytime. I mean anytime. I'll even put my mama on mute," Wellington said. His limp body didn't move.

Funny how one word had changed Jada's mood. Mama. Jada didn't want to think about her mama, at the moment. "You'd better get up and shower. You've got ten minutes. You know how punctual Simone is. She's probably sitting outside in her car watching the clock."

Jada followed Wellington into the dual shower. His

nine shower heads were on one side and her nine were on the other.

"Ba, when was the last time we took a vacation together?" Wellington asked.

"Last year sometime."

"When last year?" Wellington asked, rubbing soap on Jada's breasts.

"Valentine's Day I think." Jada placed Wellington's hand on his chest. "Or maybe it was Easter. I'm not sure."

"We've been working so hard we haven't taken time to get away." Wellington slid his fingers between Jada's thighs.

"I'll plan a trip for us soon, if you hurry and take your shower. You know that woman is outside. How about New Year's week in Paris?" Jada asked.

"It's a good thing you can't have any more children," Wellington said stroking himself.

"You got that right," Jada said. "Speaking of kids, the doorbell is ringing, he's here." To avoid saying *our son* to Wellington, Jada found other ways not to claim little Wellington as hers. She didn't want to confuse the child with acknowledging several sets of parents. Simone seemed happier since her recent engagement which meant that soon, Wellington would have to deal with another man spending more time with his son than him. Jada would support anything Wellington wanted, except full custody. No way. Jada was through with raising kids.

Wellington quickly dressed, closed the bedroom door, and went to let Simone and little Wellington in. Jada cracked the door and eavesdropped until her cell phone rang, distracting her.

Locking the door, Jada whispered, "Hi, Theo."

"Hey, babydoll. Got some bad news for you. Theo will make it quick. Got things to do. Ciara was cleared of involuntary vehicular manslaughter of one of her ex-boyfriends eight years ago in between her marriages. Rumor has it, the accident wasn't her fault."

"What? Theo, you can't be serious!"

"Wish I weren't, babydoll. The records are sealed. But Theo will find out the details."

"Vehicular manslaughter? Ciara is a murderer? Oh, my God. I've got to get her away from Darius." Jada lowered the phone away from her ear when she thought she'd heard little hands twisting the locked knob.

"Ms. Diamond. Can I come in?" The twisting continued throughout little Wellington's words. "Please."

"Just a minute baby. I'm getting dressed. Where's your daddy?" Jada sat on the edge of their unmade bed staring at the wall. She whispered into the receiver, "Ciara is a murderer." How would Jada tell Wellington? Darius?

"Babydoll, Theo's got to run. I'll be in touch. Peace." Theo was gone.

Why had Ciara killed someone? Why was Ciara chasing Darius? The thought of losing Darius resurfaced. Jada cried, "Lord, please don't let anything happen to my baby."

The dial tone interrupted Jada's thoughts. Then she heard the knob twisting again. "Ms. Diamond, you dressed yet? I wanna show you my new Leap Frog. I can read, Ms. Diamond. Please let me in."

Where was Wellington? Jada slipped into her sweats and unlocked the door.

CHAPTER 29

Ciara accepted Darius's advice and vacationed for a week, in Paris, with Allen. Elated their property settlement was finally official, Ciara had settled for a third instead of half of their assets. She agreed to let Allen have their home in Paris. The remaining properties around the world were hers, which meant Allen got a larger percentage of the stocks. Ciara owned the restaurants. Allen owned the gas stations. In three to five years, Ciara's attorney advised, Ciara could lose more than she'd gain as Darius's wife. Soon she'd divorce Darius. But not before wreaking havoc on Darius's womanizing playboy lifestyle.

Darius was smooth. But he wasn't slick. And if he weren't careful, he'd end up a statistic. Just like Gary. Poor Gary. Ciara had warned him to leave her alone. Stop harassing her. But no, Gary was stupid enough to tell Ciara if he couldn't have her, no one would. That was shortly before Gary's last trip down the back roads of South America. Rio. Ciara had no remorse. Committing manslaughter was like dating Gary, an accident. Ciara didn't mean to kill Gary, she wanted to frighten him into leaving her alone, but Gary died instantly.

Ciara decided she had enough money of her own not to continue playing charades with Darius Jones. She wasn't desperate, blind, or ignorant. Now that Ciara was back at home, she faced the facts. Ciara knew Darius was fucking Ashlee. To complicate matters for Darius, Ashlee had to find someplace else to live because Ciara was surprisingly moving into Darius's house. The phone interrupted Ciara's thoughts.

"Yes, what time will the delivery persons get here?" Ciara paused. "Between one and five. Okay, thanks."

Monica sat on the sofa watching Ciara. "Sis, I think you're losing it. Why are you buying a house full of new furniture and having it delivered to Darius's address?"

"Because I'm his wife. That's why."

Monica's eyes bucked, neck stretched, head turned, all at once. "His what! I dared you to date, not *marry* him. You didn't mention anything about marriage."

"Well, after I finalized my divorce with Allen, I married Darius. When we went to Las Vegas, I thought, why not? He's my business partner. At least this way I have easier access to the files."

"Ciara, you can't be serious! Please tell me this is a joke."

Ciara's vision blurred into the television until she no longer saw or heard the morning news.

"I thought the two of you were just dating. Since when did you start keeping secrets from me? Monica," Monica's hand rested flat above her breasts. "Your sister."

"I'm not. I just hadn't told you. Yet. The marriage was so impromptu it didn't seem real to me. I guess having money has made me do dumb things."

"Impromptu my ass. Men don't just all of a sudden decide to get married, Ciara. Darius has a motive. And why the furniture?" Monica asked.

"I'm tired of him having full access to my home and office but maintaining his privacy at his home and office. Especially after you caught him snooping in my safe. So I'm moving in with him. Today. So I can go through all of his shit while he's busy traveling out of town with Ashlee."

"Okay, this is too much. Let's rethink this."

"There's nothing to rethink or think about. Oh, yeah. Just so you'll know. I settled for a third of the assets with Allen. That equates to approximately ten million dollars."

"One third? Ciara, you deserved half. Allen barely had a pot to piss in when you married him. You worked hard to support Allen's dreams."

"Sis, I know you love me. But let's face it. Allen worked harder. Plus, I just wanted out and another few million dollars wasn't worth hanging in there for. Allen wanted to make sure he had more than me. And that's okay. It's only money. I can't take it with me."

Monica frowned. "Sis, I don't know who you are anymore. I'm serious."

"I'm your baby sister. And I'm still the same person." Ciara raced to the ringing handset she'd left on the mantel. "You'll be there within the hour. Good. I'll be waiting."

Ciara looked at Monica. "Wanna go?"

Shaking her head, Monica sighed heavily. "I think I'll pass on this adventure. I have my own issues."

"What issues? Sis, I'm sorry. I've been so caught up. Tell me." Ciara sat on the edge of the sofa next to Monica.

"Nothing that can't wait." Monica nudged Ciara. "Go. We'll talk later."

Ciara hugged Monica and handed her the remote. "I'll be back. We can talk tonight. I'll pick up dinner."

Ciara drove to Darius's house and waited in his driveway for the movers. Policing Darius's bedroom window for any kind of movement, Ciara thought: *What if Darius was fucking Ashlee? Or Kimberly? Or whomever?* Forget waiting. Ciara rang the doorbell repeatedly.

Ashlee answered. "Hi, Ciara. Darius isn't here. He's working."

"What you need to do is stop lying for Darius. I know he stayed out all night." Ciara bypassed Ashlee. "I'll wait for him." Ciara stretched her legs across the sofa so Ashlee would have to sit elsewhere. Ashlee chose the white leather chair. "Ashlee, what's really going on between you and Darius?"

"Nothing. I was wondering the same about you. He's my brother."

"Your brother?"

"Well, kind of. My dad was married to his mom for ten years."

Ciara thought about all the questions Ashlee had asked of her at the grand opening in Oakland. And how when Darius had said Ashlee was his sister, Ciara didn't believe him. Ciara walked to the front door when she heard a loud humming engine stop and a gush of air release from the truck's brakes. The delivery persons lifted the rear white metal door.

Ciara yelled, "Cancel my order!"

"Miss, we can't just cancel your order."

Ciara reached for the clipboard and signed the invoice. "Then leave everything in the driveway."

On her way home, Ciara picked up two orders of gumbo from M&Ms restaurant.

Monica was lounging, practically in the same position, snacking on grapes. "That was quick."

"I changed my mind. You're right. The last thing I need to do is move in with Darius. I'd probably end up shooting him. With a baby on the way, I have a lot more important things to do."

Monica shook her head then whispered, "A baby?"

Ciara set the dining table and waited for Monica to join her. "Enough about me. Tell me, what's your issues?"

Monica hesitated. White rice soaked in filé dripped from the spoon, splashing into the large brown soup bowl. "I was tired of not having a relationship. So I've been seeing someone. You've been so busy you haven't noticed. And, well, I want you to meet her."

Ciara snapped her crab leg in two and frowned. *Her?* Did Monica say, *her? Her* like a friend, or *her* like a lover? Ciara thought she was prepared to deal with Monica's issue but she wasn't. They'd both detoured from what their mother had taught them. Ciara had to stop Monica from dooming herself to hell. Ciara did not, could not, and would not respond.

"It's not what you think," Monica said, stirring her spoon. "She's my new friend. Mama raised us so close that, when you became consumed, obsessed, whatever with Darius, I had no one to listen to me. And I realized I had no one who needed me to listen. We're too close."

Layers of salty tears shielded Ciara's vision. Her

chest grew tighter with every heartbeat. "Monica, how can you say that? You know that's not true."

Monica stopped stirring her food. "How long we gon' keep holding secrets? Why don't we, the two of us together, tell Mama and Daddy what happened?"

Ciara stared at Monica. "No. You promised, we wouldn't tell. I'm not going to do it."

"See, that's what I mean. We're too close." Monica reached into the Prada purse Ciara had given her. "Here's your house keys. If I come over, I'll call first."

CHAPTER 30

The time had come to talk divorce. Darius had gotten all he envisioned and more from Ciara. Access to her business. Great sex. Ciara's tight pussy now snapped to his rhythmic strokes. Darius introduced Ciara to what had become one of his favorite treats. Anal sex. And more. The movie was in production. Going well. Seventy-five percent complete. Kevin brought in new business so frequently, Darius couldn't fire him. If Darius stayed incarcerated in phony matrimony, eventually he'd lose more than Ciara.

Raindrops tapped on his bedroom window. Darius closed the blinds, showered, then knocked on Ashlee's door.

"Ashlee, you awake?"

"I am now. Come in." Ashlee snuggled under the covers, looked up at Darius and said, "What's wrong? You look rather down."

Darius cracked a half smile. "Nothing that time won't resolve. You wanna go to brunch this morning?"

"No, thanks. I have plans. Actually, I've been meaning to talk to you. I'm moving out next weekend."

Darius frowned. His lungs deflated and his mouth hung open. "Moving out? Why? Where?"

"I think it's time. Besides, you need your space. I have no right to be jealous but sometimes I am. Sometimes I even get upset. Like the time Kimberly was here and Ciara barged in then passed out. That was too much. Listening to you talk on the phone about the women in your life is one thing. Living with you and seeing so many different ones pass through your revolving bedroom door, brother or no brother, is wrong. It's horrible how you treat women. You can't possibly love all of them. And there's no way you can possibly love me."

"Ashlee, you're wrong. You're the only one I trust. Can depend on. You're my friend. And I do love you. Very much. Stay. I'll stop having women over." *Who in the hell spoke those words?* Darius scratched his thigh. "You don't have to answer me now. Just think about it. I seriously want you to stay."

"I don't think I can change my mind. If I stay, I won't be happy." Ashlee lay back on the pillow.

Darius heard Ashlee say, "don't think I can change my mind." That was a good sign Ashlee probably wouldn't leave him. "I do love you, Ashlee." Darius tickled Ashlee's sides. Ashlee pushed his hands away. "I'll be in my weight room. If you want to talk some more, come see me."

Darius watched the sparkle in Ashlee's eyes gradually fade. He had no one to blame but himself. Darius should've bought Ashlee her own home like he'd done for Kimberly.

Darius went into his weight room. Time spent traveling to and from a gym was wasted minutes he could invest in lifting. Darius stacked three fifty-pound plates on each side of the bar. He slid the metal locks on each side of the bar to secure the weights.

"Uuuuhhh," Darius grunted, hoisting three hundred pounds high above his chest. "Uuh." One. "Uuh." Two. Each time he pushed the weights upward he exhaled. "Uuh." Three. Darius did eight reps. The last two Darius pushed, exerting all his strength. He stood and stretched his arms, then loaded the dumbbells for his biceps curls.

Resting his elbow inside his thigh close to his knee, Darius slowly curled his arm toward his chest. Gradually he released, concentrating on his targeted muscle. He repeated ten reps then switched arms. The mirrors which covered every wall allowed Darius to admire himself.

Darius thought about Darryl, then curled his arm tighter, releasing his frustrations. His teeth clenched. Eyes narrowed. "Fuck him. That sorry-ass bastard. One day I might whup his sorry ass just for the hell of it." *Who was really the bastard?* Darius thought.

Ashlee entered, interrupting his thoughts. "Darius, Ciara is on the phone. She said it's important that she speaks with you right now." Ashlee handed Darius the cordless.

Darius answered the phone, "I'm busy. Let me call you back." Darius hung up, then tossed the phone to the floor.

The phone rang. "Don't answer that. I call her back when I'm done." Darius turned off the ringer. "Come here. Let me teach you how to work on your upper body."

Ashlee's eyes roamed Darius's naked chest. "No, thanks. I have to get dressed. Maybe next time."

"It'll only take a minute," Darius lied, coaxing Ashlee to the Nautilus workout area.

Ashlee's cinnamon-colored silk gown clung to her curves, defining the split in her cheeks. Her hair smelled fresh. Rosy. Darius stood close behind Ashlee, raising her arms to the bar.

"Hold on. Grab each side. And when I tell you to pull down, pull slow."

"Okay," Ashlee responded, standing still.

"Now," Darius said, guiding Ashlee's arms with his, "pull slowly. Pace yourself with my movement. This will tone your triceps."

"This is light weight."

"It's okay. You need to start off learning proper form. Next time we can add weight." Darius stepped closer. This time when Ashlee's arms lowered, he brushed against her breasts. He watched her nipples harden in the mirror. "Take a deep breath and relax. You're doing good. Just keep your arms still and bend your elbows." Darius intentionally grazed again, this time touching Ashlee's nipples.

Ashlee remained silent. She inhaled deeply. When the bar retracted in place above her head, Ashlee held on. "This is a really good stretch."

Darius cupped her breasts. His lips pressed gently against her neck. "I want to make love to you, Ashlee."

Ashlee remained silent. Her fingers loosened but didn't release the bar. Her hips curved backward into Darius's thighs as Darius pressed his erection into Ashlee's back.

"You won't regret it," Darius whispered. "I promise." One finger at a time, he uncurled Ashlee's fingers from the bar. He interlocked her fingers into his then lowered her hands to the perspiration arch in her gown above her thighs. Darius pressed gently until he saw the imprint of

Ashlee's pubic hairs. Several strands threaded through her gown.

Watching their reflection, Darius lowered Ashlee's left strap, exposing part of her breast. Then he slid the right spaghetti string below her bicep. Cinnamon silk trickled to the floor, encircling Ashlee's feet. Perfect breasts. Flawless smooth skin. Bushy but neat pubic hairs. Darius kissed Ashlee's shoulders. He licked his lips and kissed down her spine to her cheeks. His thumbs settled in the crevice between her outer lips and thighs.

Darius's tongue glided down, but didn't penetrate the space between Ashlee's butt. One thumb rotated on her clit while the other entered her vagina. Ashlee parted her legs. Darius stood.

"Come over here. Stand up on the bench and hold on to this bar."

Ashlee quietly followed his instructions.

Darius parted her thighs. He squatted, lowered his lips to hers, and slowly licked her clitoris. Repeatedly Darius licked. Then sucked. "Relax. Hold on. I got cha," he whispered before inserting his index and middle fingers into Ashlee's vagina. His fingers curled forward, teasing her G-spot.

"Ahhh," Ashlee moaned her first sounds.

Darius flicked his tongue. While massaging her G-spot, he siphoned the juices flowing from Ashlee's clit until her hips swerved in motion with his lips and fingers.

"Oh, please stop. Stop. Stop," Ashlee said, pushing his locks away.

Darius stood and reached for Ashlee's hand, assisting her off the bench. He guided her body until she straddled the bench. "Sit here." Darius sat behind Ashlee with his legs on opposite sides of the bench. "Lay down," he instructed, pushing against Ashlee's shoulder blades.

Ashlee's asshole was tight. She wrapped her fingers around the legs of the bench. Darius separated her cheeks a little more. Tilting her pelvis upward, Darius flushed Ashlee's thighs against his. His dick slowly penetrated the opening of her vagina. Darius rotated Ashlee's ass in his palms and thrust his dick deeper inside Ashlee's warm pussy. She was wet. Hot. Sweet. Sweaty.

Darius wrapped his arm inside Ashlee's thigh. His middle finger moved in circular motion against her clit. Surprisingly Ashlee's muscles gripped his dick. Darius fucked her harder. Faster. His finger moved faster. Darius inserted the tip of his other middle finger in Ashlee's ass. Her hips moved away so Darius retracted his finger, grabbed her cheeks and stroked faster.

"Aw, damn. I'm cumming Ashlee. Cum with me." Darius massaged Ashlee's clit as fast as he could.

Ashlee moaned, still gripping the bench legs.

"Yes, give it to me. Damn, you're good." Darius's cum flowed in waves, flooding Ashlee's pussy. "Damn, I knew you were the best," Darius said, slapping Ashlee's ass.

When Ashlee stood, clumps of semen plopped on the bench.

"I know I'm going to regret this. I worked so hard not to cross the line."

Darius had no regrets. Not even the fact that he didn't use a condom. He thought about going to get one but figured Ashlee would've changed her mind by the time he returned. Women. They never meant what they said.

Ashlee couldn't resist him forever. She knew she wanted what all the other women wanted. Him.

Darius said, "It was destiny. Don't have regrets. We're meant for each other."

"I'm going to shower and go to bed."

Darius smiled. Was that all it took to wear Ashlee out? "I thought you had plans."

"Had plans," Ashlee said, picking her gown off the floor.

As soon as Darius turned on the ringer, the phone rang. "Hello."

"Darius I need to speak with you. You either talk to me now, or I'm coming over to your—"

Click. Darius hung up on Ciara. This wasn't a good time to reveal his divorce request. By the time Ciara got to his house, Darius would be on his way to Kimberly's.

CHAPTER 31

Ciara fluffed her pillow. Doubling the edge, she tucked the folded pillow under her head, curled into a fetal position and closed her eyes. Tossing the cover over her face, Ciara turned onto her back. She shifted onto her right side into another cuddling position. Keys? Did she hear keys jiggling in the door? The nerve of him to show up at her place. The light switch flipped. Darius slid the sheer veneer against the wrought-iron rail.

"Another late night at the office I presume," Ciara said sitting up in bed. The digital clock changed from two fifty-nine to three A.M. Ciara loosened then retied her black headscarf. Normally Ciara would've removed the wrap and combed her afro whenever they slept together.

Darius didn't respond. He unbuckled his pants, aligned the creases, and then neatly hung the black slacks on a hanger. His polished shoes he set in the closet beneath his slacks. Darius placed his Rolex and cuff links on the nightstand.

"I thought you weren't sleeping here anymore. What happened to all those words you spoke the other day? 'I want a divorce. I'm leaving you. I never should've married you.' Huh, Darius? I agree. And we will get divorced, but not until I'm ready. What I don't appreciate is you showing up at my house unannounced."

Darius remained silent. He eased under the covers and turned his back to Ciara. Oh this nigga don' lost his mind.

"Oh, you are going to talk to me. Don't think you're not." Ciara pushed Darius's shoulder until his back lay against the sheets. "So how long have you been fucking Ashlee? And don't lie and tell me you're not because she already told me you are," Ciara lied. If Ciara could perform an abortion, she'd kill Darius's child growing inside her instantly. No. That wasn't true. Ciara wanted a baby. But Ciara also wanted to slap Darius upside his head. But if he raised his hand to hit her back, she'd have to call Monica for backup. *That's right,* Ciara recalled, *Monica has a new friend.* Ciara met the woman once. She seemed nice. Said she was happily married and all.

Darius mumbled, "Then she should've told you how long. Now, may I go back to sleep."

"Back to sleep?" Ciara straddled Darius. "You should've stayed where in the fuck you were if you wanted to sleep. This my house. You hear me! My house!" Her tensed hands forced his shoulders into the mattress.

Darius calmly said, "True. But legally it's mine too."

Ciara climbed off of Darius. "Yeah, you take your ass to sleep. You'd better sleep with one eye open."

"You know every day you convince me you're certifiably crazy. If you don't come to your senses, I'm going to commit you to a mental institution."

"Commit your damn self." Ciara shoved her pillow in Darius's face. Rage surfaced to her trembling hands. *He's not worth it, Ciara. Just go to sleep. Tomorrow is another day.* "Spoiled ass mama's boy. You need to grow the fuck up!"

"Don't hate on a brother. I'm rich. I'm fine. And I'm grown." Darius turned toward Ciara and asked, "How's Donavon?"

Donavon? What? "Don't try to reverse this. This isn't about me. Or Solomon. It's about you. And your lies. And your women. And God knows what else."

Darius propped his head on his elbow. "How's Allen? Or better yet, how's Romeo? You still hooking up with him when you get to D.C. next week? For what?"

Ciara sucked in so much oxygen her lungs hurt. How did Darius know? How much did he know?

Darius yelled, "What the fuck you having some shady-ass PI follow me around taking pictures for? For what, Ciara? So you can present to the judge? What you need to know is I got pictures too. And what the hell are you going to do with Romeo? Fuck him 'til he can't cum no more? Or better yet, let him fuck you in the ass?! Huh, Ciara? Answer me! Slut!"

Ciara's heart lightened, smiling on the inside. Darius could cheat but he couldn't handle infidelity. Ciara calmly said, "If you know all of that, then you should know 'for what?'" The demon inside of her moments ago, left her body. Wow, what a trip. In a split second her frustrations were blazing so hot, she could've seriously hurt Darius.

Darius pulled the cover above Ciara's head. "Go to sleep. Or give me head."

"These lips will never touch any parts of your body again." Ciara eased from underneath the covers and went into the living room before Darius made her a liar. She sat in her favorite seat with pen and paper in her hands and wrote.

Where did I go wrong? I'm more established, more mature, and definitely more stable than Darius. When I had Solomon I didn't want him. When he left I wanted him more. After divorcing Allen I felt relieved. After marrying Darius I felt trapped. But how did I get into those predicaments? I'm not selfish. I'm fairly wealthy. I'm not undersexed. I'm attractive. I'm on my fourth husband. First pregnancy. I'm not crazy but sometimes I feel like I'm going to snap. Maybe I need to find me a friend. A female friend and confidante like Monica and leave men alone for a while.

Ciara dragged her pen back and forth until that last sentence was marked out, then she ripped the page into pieces and tossed them on the coffee table. Ciara went into the bedroom. She shook Darius's shoulder. "Wake up. We need to talk."

Darius looked at the clock. Five-fifteen. "What, Ciara? Damn, what is it?"

"There's something I need to tell you." Ciara wanted to tell Darius the truth about Allen, Romeo, and Donavon, but didn't. "I'm pregnant."

"I thought we discussed this. We agreed. No kids. That's the only reason I stopped using condoms with you."

"You said you didn't want any kids. I said I wanted two. That's hardly an agreement."

"Well, get a divorce. I mean an abortion. Because I don't want any kids."

"You don't want kids, or you don't want a family with me?"

"Pick one. I don't trust you, Ciara. I don't even know who's the father. Donavon? Allen? Romeo? Me? Do you know? I'm not raising some other man's child."

"Of course I know. It's yours." Tears streamed down Ciara's cheeks. "And regardless of how you feel, I'm having our baby."

Darius sighed heavily. "It's six o'clock. I've got to go. Don't call me at my office with this foolishness. And don't be late for our meeting with Parapictures."

"What? I'm the one who's acting foolish? Whatever." Ciara shook her head. She sat on the edge of the bed and waited until Darius showered then left. Ciara showered and left too.

CHAPTER 32

First-time home buyer, Kevin Williams, strutted about his new home and smiled so wide his jaws ached. Three thousand square feet of jet black and cobalt blue furniture was arranged by a professional interior decorator. A few gold fixtures were accented throughout his house. The living room, two loveseats, one black, one blue on opposite ends of the gold-trimmed coffee table. Two high-back suede chairs, one black, one blue, were situated to the left of his fire-place. A glass-top table sat between the chairs with a glass chess set on top.

Soon Kevin would transition from Somebody's Gotta Be on Top to Parapictures. Leaving Darius's company meant no more lump sums of cash for NyVek. Tony offered a top power position in the movie production department. Whenever Kevin accepted Tony's offer, if Darius wanted Somebody's films to top the box-office charts, Darius would have to depend on Kevin.

Bing. The sweet sound of authentic crystal wine

goblets. The cellar, stocked with libations, awaited his guest's selection.

Striking a match, Kevin lit each of the seven tall gold candles on his dining room table. Seven upholstered dining-room chairs, four black, three blue, surrounded a rectangular glass-top table situated atop a life-sized stuffed lion. Never would Kevin have two heads of his dining room. Carefully Kevin basted the duck, stirred the potatoes, then reduced the heat under the steaming carrots and snow peas. Thankfully there were no rodents or roaches since he'd moved in.

Kevin spread his arms east and west. "This is living." He kissed his fingertips like Tony. "Mmmmm."

Ding-dong.

"She's finally here." Kevin hurried to the door, admired his black slacks and long-sleeve shirt in the foyer mirror, and smiled. His fingers turned the knob to greet his first houseguest. "Welcome to my home. Come in. You look beautiful."

Fortunately Ashlee hadn't seen his Compton apartment. Afraid he'd transport undesirables, Kevin had left everything he owned at his Compton residence, except his new wardrobe which he delivered to the dry cleaners and shoe shop before storing it in his master walk-in closet.

Ashlee moved one foot length at a time on the plush gray carpet. "Thanks. For inviting me. Smells good. I didn't know you could cook."

Kevin hadn't cooked. He hired a mobile chef to prepare the meal and make it appear he'd done everything himself. "There's lots of things about me you don't know. But give us time. That'll change." Kevin ruffled the shingles on Ashlee's red poncho. "Nice pullover. I noticed after the rain, August nights can get a little cool."

"Yeah, it doesn't take much for me to get cold. I'm glad you invited me. I needed a break from work. So promise me you won't discuss work."

"Okay, after this one quick question. Have you cut this week's check to NyVek? I haven't . . . I mean they haven't received the check and I haven't seen the invoice yet."

Ashlee frowned. "They called you?"

Kevin shook his head. "Naw, Angel transferred them to my extension because you were out of town with Darius."

Four lines creased Ashlee's forehead. "The check is in the mail."

"Cool, you hungry?" Kevin asked, rubbing his stomach. "I'm starving."

Yes! Kevin knew he wasn't smart enough to outsmart Darius forever. The main reason most crooks got caught was because they didn't know when to quit and move on. A few more disbursements and Kevin would quit before Darius realized what happened.

Ashlee selected a bottle of merlot. Kevin pulled out her chair. Ashlee's knees grazed the lion's mane. "Wow, this is interesting. I don't want to know if he's real."

"Yes you do. And no he's not."

"Whew. Coulda fooled me," Ashlee said, relaxing.

As instructed by the chef, Kevin placed the platters on the table mats along with the proper serving utensils. After holding Ashlee's hand and saying grace, Kevin asked, "So do you enjoy working for Darius?"

"Sometimes. Most of the times. But we agreed not to talk about work."

"Fine. Then let's talk about us. How do you feel about exclusively dating me?"

"Whoa, that's a lot to ask. Right now I could use a really good friend. Umm. The vegetables are tasty."

Kevin smiled while biting his bottom lip. "Are you seeing anyone?"

Ashlee's eyes traveled toward the ceiling then back to her plate. "No, not really."

"What's that supposed to mean? Either you are or you aren't. I'm interested in you."

Ashlee shook her head. "No, I'm not."

"Good. Then give me a chance to prove myself to you. I'm living in this big-ass house all alone. Move in with me."

"I can't. I'm in the process of looking for a place to buy of my own. Besides, I need my space and we barely know one another."

Kevin carried the plates to the kitchen and returned with two slices of chocolate triple layered cake a la mode.

Raising the fork to Ashlee's mouth, Kevin said, "Let me feed you."

"Whoa." Ashlee gripped his wrist. "No, thanks."

"Fine. Let's go to the family room."

All the money Kevin had spent on the meal and Ashlee ate the vegetables, sampled the duck, and never touched the potatoes. Her red wine sat in her glass on the kitchen counter. She didn't want to talk business. She didn't want to talk personal. If Ashlee didn't want to have sex with him, she might as well leave and stop wasting his time and money.

"Okay. But do you want me to help with the dishes?"

Hell, no. Either do the damn dishes or leave them

alone. Help? Kevin said, "It's cool. I'll put them in the dishwasher later."

The way Ashlee acted, Kevin may as well ask, "Have you had sex with Darius?"

"What? What kind of question is that? He's my brother. Of course I haven't. What's it to you?"

"Darius is as much of your brother as I am. Can't you see I'm seriously interested in getting to know you better? A whole lot better." Kevin leaned to kiss Ashlee. His hand cupped her breast. Ashlee placed his hand in his lap, and then quickly turned away. "I apologize. I shouldn't have done that. It's just that you're so beautiful." *And either we have sex or leave my damn house.*

Ashlee stood, massaged the nape of her neck and said, "Thanks for inviting me over for dinner. I have to go."

Kevin politely escorted Ashlee to the door and retrieved her red pullover from the coat closet. "I apologize if I offended you. I thought we were both consenting adults. I'll see you at work Monday. And don't mention any of this to Darius."

Ashlee looked back at Kevin standing in the doorway and said, "I do like you. Maybe next time. Good night."

Ashlee had mentioned she needed a friend. So instead of trying to date Ashlee, Kevin decided he would work on becoming her best friend. If Ashlee learned to trust him, she could also learn to love him.

CHAPTER 33

Life had become more like the Universoul Circus. Kevin was jumping through hoops for Tony and damn near standing on his head trying to entertain Ashlee. Ciara had vanished. She wasn't at the meetings. No phone calls. She wasn't at her home or office. Monica and Megan claimed they had no idea where Ciara was. Liars. Darius's mother had become a mime. Each time he saw her Jada was speechless, at least toward him. Wellington by default was proclaimed the ringleader.

Darius tapped on Ashlee's door. "You ready?"

"Yeah, but I don't understand why you insist I accompany you on this trip to San Francisco. I just got back from San Francisco last week."

"I told you. I need you. Isn't that enough?"

Ashlee remained silent. Pressing the lever of her carry-on suitcase, she lifted the handle and left her bag in the doorway for Darius. "I'll be in the car."

"I'm right behind you."

How had Darius managed to screw up his relationship with Ashlee? Understandably, he hadn't located Desire but where in the hell was Ciara? Unbeknownst to Ashlee, this trip to San Francisco was primarily pleasure. Darius had to distance Ashlee from Kevin to renew Ashlee's faith in him. Lately Ashlee spent more time away from his house. When Darius came home late nights or early mornings, Ashlee's bedroom door was open but she wasn't in the room.

Ashlee sat so close to the limousine door, if the driver would've made a sharp turn, Ashlee would've fallen out of the car.

"How's your dad?" Darius asked, breaking the silence.

"That's funny, you inquiring about Lawrence. He's fine. Wants to know if I'm coming home for Thanksgiving or Christmas and if I'll stay."

"And? What did you tell him?"

"I don't know. Labor Day hasn't passed yet. My dad wants to take me to Vancouver." Ashlee continued staring out the window, watching the summer sunrise cast orange, red, and yellow hues up into the sky. "He says I don't seem happy."

"Well, are you?"

Ashlee turned toward Darius then looked away. Darius knew the tears in her eyes reflected the pain he'd caused.

Sliding closer, Darius hugged Ashlee. "What's wrong?"

"Everything."

The driver parked in front of the skycaps at curbside check-in. He stood outside the door but didn't open it.

"Do you need a raise? What?" Any reason except Darius being held responsible for Ashlee's sadness was acceptable.

Ashlee folded her arms. "Darius, you are so selfish. You never admit when you're wrong. You're always right. And everyone else is always wrong. You're a pathological liar. You lie all the time." Ashlee sniffled. Tears rolled down her red cheeks. Refusing to look at him, Ashlee kept staring out the window. "Darius, you lie so much I don't think you know how to tell the truth. We're not kids anymore. I'm a woman. A woman with feelings."

Darius placed his hand on Ashlee's chin. Turning her face toward his, he kissed each eyelid. "I'm just trying to play this game of life. It's hard for a black man to stay on top. I gotta be hard. Or everyone will think I'm soft. And since I control what people think about me, I can't allow anyone to believe that Darius Jones is a weak man."

"You don't have to be weak to be honest."

"You don't understand. Honesty has no place in this world. I can't trust anyone. Not even my own mother." Darius paused as Ashlee's big red-and-brown eyes pierced into his. "Of course I can trust you. But only you. Why do you think I want to marry you?" Damn, he didn't mean to slip and say that.

"Marry me? Darius, you can't still be serious."

"Why not? We already had sex."

"See, that's what I'm talking about. To you we had sex. To me we made love." Ashlee shook her head then whispered, "And we made a mistake."

Darius objected. "No, you're wrong. We didn't make a mistake. We did make love. It was beautiful. I want to make love to you again. I love you."

"Stop it Darius Jones. Just stop it! You're telling me what you think I want to hear. Not what's in your heart. Sometimes I don't think you have a heart."

Darius tapped the window. The driver opened the door.

"We'd better go before we miss our flight," Darius said, drying Ashlee's face with his white monogrammed handkerchief. The initials DL—representing *Darius's Law*—were engraved in gold to constantly remind him of his ten rules.

Darius rocked Ashlee in his arms from takeoff until landing. From Los Angeles to San Francisco. One hour and ten minutes. And again in the limo until Ashlee fell asleep.

Ashlee opened her eyes. She squinted. "Where are we going?" Her head rested on Darius's shoulder.

Darius lounged on the long leather seat. "It's a surprise."

Ashlee read, "Welcome to Napa Valley?" as they rode past the sign. "Darius, I'm not spending the night with you in Napa."

"If you don't want to spend the night, we'll leave. But let's enjoy the mud baths and massages I've scheduled."

Darius had their bags delivered to the room while the receptionist directed them to the spa. Darius removed all his clothes, put on the thick white cotton robe, and entered their private room where Ashlee was already waiting. She was beautiful. Her hair was tied behind her head with one of those pink stretch bands. Her robe was wrapped tight. Darius stood behind Ashlee and untied her robe. Gently he slid the soft cotton over her shoulders, down her arms, off her body.

"You are so beautiful." Darius turned, removed his robe, and hung both on the electric warmers.

Smack! A hunk of mud clung to his butt. Darius smiled.

"No!" Ashlee yelled, racing around the tub. "Not my hair! Anywhere except my hair!"

"Anywhere?" His eyebrows lifted. Darius smiled, then smeared mud all over Ashlee's shoulders avoiding touching her breasts.

Ashlee covered his chest. He painted his name across her belly button. She saturated his abdominals. Darius smeared her butt. They took turns until each of them was blanketed in mud from head to toe. Darius embraced Ashlee. When he released Ashlee, their bodies suctioned apart.

"So much for relaxing in the tubs of mud," Ashlee commented.

They showered together. Darius washed every grain of dirt off of Ashlee. Carefully he rinsed between the folds of her lips. She did the same to him, carefully removing the particles from his locks and hairs. Hours passed like minutes.

Darius buzzed for the assistant, who led them to a huge room with a Jacuzzi and two massage tables.

"Your milk-and-honey bath is ready. Press this button to turn the Jacuzzi on and off. Mr. Jones, the temperature is set to seventy-five as you requested. You can adjust the water to your liking. The thermostat is on this wall. Have fun." She smiled and left.

Darius asked Ashlee, "So how do you feel?"

"I'm fine. I must admit I am having fun."

"Good." Darius disrobed Ashlee and held her hand until she was safely in the bubbling water.

Darius massaged Ashlee's feet.

"That tickles."

"Relax. Take a deep breath and concentrate on the touch that makes you feel good. Eventually, it won't tickle anymore."

Ashlee whispered, "You're right."

Darius wanted to sex Ashlee so bad pre-cum flowed from his dick into the water. He was careful not to let Ashlee's feet touch his erection. She was so innocent. Pure.

After their massages, Darius escorted Ashlee to their room. "I'll be right back."

"Where are you going?"

"I need to make a call. I'll be right back."

"You can't make the call from our room?"

"I said, I'll be right back." Darius closed the door then walked to the lobby. He dialed Ciara's home number.

"This is Monica and no Ciara isn't home."

"What the hell did you do? Transfer her calls to your number?"

"What's it to you? I don't have to answer to your pathetic ass. You don't want to be a father to your son. But I guess considering your real daddy abandoned you, that's what you're going to do to your son too. Just leave Ciara to raise to your baby boy on her own, huh? I'm sorry I told her to date you."

Click.

Darius sat in the lobby staring at the waterfall. *A boy.* Was Monica just saying that or was he really having a son? The last thing Darius wanted was to treat his son the way Darryl had treated him. Crying is for girls and sissies. Darius forced back his tears.

"Damn, I'm going to have son. I'm going to be a father."

Darius would try contacting Ciara again tomorrow.

CHAPTER 34

Darius hesitated. He picked up the cordless. Placed it back on the base. His hands traveled over his locks. Darius held the phone staring at the buttons. He hung up. Darius slipped into his charcoal gray suit and black shoes. He looked at the cordless lying in the center of his bed, then closed his bedroom door behind him. Exiting through the garage, he drove to work in a daze.

Why did he feel the need to call Darryl today? Darius redirected his thoughts to this morning's production meeting. Finally, he'd have an opportunity to talk with Ciara. As Darius walked into his office, Angel handed him his schedule along with a note. Darius unlocked his door then unfolded the message.

Ciara Monroe won't be attending the meeting today or next week.

"Damn!" Darius balled the note and tossed it into the trash. He buzzed Angel. "Angel, did Ciara say anything that you didn't write on this note?"

"No, Mr. Jones, she didn't."

"Did Ciara call? Or Monica?"

"Ciara."

"Did you get her number from the caller I.D.?"

"The number was blocked."

"Okay, thanks." Darius hung up the phone.

Kevin tapped on the door. "What's up, mein? You ready to discuss the agenda for the meeting?"

"Yeah, sure. Come in." Darius dialed Ashlee's extension. "We need to review the agenda in my office. Now." Darius hung up.

During their trip to San Francisco, Darius had sensed that Ashlee was withholding information. Not something simple like a vacation request or time off. Whatever worried Ashlee consumed most of her thoughts. First she had started out to the airport upset. Then in Napa, Ashlee was happy. Darius needed to make love to Ashlee that night. She agreed that would be their last time but didn't say why. By the time Darius checked out the next day, Ashlee was upset again. Almost depressed. Women.

Ashlee entered and quietly sat at the round conference table across from Kevin.

"Good morning, Ashlee. You look nice as usual." Kevin nodded. Smiled. Nodded.

"Good morning," Ashlee replied.

Kevin squinted. His meaty forehead buckled. He asked Ashlee, "You all right?"

"Yes," Ashlee nodded. "I'm fine."

"Okay," Darius said, sitting between them. What was up with the nodding and bobbing? "Ashlee, brief me on the finances for the film."

"Our resources are low. We need to cut the budget in order to make it through this final phase of production."

Darius scanned his copy. "Low? Why? I thought the funds Ciara and I contributed were more than sufficient."

"They were," Ashlee said. "Until you contracted with Ny—"

"Um, um," Kevin cleared his throat. "We can make it through production without adding any new expenditures. And we can take a look at where we can cut the remaining budget. I'll get with Ashlee and we'll prepare a proposal for your review."

Darius looked at the clock. Ten minutes before their next meeting. "Don't either of you leave the office today. We'll continue this discussion immediately after the meeting. Ashlee, I want a detailed report of every single expense item disbursed from my account along with a brief explanation of everything and bank records of all deposits for this movie production. I want it on my desk Thursday morning. I refuse to leverage funds from *The Honey Well's* budget. And, I'll be damned," Darius's fist pounded the table, "if I'm going to contribute another dime! I want to know where my damn money went. You hear me!" Darius stared at Kevin then Ashlee.

Where in the fuck was Ciara? Who gave a shit about Darryl? Him. Mama. Fuck 'em all! Darius screamed in his head. "And I'm scratching finance from the agenda," Darius said, staring directly at Kevin. "We'll discuss finances at the next meeting when I'm better prepared."

"Thursday is only three days away and I have to do payroll on Wednesday."

"I'm depending on you to make it all happen," Darius said.

"Don't worry Ash, I'll help you," Kevin said.

Darius stared at Kevin. "I'm not paying you to help

Ashlee. Ashlee can handle it. Alone. I'd better not, between now," Darius's pointing finger hit the table, "and Friday, see you," he pointed at Kevin, "in her," Darius pointed at Ashlee, "office."

Darius gathered his papers. He handed Angel the revised agenda. "Delete item number one and bring clean copies to the conference room."

"Certainly, Mr. Jones." Angel smiled.

If she weren't his secretary, he'd tap that ass. The intrigue turned him on more.

Darius headed into the conference room. "Good morning, Candice. Tony. Everyone."

"Jones, you're late," Tony said. "I have another meeting to attend. Production is lovely." Tony kissed his fingertips. "This movie should be a wrap by Thanksgiving and on the big screen right before Valentine's Day."

"There's one thing we need to be aware of," Kevin said, commanding everyone's attention, especially Darius's.

"What's that, Williams?" Tony said.

"Don't add any, I mean *any* expenses to the last quarter statement without submitting a request to Ashlee, first."

"Williams, you run a tight ship. I like that. Jones, it's a good thing Williams is your family. I gotta go. Angel, e-mail me the minutes as soon as possible, would you darlin'?"

Angel smiled and nodded.

Candice spoke. "Darius, I have a question for you."

Darius looked at Candice.

"Now that we are close to the completion of production and since Terrell did not get the part, how is it that

Black Diamonds is on the agenda as the recommended PR firm to handle publicity?"

"It's simple. Black Diamonds submitted the best proposal. And for this film nothing but the best will do."

Candice's eyes scrolled to her left corners, then right, and finally in a circle. Then back at Darius. "Well, it's a conflict of interest."

"Actually, it's just the opposite. Black Diamonds has a vested interest."

"Well, all I can say is you'd better consider option number two." Candice stormed out of the room.

"Don't worry man. She just blowing off steam," Kevin said. "I can handle her. She'll sign the agreement."

Angel excused herself from the room. Darius's eyes trailed her long legs until they were out of view. When he noticed Ashlee staring, he smiled. Angel returned a moment and said, "Mr. Jones, Ms. Monroe is on the phone."

"Don't continue without me. Take a break." Darius raced to his office and shut the door. "Ciara, where are you?"

"This isn't Ciara, it's Monica. I told you Ciara doesn't want anything to do with you. I'll be by tomorrow to pick up a copy of the minutes from this morning's meeting along with a copy of the budget. Until further notified, I'm taking over all of Ciara's business."

"You can't do that!"

"I can. And I will. I'll deliver a court-certified copy of my power of attorney tomorrow. And you need to notify me of every meeting and keep me abreast of all contracts. Good day, Mr. Jones." Monica hung up the phone.

Darius gnawed his bottom lip. What in the fuck was Ciara trying to prove? Darius dialed his attorney's office.

"Hello, Mr. Jones."

Darius didn't respond with a greeting. "I need to file for divorce. I'll be at your office this afternoon. Bye."

Darius sat swirling his pen in circular motions. He needed a private investigator to locate Ciara. Theo could get the job done. But once before Theo had refused his request to trail Maxine. Maxine. Two kids. And a husband. Refusing to accept no for an answer, Darius dialed Theo's number.

"Speak to me. What's up, Darius?"

"I need you to find Ciara. She's missing. We're concerned."

Theo dragged Darius's name off his tongue, "Da-ri-us. You know I only work for your mother. That would be a conflict. Can't do it."

"But my mother has no affiliation with this matter. Can't you help me out this once?"

"Nope. Gotta go. Peace." Theo hung up the phone.

Darius could easily find another PI but finding one he could trust was the problem.

CHAPTER 35

After meditating and praying for several days, Jada's vision to help her child was clear. Her stomach churned in knots. Undeniably, Darius's pain hurt her too. Darius stopped returning her phone calls. Didn't visit on weekends to see or pick up his little brother. No recent voicemails saying, "Ma, I'm okay. Tell Dad I said hello." Hopefully Darius received her message to meet for lunch at eleven.

Jada stood in the doorway. She tilted her neck. Yes, her legs were there but her limbs were numb. The restaurant was quiet as she'd hoped but in about an hour or less that would change. Jada had come too far to leave. Her comfort level wasn't important.

"Soon this will be over," she mumbled, then approached the host.

"Tanner reservation."

"Welcome, Ms. Tanner, would you like to be seated or do you prefer to wait for your party?"

Somberly, Jada replied, "I'd like to be seated."

"Certainly. Are you still expecting two guests?" he asked, reaching for the menus.

"Yes."

Jada followed the waiter along the rail, up three stairs, to a square table set for four in the corner. Good. No windows. No unnecessary distractions. No other diners nearby. He swiftly removed one place setting from the white linen cloth.

Jada glanced at the menu. No appetite. Maybe she'd order soup or a leafy green mixed salad.

Jada overheard the waiter say, "Yes sir, she's here."

Unable to see the front entrance, the next voice she heard was Darius's. "Man, I'm not wearing that shirt."

"Sir, this is formal dining. No button-down shirt with a collar, no service. Please, wear the shirt."

Darius approached the table wearing a blue cotton collared shirt over his NBA jersey.

Jada smiled. "Hi, honey. How's everything?"

Jada tried creating a gleam of excitement in her eyes but so many disappointing events had occurred between them, Jada doubted if a twinkle surfaced.

Darius flopped in his seat and said, "What do you care? You barely speak to me. You get upset when I don't call. Then you invite me to lunch. What for?"

"I've told you, honey, when people stop responding they feel there's nothing else they can do. You pushed me away. It seems you intentionally hurt me." Jada wanted Darius to object. He didn't. "I love you but I can't resolve your problems. You're too stubborn. How's work?"

"Fine, Ma. Now that I've dug in that ass, Kevin is working out well. Ashlee too. Fine. Everything is fine."

Didn't take long for the attitude to arrive. Jada ignored Darius's comments. Had Darius dug in Ashlee's ass? What did Darius mean?

"Honey, I don't trust Kevin. He has bad vibes."

"You don't even know my brother. He works for me."

Jada glanced toward the entrance. "Well, I might as well tell you before he gets here. I invited Darryl to eat with us."

"Why? I don't need him."

"Yes, honey. You do. You need to develop a stronger relationship with him or hear him say to your face that he doesn't want anything to do with you."

Darius removed the starched shirt. "There you go again. Trying to decide what's best for me. Every time you do this you make my life worse. Miserable." Darius tossed the blue cotton across the back of his chair and stood. "I have better things to do with my life."

"What if I told you he honestly acknowledged he'd been an asshole and he was thankful I'd called? Baby, I know you want to bond with your father. And he wants the same. If you walk away now, he may never try again."

Darius stopped, returned to his mother, and stood in silence.

Darius's eyes shifted left to right. He ran his hand over his locks. Finally he put on the shirt and sat. "Ma, you just don't understand the void you've created in my life. I mean, I could've been an NBA all-star. I never wanted to run a company. Basketball was my dream. My life. And you held on to your lie for so long. So long that, thanks to your selfishness, my dream is now out of reach."

"Baby, you don't know how sorry I truly am for hurting you. But you should never give up on a dream. Never."

"She's right," Darryl said, walking up to the table. He pulled out a chair, turned it backward, straddled his seat, and sat directly across from Darius and next to Jada. Darryl's chin rested on his long hands which covered the top of his chair. "Did I ever tell you how I got into the league?"

Darius stared at Darryl. No nod. No words.

The waiter approached the table. "Would you like for me to come back?"

Darryl answered, "Please."

"I'll be in this area. Just let me know when you're ready."

Darryl wasn't going to get away without telling the story Jada never heard. Jada said, "No, you didn't tell us how you got into the league."

"Well, because I was six-nine in high school, everyone wanted me to play ball. I mean, I loved the sport, don't get me wrong. But it wasn't my dream. I wanted to own my own business. Like your mother. Work for myself. Like you. But everyone, my mother, father, aunts, uncles, cousins, you name it, they all wanted me to go to college on a scholarship and save them money. Play ball. And go pro and then give them money."

"So what'd you do?" Darius asked.

"I played at TSU for two semesters then I tried to quit. Just like you quit after your freshman year. But they went ballistic. Even my mother. I couldn't believe how angry everyone was with my decision. So I stayed."

Jada thought, *then maybe Darius and Darryl understand how I feel about the screenplay.*

Darius looked at Darryl and said, "I quit because you benched me."

"Let's get that straight. You benched yourself. I wanted to see how serious you were. You were preoccupied with women so I figured you were forced into basketball too. So I decided I wasn't going to push you someplace you didn't want to be. If you really wanted your starting spot, you would've worked harder. Not quit. Winners never quit."

"Why didn't you tell me you were my dad when you autographed my shirt at my AAU game when I was a teenager?"

Jada looked up at Darryl, waiting for a response.

"Darius, I was so proud of you. But I was jealous of your mother. She never needed me. She rolled up at that game in her new Benz. Her new man sat to her left. Her old man on the right. Always so independent. Miss I Can Handle Everything on My Own. She didn't need me like those other women. I mean, look at her. Still beautiful. Successful. Getting ready to expand her company. Then when she said Wellington was the father, I knew she didn't need or want me."

Jada had to speak in her defense, "Wait one minute. You were the one who told me 'I'd better tell Mr. Wellington, loverboy Jones my baby was his.' "

"Jada, I know. And I apologize."

What? Darryl apologized. That was a first!

"Plus, my boy Terrell planted the seed that Darius might not be mine. What can I say? I was young. And dumb. I did what was convenient for me."

"Darryl, you weren't young. You were thirty-five years old when I told you I was pregnant."

"I know. But you black women just don't get it.

Without a real woman—a woman who believes in her man, supports her man even when he's wrong . . . and one who's not always attacking her man or trying to be the man. From our mother's arms into a woman's arms, some of us are still looking for a superwoman to replace our supermom. Man, my mama cooked, cleaned, worked, and took care of us. Helped pay the bills and never complained."

Jada commented, "Well, my daddy worked. Mowed the lawn. Washed the cars. Spoiled my mom. Spoiled me." Jada's neck swerved side to side. "And my mother never had to go out at night to find him or stay up all night because he didn't come home. My mother worked because she wanted to. Not because she had to."

Darryl laughed at Darius's expression. Darius's head was buried in his hand.

"Jada, calm down. This isn't about you. You've had your turn over and over again. This is about our son. My son. Everybody knows you're spoiled. Jada, because of what we've done, Darius doesn't know who or how to trust. Your role is more important than mine because until he learns to trust you, he'll never trust anyone. Including me. Where was I? Oh, yeah. My point was, I guess some men don't know how to grow up. Others just don't want to. I guess that's why I'm here. It's time for me to grow up. Stop running. Stop blaming everyone else. Darius, look at me, Son."

Darius looked at Darryl.

"I do want to get to know you. I know it's late but it's not too late. And if you're serious about realizing your dream, I can train you one-on-one. We can get you back into college, on one of the top teams. I have enough contacts to get you looked at by the pros, but it's going to be up to you to put in the work."

Darius shoulders rose below his ears, almost touching. "I don't know what to say, man."

"You don't have to say anything. Just think about what I said, and if you decide to go back to college, know that I'm ready to help you." Darryl stood and opened his arms to Darius.

Darius stood but didn't open his arms.

Darryl hugged Darius tight. "I know, Son." He grabbed the back of Darius's head and pulled Darius in closer, then Darryl kissed Darius's forehead and said, "I love you too. I'll be in touch. Soon." Darryl placed money to pay the bill on the table, then left.

Jada sat at the table with Darius. She wanted to question him about Ashlee but couldn't. Not wanting to interrupt Darius's thoughts, Jada motioned for the waiter to wait a few more minutes before taking their orders.

CHAPTER 36

Darius reflected on his conversation with Darryl. Darryl kept his promise and phoned sooner than Darius expected. The next day, in fact. Their relationship was awkward yet evolving and, although Darius wouldn't admit it, gratifying.

If he could turn back the hands of time, Darius fantasized seeing himself . . . at five years old, proudly riding on Darryl's shoulders seven feet in the air. At ten, happy having Darryl coach his fifth-grade, Catholic Youth Organization team. At sixteen, instead of getting an autograph from Darryl Williams, Darius would've had Darryl talk to all the college basketball coaches that were blowing up his cellular and home phones. At twenty-one, Darryl would've had courtside seats to his NBA games. Maybe in a few years, Darryl would still have those tickets. What a difference having his real dad would've made in his childhood development. And all the things Darius dreamt of would've only cost Darryl time. Time. Time.

Angel stood in his doorway wearing a black velvet hoodie dress with knee-high boots. "Mr. Jones, Darryl Sr., is on the phone. He says it's important."

Darius's eyes roamed Angel's protruding breasts squeezed between a low V-cut neckline. "Thanks." Watching her butt sway, he shook his head then answered the phone, "Hey, what's up?" Darius wasn't sure if he'd ever become comfortable calling Darryl *Dad*.

"Hey, Son. I want to invite you to the Cal, Stanford game in November. You think you can be in Oakland?"

Darius's bright eyes matched his smile. "Whoa, of course. But that's eight weeks away."

"I know. But I need to start lining up your schedule to meet the head coaches. Once we get you on a team next year, it'll be easier for me to get you into the NBA draft the following year. You know, give the pros a chance to see they need you. The University of San Diego and UCLA are good NBA feeder colleges."

"Okay, I'll be there whenever I need to. Just let me know. Maybe I can help you start your business."

"You've done enough helping Kevin. Thanks to you, Kevin has really grown a lot. He's more confident. He's happy. He's successful. And I believe, for the first time, he's even falling in love. Son, remember this. Very seldom will you help the person who helps you. But you must selflessly help somebody. Whatever you put into the universe, you shall receive."

Darius instantly thought about Ashlee, Kimberly, Desire, and Ciara, realizing the way he'd treated each of them was wrong. In time, with time, Darius would do what he'd never done before: apologize.

Why couldn't Wellington, with all his love and concern, do in twenty-one years, what Darryl had done in two weeks? Make Darius Jones recognize, like other men, that in addition to anger and outrage, he too had feelings. Emotions. Compassion. All Darius ever wanted to do was star in the NBA. And now that his dream was back on track, fear intertwined with his excitement. What if his best game wasn't good enough?

Darius vigorously shook his head. "Okay, by—"

"Wait, is Kevin there?"

This time Darius didn't mind transferring Darryl. Knowing Kevin was on the phone, Darius visited Ashlee's office and sat on the corner of her desk.

"I need you to go out and celebrate with me."

Ashlee frowned. "Celebrate what? When?"

"Tonight. After work. For you I'd better say after six because you don't know how to leave this place."

"Darius, I can't. Not tonight. I have plans tonight."

"Reschedule until tomorrow. I need to talk with you."

Ashlee whispered, "Darius, I can't reschedule with him. Not again."

"Who is it? I'll have Angel call and cancel for you." Forget rescheduling with that fool.

Ashlee said, "It's—"

Kevin interrupted, "Hey, no one invited me to the party." Kevin entered and sat at Ashlee's desk. "The old man is finally coming around, huh? That's good. He told me about the Cal, Stanford coaches. Ashlee and I should take you out to celebrate your embarking career. Ashlee. You wanna change our plans to take out the boss? Before you know it, my dad is going to introduce Darius to all the head coaches, and we'll have to run Somebody's Gotta Be on Top." Kevin smiled.

Ashlee sighed, then looked away from Darius. "You guys go without me. I'll stay here. Besides, I have some paperwork I need to review."

Darius waited for Kevin to leave but Kevin leaned back and clamped his hands behind his head, then placed his ankle atop his thigh.

"Kevin, I need to see you in my office."

"Sure thing, boss. I'll be there in just a sec. I have some exciting news to share with Ashlee, mein."

"Now," Darius said then left.

Kevin arrived in Darius's office ten minutes later and sat at the conference table with two packages. "Mein, check this out. I got two," Kevin held up two fingers, "new movie deals in the works. Parapictures was so impressed, Tony offered us contracts on his upcoming films."

"Let me see this." Darius couldn't believe what he'd read. "Our percentage yields a grand total of fifteen million dollars."

"Yeah, mein. Can you believe that shit?! I want a fat bonus with incentives," Kevin said, rubbing his palms together.

"We can talk about that later."

"Naw, mein. No need to talk. I already factored my compensation into the budget."

Darius picked up his package and sat behind his desk. "I'll review the entire proposal and we can discuss this tonight. And, I told you not to talk to Ashlee."

"Mein, you crazy. Ashlee is fine. Single. Intelligent. And we work in the same field. Plus, she's your family or otherwise I know you. You would've tapped that ass a long time ago."

"Yeah, but she's family. My family. Is your family too."

Angel stood in the doorway. Both Darius and Kevin looked up. "Mr. Jones, Candice is in the lobby. I told her you were busy but she insisted on waiting."

Slowly shaking his head, Darius exhaled. "Send her in. Kevin, we'll talk later, man."

As Kevin exited, Candice jerked the door and stamped into Darius's office. Bracing herself with one hand on the desk, the other on her hip, Candice leaned forward and said, "If you don't remove Black Diamonds from my contract today, I swear this film will never make it to the big screen."

"Candice, I'm a busy man. I don't have time for this. I just got two bigger contracts. Talk to my mom and work something out."

"Oh, you don't have time. We'll see about that after I talk to Monica."

Darius would talk to anyone but Monica. "Candice, wait. Have a seat."

"Um, hum. I knew that would get your attention. Maybe I should write a screenplay about you."

"Leave my life out of your head. And to make myself clear, I'm not asking you. Now what is the problem between you and my mother? You two are driving me insane. Nothing would make my mother happier than to see this movie end up in a slush pile. And nothing will make you happier than to have my mother's life story make you filthy rich as long as my mother doesn't share in the profits. I don't get it."

"See, I told you the conflict of interest was a problem. She's trying to sabotage my movie."

Since Jada had helped Darius's relationship with Darryl, maybe Darius could help his mom reunite with her best friend.

"Candice, meet me in Oakland. Tomorrow. My house at two o'clock."

Women.

CHAPTER 37

What did the words "I love you" truly mean? Darius wondered if the times he'd spoken those words to his mother, was he sincere? Maxine? Ashlee? Ciara? Had he told Ciara he loved her? He couldn't remember. His friends? What friends? Friend. K'Nine. Wellington? Darius's list of potential friends could fit on a one-by-one-inch sticky. Females. Lovers. Naw, he definitely didn't love them. But he shouldn't refer to them as whores. In addition to all-stars, maybe he'd start calling the females he fucked *jewels*. And the polished ones, like Kimberly, *gems*. The next time Darius said "I love you" he'd mean it and tell the person why.

"Kimberly. Let me put Slugger in your ass missionary style in the hammock." Darius stroked Kimberly from behind, pushing her down 'til her titties touched the mattress. "Hold on to my nuts, baby." Darius glanced around the hotel suite. The suite with the hammock was their favorite. Included in the cost, a new hammock was hung each stay and available to take home afterward.

Kimberly reached between their thighs and grabbed both of Darius's balls.

"Ah, yes. Squeeze 'em." Darius deliberately slid his dick all the way in Kimberly's pussy. He pulled out. Then he re-entered Kimberly as she re-gripped his nuts.

Kimberly moaned, "Mmmmm. Your dick is so big. I love it." Kimberly always moaned during sex whenever any part of his body touched hers. Something about her moans kept his dick hard.

Kimberly confirmed what Darius had suspected. The women, most of his jewels and gems, when they said "I love you" what they really meant was they loved *it*. Slugger. His dick. Had to be true because the females didn't know enough about him for their expressions to be directed toward him. Kimberly was different. She said what she meant. Nothing more. Darius learned that Kimberly didn't tell her personal business.

"Massage your pussy, daddy."

Darius dripped saliva onto his fingers. Up and down, sandwiched between his longest fingers, Darius massaged Kimberly's shaft. Teased her clit. Stroked her shaft. Teased her clit.

"Oh, yes daddy you know how she likes it." Kimberly arched her back, then rotated as deep as she could onto his dick. Tightening her pussy, Kimberly relaxed her back then arched again.

Darius rewet his fingers. This time he massaged her shaft faster and in circular motion.

"Mmmmmm, yes daddy. Fuck me harder. She's cumming. Damn, you. Damn, you. Damn, you, Darius. I love it when you fuck me hard, daddy."

Darius moved his knees and pelvis closer. He

paused for a moment so Kimberly could work her spot. She was in the zone. The palm of his hand slapped Kimberly's ass three times. The sting made Kimberly cum harder. In waves with his waves, Darius felt Kimberly cum on his dick.

"Incredible," Darius said, withdrawing himself. "I'm glad you agree to see me whenever I want my pussy."

"Only you, daddy."

Of course Darius still paid the Visa in Kimberly's name through his online banking, paperless statements. If Darius ever married, his wife would never know how much he spent on Kimberly. Kimberly was the only one with his credit card. The rest had strictly cash. The corner of Darius's mouth curved. That's right. He did have a wife. Wherever the fuck Ciara was, she was probably fucking some other guy. After Ciara disappeared, Darius's visits with Kimberly had increased to three days a week: Thursday, Friday, and Saturday.

"What's wrong, baby? All of sudden you seem out of it. Let's do the missionary position you love." Kimberly lay on her back, raised her legs above her hips and spread her thighs.

Darius stroked his dick and said, "Later. I've got to go home. Shower. Change. And get to work. I'll be back around noon. Have her ready and waiting for me."

"Anything for you, daddy," Kimberly said, closing the bathroom door.

Wearing yesterday's suit, Darius walked through his front door at seven.

"Good morning. You look nice," Darius said, admiring Ashlee's white lace crew top and navy knee-length skirt as she closed her bedroom door.

The next sounds Darius heard were the garage door opening then closing.

Darius undressed, showered, and re-dressed. Grabbed a V8 Splash from the fridge and left. En route to work Darius thought about Ashlee. How she didn't speak to him this morning. Once Darius started traveling with the NBA, Ashlee was gonna wish she had spoken to him. Was Darius pushing Ashlee into Kevin's arms? Ashlee could forget about moving in with Kevin. Darius was boss. He could overrule any of Ashlee's or Kevin's choices, professional and personal. Darius should spend more time in the office and less time enjoying his money and his women.

Darius unlocked his office door. The sensor lights flashed on. The papers in his in-box were shuffled. Not neat and even like he'd left them last night. Standing in front of his desk, Darius glanced around his office. Everything else was in order.

"Excuse, me. Good morning," Angel chimed, standing in the doorway. Ankle-high boots. Black leather capri pants. And a black wool crew-cut sweater that loosely clung to her breasts. "Mr. Jones. You have a messenger in the lobby. He said you have to sign for the package."

"Fine, escort him up."

While waiting, Darius scooped his papers, tapping them on his glass-top desk until they were even. Darius thumbed through the pile. All of the papers were there.

"Excuse me, sir," the man dressed in navy shorts and a navy polo-style shirt said. He punched a few buttons. "Sign here."

Darius scribbled on the electronic pad. "Thanks." Darius rattled the small cardboard box. "Well, it didn't explode. Actually it feels empty."

Darius shook the box again. The return address was a post office box. In Iowa? He frowned then sat the box aside. His meeting with Candice and his mother was in a few minutes. Terrell had insisted since everyone lived in the LA area, Candice wasn't flying to Oakland. That was cool but Darius insisted that Terrell not attend the meeting.

Angel stood in the doorway. "Mr. Jones. They're here. I think you should join them now." Angel nodded. Her eyes widened. "What was in the box? A watch?"

"I haven't opened it," Darius said, exiting behind Angel.

When he entered the conference room, his eyelids stretched toward his hairline. His mother was at one end, and Candice at the other. Darius shook his head and sat next to Candice.

"Mom, would you please come sit down here with us?" Darius paused. "Please, Mom."

Jada slowly gathered her purse and palm pilot. "Okay, if you say so. Make this quick because I have to get back to my office."

"I don't believe this. You two are acting my age. Y'all were friends before I was born. Nothing can replace friendships." Darius wished he had a male friend he could trust. K'Nine was cool but Darius hadn't called him since the night he'd used K'Nine's house to entertain Desire and her friends. Maybe after Darius started ballin' again, he'd become closer to K'Nine.

"Jada, I'll get to the point. You don't want my screenplay to be successful so Black Diamonds cannot represent me."

"I once felt that way too. But after talking to Wellington, it makes perfect sense for Black Diamonds to handle the publicity. We're best qualified and I've set aside my personal feelings."

"Oh, is that so," Candice said, staring blankly at Jada. "Well, I don't believe you."

Jada returned the same stare. "Well, I don't trust—"

"Ladies. Please. Stop it! We should all be celebrating. Not hating."

Candice rolled her eyes toward the ceiling. Jada grabbed her purse.

"Honey, I'll call you later." Jada looked down on Candice and said, "Good day. Trader thief."

Darius shook his head as Candice left him sitting at the table alone. Women.

Returning to his office, Darius picked up the box, shook it again then noticed two more identical boxes sitting on his round table. Darius dialed Angel's intercom.

"What are these other boxes?"

"I don't know. They were delivered without signature requests while you were in the meeting."

Darius hung up, palmed his scissors, and slid the edge underneath the tape. *What the shit?* When the box tumbled to the floor, ashes that reeked of sweet perfume covered the plastic mat beneath his chair. A black envelope dropped near his shoe. Darius hesitated. Cautiously he slid his letter opener across the top. Pinching the corners of the card, Darius sneezed, then read the silver metallic handwritten words, "Ashes to ashes. Dust to dust."

Repeating the words, Darius stared at the other boxes. *What? Why?* Some idiot, playing games. He was more careful opening the other boxes and letters. The second note read, *Ashes to ashes. Dust to dust.* The third, *Ashes to Ashlee. Dust to dust.*

What the fuck?! What kind of sick-ass shit was this?

"Ashes to Ashlee?" Was that a death threat to him? To Ashlee?

Darius calmly strolled into Ashlee's office. "I need you to do a sixty-day detail in San Francisco."

"What?"

"I just need you to do this, for me. It's only two months."

Ashlee frowned. "When?"

"Starting Monday."

"No way. That's too soon."

"Okay, how soon can you leave?"

"The end of the month."

Darius shook his head. "That's two weeks away."

"I know. Why the rush?"

Darius bit his bottom lip. "Just need to get the office structured before the year end. That's all."

CHAPTER 38

Small brown boxes continued being delivered. Two. Three. Sometimes five a week. The contents the same. Darius stacked the boxes in his storage cabinet as evidence to aid the police in capturing the deranged idiot. Darius prayed *Ashes to Ashlee* was a typo because all the other letters read *Ashes to Ashes*.

Angel stood in the doorway. "Mr. Jones, there's a sheriff in the lobby to see you. After you're done talking with him, we need to go over your weekend itinerary."

"Did you say a sheriff?"

Angel nodded.

"Oh, good. Maybe they've found that fool." Darius walked beside Angel until he reached the man dressed in uniform on the first floor.

"You Darius Jones?" he questioned.

"Yes, I'm Darius Jones. I hope you have some good news."

"Sir, you're being served with a restraining order. You must stay at least one hundred feet away—"

"Wait, wait, wait, hold up a minute," Darius objected, raising his hands. "A what? For what?"

"A restraining order, sir. From a Mrs. Ciara Monroe."

Darius laughed. "You got jokes. I haven't seen that bit . . . her in months."

"Then staying away shouldn't be a problem, should it, sir?" The officer handed Darius the papers and promptly left.

What was Ciara up to? Playing childish games. Ciara probably wasn't pregnant. A restraining order? The only time he touched Ciara was during sex: doggie style, missionary style, free style, or forcing her head down so she could deep throat his dick like his other freaks. Oh, he'd meant *jewels* and *gems*.

Thinking of freaks, Monica had been quiet lately. Busy trying to legally restore Ciara's controlling interest. Darius considered transferring his fifty-one percent interest in Monroe, Jones and Company to Kevin but he couldn't trust the way Kevin crawled on his belly to please Tony.

Darius crumbled the restraining order, flipped his wrists, and scored two points in his trash basket. Ciara wasn't serious. And Monica was abusing the power of attorney that Ciara had signed. Darius should have an expert compare Ciara's signatures on the restraining order and his marriage certificate. Darius looked at the restraining order in his trash can.

Angel pecked on the closed glass door.

"Come in," Darius said, powering up his palm pilot.

Angel crossed her bare legs then leaned forward. "Your flight to New York is at one on Jet Blue, gate 5C. Before you leave, Kevin needs you to sign these documents. The contractors have completed installation of security cameras in every office and on each floor. To view what everyone is doing, including me." Angel walked behind Darius and held his mouse. "Click on this icon. You need to establish your password and it's advised one additional person have the password." Angel waited until Darius selected a password. "Now if you click on an employee's photo, name, or you can view by office number, you can monitor each room, conference areas, and such. Except the restrooms. You can't see inside those." Angel smiled. "If you want the remote feature, they can also program your palm pilot so you can monitor the office at any time."

Darius clicked on Kevin's picture. Was he growing locks? Kevin dug into his nose. Darius's eyes stretched when Kevin put his finger in his mouth then dug in his nose again.

"Okay, I've seen enough. For now. No one will have access to the system until I'm comfortable with how the cameras work. And yes, I definitely want the remote monitoring feature."

"Oh, yeah. One more thing. The cameras record up to seventy-two hours. That way while the office is closed for weekends and holidays, if anything happens, you can view the DVD later. And all DVDs are backed up by the service provider. Just in case you lose or damage any of them."

Angel's body and fragrance caused blood to start to flow into Darius's dick. Darius mentally controlled Slugger then said, "Thanks, Angel. Tell Ashlee I'd like to see her in my office."

Ashlee walked in, no makeup. Slightly red eyes. No manicure. She sat in the chair in front of Darius's desk.

"Ashlee, you ready?" Darius asked, looking at her

picture on his desk then at her face. Since Ashlee started working late she'd become overly friendly with Kevin. Too friendly. And she appeared tired all the time, like Ciara before she disappeared.

Their business and pleasure trip to New York should pep Ashlee up. Darius couldn't risk having anything happen to Ashlee because of that anonymous idiot or Kevin.

"Yeah, give me a few minutes."

Kevin strolled in. "You two off on another trip? I'll see you when you get back, Ashlee. Don't forget to get my care package from my boy Lamont while you're in Harlem."

"We're going to Manhattan," Darius replied.

Kevin shook his head and smiled. "It's all the same, mein."

Darius continued, "On business. Ashlee, get your things and let's go. The driver is downstairs."

Darius escorted Ashlee to the car, left the bags on the sidewalk, and sat next to Ashlee. Ashlee refused to allow Darius to touch her en route to the airport.

Breaking the silence, Darius said, "I'm buying a second home in Oakland and need you to travel with me next weekend, so keep your schedule open."

"No, Darius. I can't. I won't. It'll just have to wait until my detail starts."

"Maybe, we'll see." Darius exhaled. "I haven't been completely honest with you, Ashlee. The reason I want you to go to San Francisco on detail is because I need to distance you from Kevin. He's my brother and well . . ."

"Well, I'm your sister."

"No, you're not. Not to me. Besides, mixing business with pleasure creates unnecessary problems." Darius reached inside his pocket. He retrieved a small black box and opened it. "Ashlee, I want you to marry me. You don't have to answer. Just wear my ring and think about it."

Ashlee shook her head. "You really are disillusioned. I cannot marry you. I will not marry you. The answer is no and keep your ring."

Rule number four: never accept no. "When you change your mind, let me know. The ring is yours," Darius said, folding the solitaire in Ashlee's hand.

Darius stopped at the ticket counter. "Can't be."

"What?" Ashlee said, trailing Darius's eyes.

Darius stared at the woman getting on a nearby elevator. Darius could spot those huge breasts anywhere. Darius yelled, "Ciara! Wait!"

Leaving his luggage, ID, and wallet at the counter with Ashlee, Darius raced toward the elevator. Ciara frantically pressed the button and vanished beyond the doors. Darius ran toward the escalator, rode halfway down, then jumped over several moving steps. Ciara briskly crossed the car and shuttle lanes. Darius ran faster shouting, "Ciara! Wait! Ciara!"

Ciara started running. She stopped by a San Francisco police officer, pulled out a piece of paper, and pointed at Darius. Darius stopped as he watched Ciara disappear into the garage.

"That bitch!" Darius would catch her conniving butt eventually. Ciara couldn't hide forever. And what was she hiding from? Certainly not him.

Returning to check-in, Darius retrieved his wallet from Ashlee.

"What was that all about? Why were you chasing her like she stole something? Why did Ciara run away?"

"I'll explain it to you later," Darius lied. "You got my boarding pass?"

Ashlee nodded.

"Good. Let's go."

CHAPTER 39

Kevin successfully swindled his first million a lot sooner, and easier, than expected. With Darius out of town, Kevin had ample time to manipulate the financial records. Poor little rich kid. So busy being important he neglected to balance his checkbook. Darius's mommy could bail him out with another million. By the time the auditors completed Darius's fiscal year-end financial analysis, Kevin would accept Tony's offer. Kevin parked in the outdoor lot at Parapictures. To his right, the studio. Ahead, the twenty-one story office building where he'd soon work.

Kevin greeted Tony in the studio. "Tony. How're the new projects coming along?" Kevin wrapped his arm around Tony's shoulder as they walked through the props at Parapictures.

"Williams," Tony said, peeling Kevin's fingers away, "you do good follow-up. You know that's where a lot of businesses fail. They get a contract and don't follow up. Learning the business. Making great suggestions.

You sure you won't accept my job offer? You're here almost every day. I could use you on my staff."

"Actually, I've been thinking about a career transition. There's no growth potential for me at Somebody's."

"Whatever Darius is paying you, I'll double it. And offer you an incentive package. Think about it. I gotta go." Tony patted Kevin on the back then shouted, "Hey, Joey! Hold up! I'm coming!"

"Peace." Kevin said, continuing to stroll the deserted set. The cast for Darius's film was shooting the last scenes in Oakland. Darius and Ashlee were in Oakland again. There was nothing to think about in regards to Tony's offer. Kevin hadn't accepted because he didn't want to appear anxious. And the longer Kevin waited, the more money Tony offered.

Kevin sat in the director's chair, pulled out his cell phone, and called his dad. "What's up, old man? When you coming to see my new house?"

"I'll be in LA soon. UCLA, Santa Barbara, and the University of Southern California coaches want to meet Darius."

Darius. Darius. Darius. That was all Darryl talked about lately. "Still steadfast on making one of us an NBA star, huh?"

"Darius is the only one of you that has the talent and skills to make it. Darryl Jr. could never dribble well with his left hand and you were never consistent with your outside shots."

Fuck Darius. "I'm going to ignore that comment. Look old man, you can stay with me or stay with Darius." Kevin paused. "Hey, why the sudden interest in Darius?"

"Can't make up for time lost but I'm tryin' to do the

right thing before it's too late. Now that I'm no longer envious of Darius or Jada, I'm proud of my son. And you should thank Darius. You wouldn't be where you are if it weren't for Darius giving you the opportunity."

Proud? His dad said he was proud of his son. Kevin wished the words were intended for him. Kevin studied the set design. "Me too. I'm tryin' to do the right thing. I'll mail you a key in case you decide to come over, stop by, whatever, and I'm not home. But call first. I might have Ashlee over."

That was another thing pissing Kevin off. Every time he made plans with Ashlee, Darius took Ashlee with him on the road. At first Kevin's attitude toward Ashlee was ill intent. Not anymore. He really did love her. There was something about Ashlee that was pure. Genuine. Romantically magnetic. After Kevin had apologized to Ashlee for disrespecting her and promised he'd never do that again, their friendship grew.

Kevin slid back his sleeve and looked at his Rolex. Oh, shit! Kevin had forgotten that his homeboy from Harlem's plane had arrived into Long Beach airport thirty minutes ago. Kevin's house was forty minutes away from Parapictures.

"Hey, old man. Let me call you later. Bye." Kevin ran to his Cadillac.

With one hand on the wood-grain steering wheel, Kevin speed dialed Lamont.

Lamont answered, "Nigga, where you at?"

Kevin darted through traffic, constantly switching lanes. "I'm on my way. I was tied up at the office. Where you at?"

"Figured as much. That's why I didn't hit you up. I'm chillin' in front your crib. Nigga I know you gave me the wrong scrillers. This ain't yo' shit. But a brotha ain't got it good like you I gotta go befo' my celly hit that next—" Lamont hung up.

When Kevin cruised in front of his home leaning out the window, Lamont was sitting on his suitcase blocking the driveway. Kevin tapped his horn and fanned his arm.

"Get out the way, nigga."

Lamont smiled. Leaving the suitcase, he walked up to the window. "Man, what bank did you rob? This you playa?" Lamont pointed at Kevin's sports utility vehicle, then the house.

"That ain't all, mein," Kevin said, still pronouncing *man* like he was ordering Chinese food. Grinning, Kevin turned off his engine. "You are looking at a certified, true-and-tried, millionaire mein." Kevin pinched the tips of his white collar then snapped his wrists.

"You lyin'. Yo' ass did rob a bank. You know I ain't never been to jail and I swear if the cops show up here, I'm tellin' 'em everything I know."

"Which ain't shit."

They entered the house laughing.

Lamont sat his suitcase in the living room and gave himself a tour. Lamont returned with the same smile plastered across his face. "Four bedrooms? Maybe you can hook me up with one of dem jobs. I can move in with you."

"Mein, your wife ain't lettin' you go nowhere and you know it. Make yourself at home. Your guest bedroom is on the left. I need to run to the office right quick. I should be back in about two hours."

"Cool, man. You got any LA freaks to introduce me to?"

"The sistahs will be here at ten. Sistah, sistahs,

mein. They do everything together. You better get some rest, call your wife early, then cut off the celly," Kevin said, opening the door.

"Now that's what I'm talkin' 'bout." Lamont bobbed his head.

"Peace." Kevin pinched his collar, snapped his wrists.

Heading toward the door, Lamont yelled, "Is that a real Rolex boy-ie!"

Kevin swiftly closed the door. His basketball shots weren't that off. Darryl should've put in more time practicing with him. Kevin arrived at the office. Making sure Angel was gone, he entered Darius's office through the back door. What were all those boxes stacked on the round table? Kevin shook one box. Then another. The box felt but didn't sound empty. Kevin opened one of the boxes.

Kevin pinched his nose. "Oh, shit! Damn, this cheap ass perfume stinks." He stared at the postcard on the floor. A closed casket. Black. Long. Kneeling over the picture, Kevin flipped it over with his pinky nail and read, "Ashes to Ashes." What the fuck did that mean? Why hadn't Darius said something? Was someone plotting to kill his brother? Who? Why? That's what Darius deserved for fucking over so many women. Maybe Kevin would stay at Somebody's longer. If Darius were killed, somebody had to take over the company. Kevin smiled. Moving to LA was the best decision he'd made in his life.

CHAPTER 40

Riding in her Benz with Monica driving, Ciara felt centered again. She was back home but not back to work. Ciara's sabbatical to the Redwood Mountains resort was a spiritual awakening which allowed her to accept Solomon's death. Regardless how insane her relationship with Solomon may have appeared to others, Ciara loved and missed Solomon.

Witnessing God's beautiful creation of rolling mountains of natural hues, brown, red, orange, strategically placed by Mother Nature enlightened Ciara that everything and everyone has its place. Its time. Over time the mountains, although breathtaking, had begun to corrode. Like mountains, with time, people inevitably had to expire. Death was as natural of a progression as life. And God controlled the start and stop watch for every living organism.

Never again would Ciara kill. A spider. A fly. An ant. A human being. At least not intentionally. But Ciara had every intention of scaring the hell out of Darius.

She wanted to make Darius think about life. His. Hers. Their son's. Ciara prayed daily for a baby boy.

Talking over dinner last night at Monica's, their sisterly bond was reunited. Monica had apologized and said, "I wanted you to feel how I was feeling and words, regardless of how I expressed myself, had no impact." Ciara remembered commenting, "Yeah, you were right. I'm sorry for shutting you out. Mama always said treat people the way they treat you and soon they will hear. Tell them what you don't like—" Monica had finished Ciara's sentence. "And they'll only hear what they want to hear."

Ciara's heart raced. The closer Ciara got to Darius's home, the more her calm demeanor converted into nervous energy. Maybe she shouldn't have showed up at Darius's house. This was the first time Monica insisted on being a part of the plan to pay back a man. Darius Jones, if he was lucky, would have all of his limbs when they left his house. Monica parked in front of Darius's house and left the engine running in the sports car.

Ciara knocked with force on Darius's front door with her boot. *Bam! Bam! Bam!* Ciara raised her boot and kicked again. *Bam! Bam! Bam!* Ciara wanted Darius to know this was not a pleasure trip.

Darius's door flung open. Holding the outside knob, Darius opened his mouth wide but before any words escaped, Ciara drew back her hand as far as she could and slapped Darius's face.

Monica whispered, "As Missy Misdemeanor would say, 'Run for cova muthafucka.' You done fucked with the wrong bitch!"

Ciara stood outside Darius's door. With every deep breath, her breasts heaved up and down. When Darius motioned to close his door, Monica swiftly put her foot between the crack and rammed her shoulder into the door so hard it flew open again.

Darius yelled, "What the fuck!"

Monica aimed a fully loaded gun at Darius's face. Ciara's eyes bucked. Ciara had no idea Monica had brought a gun. What if Monica killed Darius? Ciara and her sister would be divided by jail cells. Darius would join Solomon. And the one thing Ciara longed for would be stripped away from her bosom at birth.

Darius stood, eyes bucked, blocking the entrance. He rubbed his mouth. Blood stained his hand. He wiped the redness into his espresso-colored pajama pants. Darius casually said, "It's over, Ciara. I want a divorce."

Ciara snapped with fury. "I say when we get a divorce. And we will not get divorced until I," Ciara pointed toward her chest, "get my companies back and you," Ciara pointed her finger up toward Darius's face, "compensate me for the damages."

"This is bullshit," Darius said, stepping away from Monica's barrel and Ciara's finger. "Those are my companies. And this conversation is over. Leave my house or I'm calling the police. And what happened to your restraining order? Doesn't that mean you need to stay away from me too."

"This conversation ain't over," Monica's voice escalated, "until my sister says it's over."

"Look, Bonnie and Clyde." Darius laughed. "You two are a joke." Darius motioned to close the door again.

Monica fired two shots in the air then pointed the gun at Darius's dick.

Ciara gasped, never having intended for the situation to escalate to a life-and-death matter. Thinking back, Ciara recalled how all of the heated arguments never started off that way. Who allowed the situation to get out of control? Was it her for initiating the first words of anger? Was it Darius for mistreating her? Was it Monica for secretly bringing a gun?

Darius froze. "Oh, shit! What the fuck! You crazy ass." Darius paused. His eye widened.

Click. Monica cocked the gun, still aiming at Slugger.

Ashlee came running to the door. "No, Ashlee go back! Call the police."

"I save the best for last," Monica continued whispering. "Move again without my sister's permission and I'm going to make a lot of women happy and sad at the same time."

Darius stood still. "Y'all crazy." His blood-filled nostrils flared as his chest expanded and deflated several times.

Ciara knew he wanted to call them bitches but had enough sense to know this wasn't a good time. "Darius, all I'm demanding is restoration of my companies and reparations for any damages. You've got five days. That's all. Oh, yeah." Ciara rubbed her protruding stomach. "And you will take care of your son."

"If you don't kill him first," Darius replied.

Monica held the gun with both hands and said, "Keep messing with my baby sistah and I'm gon' tell our daddy. And trust me. You don't want me to tell Leroy." Then Monica whispered to Darius, "Five days. Or run for cova muthafucka."

Ciara turned and walked to her convertible, glad no one was seriously injured. Monica stepped backward until her butt touched the car, she opened the driver's door, and drove off. Smoke trailed the screeching tires.

"Monica, you are crazy." Ciara laughed until tears rolled down her cheeks. "I was praying you wouldn't shoot the dick. Shoot him in the ass but not the dick."

"What do you care?" Monica wasn't laughing. She was mad. "I should've shot between his legs and made him shit on himself. Always putting his dick in somebody's face. Muthafucka. I hate him!"

Ciara rubbed Monica's arm. "It's okay, Monica. Uncle Ray can't hurt us anymore. He's dead."

"You know I almost had a flashback. I really could've killed Darius. And it would've had nothing to do with Darius."

"We gon' be alright. I don't have to leave for Trinidad today. I can stay here with you or you can come vacation with me." Tears of sadness rolled down Ciara's face. She remembered all the bad things Uncle Ray had done to them. Uncle Ray especially liked Monica because Monica was older and her butt was bigger. Uncle Ray liked Ciara because her titties were big even when she was a little girl. Uncle Ray said, "If either of you tell a soul, I'm telling the police how your daddy, crazy Leroy, killed our brother. It wasn't an accident. Oh, no he meant to kill Slim." After Uncle Ray died of a heart attack, their daddy had become depressed. Ciara and Monica decided the rapes weren't worth talking about or telling Daddy. But Ciara knew the nightmares still haunted both of them. And perhaps that's why neither of them knew how to sustain healthy relationships with men.

Monica parked at LAX passenger departure. The patrol officer blew her whistle several times. Ciara dried Monica's tears with a tissue. "You sure you're gonna be okay, Sis?"

Monica blinked several times, washing away her tears. "Yeah, Sis. I'll be okay. Now, go. Enjoy your vacation. I'll pick you up in five days."

Ciara motioned to the patrol officer to stop blowing that damn whistle. "I love you. I'll call you as soon as I get in."

Monica nodded then drove off. Ciara wheeled her carry-on to the counter and handed the ticket agent her passport.

Ciara boarded her plane and propped the pillow against the window in first class. She refused to entertain Darius's request for a divorce. Maybe she'd hire a private investigator to work internally for Darius's company and sabotage Darius's business. Kevin claimed he had no knowledge of the takeover but Ciara didn't trust Kevin any more than she trusted Darius. Maybe she'd report Darius to the Internal Revenue Service for tax evasion. Even if the IRS didn't uncover any wrongdoings, the costly investigation would take months.

Dozing off, Ciara smiled thinking about her return home to Monica in five days.

CHAPTER 41

At Jada's request—a formal invite sent via the United States Postal Service—Candice agreed to meet for lunch at Alex's. The filming was complete. Editing was scheduled to begin next week. Darius had insisted that Jada fly to Oakland and view the taping of the last scenes. Watching Morris and Kenya reenact the breakup of her relationship with Wellington made Jada cry, wishing she'd never left. They'd lost twenty years. Years that could've been filled with loving memories as husband and wife. Twenty anniversaries.

Candice must have designed the set of Jada's penthouse in the Oakland Hills. The backdrop with the tall evergreen trees. The living-room fireplace. The packed boxes. The sofa and unpacked throw pillows. Then it happened. Kenya gave Morris the soul mate ring. The same ring Jada had given to Wellington the night their relationship ended. Jada watched intently when Morris kissed Kenya. Then they made love. Jada relived her orgasmic moment. Hearing Kenya speak

Jada's last words to Wellington, "I don't know where we go from here . . . but I do know I've renewed my lease on life. I have a business to start and a plane to catch to Los Angeles. Maybe I'll call you. Maybe I won't." Jada recalled feeling empowered and empty at the same time. How many people were fortunate to have someone turn their life into a movie? Being on the set for five days, Jada realized she may not have another twenty years to live. But if she did, she didn't want to live them without her best friend.

Jada sat in her office brainstorming how to best promote the movie and Soul Mate jewelry line. Jada's secretary buzzed the intercom.

"Mrs. Tanner, you have a Mr. Reynolds on the phone. He will only speak with you."

"Reynolds? What company is he with?"

"I don't know and he won't say."

Another person trying to get to Darius through her. Jada imagined when Darius did join the NBA she'd have more strangers and clients trying to get tickets, hopefully to the Lakers' games. "Thanks, put him through."

Jada glanced down at blank sheet of paper. Lost in thought, great ideas floated in her mind. This Mr. Reynolds guy would delay progress.

"Hello, Mr. Reynolds. How may I help you?"

"Thanks for taking my call. The reason I'm calling is your company came highly recommended by one of my long-term clients. I'd like to discuss contracting with Black Diamonds to do PR for my upcoming film festival."

"I'm listening."

"Specifically, I'll need two full-time staff persons for six weeks to focus on our print ads, radio announcements, TV commercials, and internet promotions."

"My company can handle that. Let's schedule a meeting to outline the details."

"One more thing. Are you part owner of Somebody's Gotta Be on Top?"

"No, I'm not," Jada lied. "That's my son's company. Why do you ask?"

"Great! Then can you facilitate a meeting with my company and your son's? We really want his input for our featured film."

"I have a client on the other line," Jada lied to get Mr. Reynolds off the phone. "I'll give Darius your information today, and I'll speak with you tomorrow. Good-bye Mr. Reynolds."

Jada stared at the blank page. Tiny black dots formed each time the pen tapped. Who was this Mr. Reynolds? She'd never heard of him before. What film festival? Did he really want her assistance or was he trying to find out more about Darius's company?

Jada left her office and drove to Darius's home. She parked in his driveway. Slowly she approached the door and rang the doorbell. Waited. Knocked. Waited again. Jada fumbled through her purse and retrieved her keys to Darius's house. Slowly she unlocked the top, then the bottom.

Pushing the door, Jada said, "Hello. Is anybody home?"

No answer. Music was playing softly throughout the house. Jada tapped on Ashlee's door. The guest bedroom door. The other doors. Then Darius's bedroom door. No answers. She opened Darius's door. His room was designed for a king. Royal purple smothered in a rich gold and deep black covered his bed.

Jada shuffled through the stack of papers on Darius's credenza. Neatly she searched every drawer. His nightstands were filled with condoms. Jada noticed a black briefcase peeping from underneath the bed. She retrieved the case, slid the gold latches, and was happy they released. Jada opened the case. Photos of naked women spilled onto the carpet. Black. White. Asian. Latino. Some nationalities she couldn't identify.

"Jada? Is that you?"

When Jada looked up, Ashlee was standing in the doorway. "Oh." Jada hurriedly stuffed the pictures back inside, closed the case, then pushed it under the bed. "Yeah, I just lost my earring."

"Underneath Darius's bed?"

Jada stood, brushed her pants, and walked over to Ashlee. "Yes. That's all."

"What were you looking for?"

"Ashlee, come here. Sit." Jada patted the sofa in Darius's bedroom. "I need to speak with you."

"I don't think we should be in Darius's room. He likes his privacy. Besides, I came by to get a few things I'd left. I'll talk with you in the living room."

"Fine." This child really needed professional help, Jada thought. Ashlee was in denial of her true feelings for Darius. Jada glanced around Darius's room, making certain she'd left everything in its place.

"Is something wrong?" Ashlee asked.

"Yes, there is. I need to know what you know about Ciara."

"Darius told us not to discuss business-related issues with anyone who wasn't involved."

"Ashlee, look at me. I'm Darius's mother. And I was once like a mother to you. I am involved." Jada couldn't believe she was so desperate to save her son that she was snooping behind Darius's back.

"I know," Ashlee said. "But it's confidential. I can't."

"What's really confidential between you and Darius? I've seen the way you two look at one another."

"If you mean are we intimately involved, no. If you mean are we in love, yes."

"Ashlee, how could you? Darius is your brother."

"I know it's not right. But I can't help how I feel about him. Or how he feels toward me. That's why I moved out. I'm going on detail to San Francisco."

"Ashlee, let me tell you something about love. If in your heart you feel a relationship is not right, don't go there. Love is sacred, not selfish. You and Darius have a special kind of love. One that allows the two of you to depend on each other no matter what. That's what you want to preserve. Your friendship of love. You were smart to move out of Darius's house. Because if you ever cross the line with Darius, he'll hurt you just like all the rest. You know how Darius is. He loves women." Jada thought about showing Ashlee the pictures. That was a bad idea. "Darius needs your love. But he doesn't need to be your lover. I've got to go."

En route to the restaurant, Jada thought about what she'd tell Darius if Ashlee told him she was searching through his belongings. Jada valet parked at Alex's. Stopping at the host, Jada saw Candice waving and said, "Never mind. I see her."

"Hey, girl. I'm glad to see you."

"Me, too," Jada said, wrapping her arms around Candice's shoulders. "Two mimosas please."

"This is just like old times. I missed my friend." Candice smiled.

The waiter placed two champagne flutes on the table.

Jada raised her glass and said, "A toast. To success. Your film. My life. Our money."

When the crystal clanged, Candice said, "Jada, I just want you to know. I never stopped being your friend."

Jada looked at Candice and said, "I know."

CHAPTER 42

Darius lay across his bed waiting for Kimberly to finish her shower. The day was long. The evening was early. Six o'clock. The fifth day of Ciara's threat. Darius didn't trust driving his car, or working in his office. But no woman could punk him out of being at his own house. Ashlee's flight was departing to San Francisco in four hours. Ashlee insisted on taking a late-night flight and traveling alone. Maybe she was spending time with Kevin. Darius tried clearing his mind and thinking about nothing like his mother did when she meditated.

Darius hurriedly answered his cellular, "Yeah, what's up?"

In an already disappointed tone, the familiar voice of Crystal on the opposite end replied, "Hey, daddy. What time you coming home to mama?"

Darius sensed the underlying tension in her voice. She knew he'd lie to her again and couldn't understand why she kept subjecting herself to unnecessary pain.

At the moment he was too busy to care and replied, "I told you I'm working late. Why do you keep calling and asking me the same annoying-ass question? Maybe you're right. Maybe you are losing your damn mind."

Silence lingered. He could picture the tears welling in her sad brown eyes. Darius couldn't remember when he'd begun treating Crystal badly but his patience had grown shorter by the day. And any day the shit was going to explode because he was tired of Crystal calling him all the damn time.

"Look," he continued, breaking the stillness. "I gotta go."

"But—"

Darius hung up, rolled over, then kissed Kimberly on the ass. "Give daddy some brain." He needed more than just head. Darius wanted Kimberly to suck him unconscious so he could forget that Crystal existed.

At least Kimberly knew what she was doing. Not like the college student he'd fucked last night. Whatever her name was. Any female that sucked his dick within four hours of meeting him wasn't worth remembering no matter how fine she was.

Kimberly worked her magic. Slurping. Stroking. Nibbling on his head until waves of semen flowed. Just as the last wave disappeared into her mouth, his cell phone rang. Darius ignored the call.

"Get daddy a hot towel and some juice."

Kimberly bounced her booty until she was out of his sight.

Darius's phone rang again. Blocked call. Darius massaged his drooping penis. Kimberly cleaned his pubic hairs, balls, and dick.

Darius yelled into the phone, "What? Crystal, I told you—"

"Hey, mein. This is Kevin. Your office is burning down. Get over here. Now!"

Darius leaped from the bed. "What the fuck did you just say?"

"Get over here right away, mein. Somebody's Gotta Be on Top Enterprises is up in flames!"

"What's wrong?" Kimberly asked, sitting up in the bed.

"My office building is on fire," Darius answered, hopping on one leg to put pants on his naked body.

"Did you know you were calling Ciara's name in your sleep?" Kimberly asked, pressing the power button on the remote.

Who gave a fuck! Women. His office was burning down and all Kimberly could say was he called Ciara's name in his sleep. Fuck Ciara! Darius heard Monica's voice, *"Run for cova muthafucka."*

"Aw, shit!" Darius mouthed, "Ashes to Ashlee." *So that's what that meant.*

Darius raced out the door, dialing Ashlee's number from his cell. Ashlee was the only woman alive worthy of becoming his wife. And as soon as he divorced Ciara, he was going to do right by Ashlee.

The call dropped immediately when he closed his car door. "This is bullshit!" Darius hit redial. The call dropped again. The third time he heard, "Hi, you've reached Ashlee Anderson of . . ." Fourth. Fifth. Sixth. Seventh. Darius tried again.

Darius drove as fast as he could until he arrived at his office. Flames surrounded the perimeter. Firefighters raced out of the burning building. Darius ran to Kevin shouting, "Where is she, man?" For a second, Darius thought about his palm pilot and how he'd seen Kevin sneaking into his office from the back stairway.

"I spoke with her a few hours ago. She should be en route to the airport," Kevin replied.

"Whew!" Darius's back hand swiped his sweaty forehead. "So this is what those messages meant," Darius mumbled.

"What messages, mein? The ones in all those boxes stacked in your cabinet?"

Darius shifted his eyes toward Kevin. "Yeah, you know. The ones you searched every time you snuck into my office. I should whup your ass." Darius closed his eyes and prayed, thanking God he'd sent Ashlee to San Francisco. Yeah, it was eight o'clock. Ashlee was at the airport. Darius's insurance company would cover all damages.

"Mein, look out!" Kevin yelled, pushing Darius aside. A computer chair flew out from the top-floor window.

"Help," the voice was faint. Ashlee stood in the window, then suddenly disappeared coughing behind a cloud of smoke.

"Ashlee! I'm coming to save you!" Darius yelled. "Kevin, give me your shirt and socks." Darius wrapped the cotton shirt around his face, placed the socks on his hands, and then raced into the flames.

"Stop!" The firefighters restrained Kevin, but were unable to catch Darius.

What have I done? I'mma die in here. I can't see shit, Darius thought as he crawled up the back stairs to the third floor. *Lord, please, Jesus. I know I'm not supposed to open this door. If it's my time.* Darius ripped his pants leg, double wrapped his hand, reached up and turned the knob. He stumbled over Ashlee's motionless body lying in the hallway. Through the smoke, water, and flames, Darius gasped for air. His legs buckled when he tossed Ashlee over his shoulder.

Darius thought, *Ashlee, I got you into this. And I swear I'll get you out alive even if it kills me.*

CHAPTER 43

The hospital's waiting room was quiet. Kevin discreetly observed Jada. She was fine for an older woman. Wellington. Looked like money. Candice, in her younger days, she was probably fine as hell. Not now. Terrell. Aging actor trying to stay young-looking. Darryl sat next to Kevin eyeing Jada.

The ambulances had rushed Darius and Ashlee to emergency. Grateful those firemen caught him, Kevin questioned his love for Ashlee. He had no intentions of making it past the firemen like Darius but he had to pretend, so he could lie to Ashlee about how he tried to save her life.

Kevin whispered, "Dad, stop staring."

"I'm not. Unless I close my eyes, I have to look someplace. Right?" Darryl's red eyes shifted to Kevin. "I'm so glad Darius didn't die in that fire you know. We're really bonding. He's actually quite funny when he's relaxed. And he handles that basketball like he handles his business, intelligently. I pray this accident doesn't ruin Darius's chances of going pro. "

If Darius was so intelligent, why didn't he keep better account of his money? Kevin shook his head, doubting Darryl would've taken the first flight out to LA if it were him in the hospital.

The nurse entered, interrupting his thoughts. "Is anyone here from the Anderson family?"

Kevin glanced around the room. Jada was curled on the sofa sleeping in Wellington's lap. With the support of a pillow braced behind his head, Wellington was also asleep. Kevin glanced around the room again. Ashlee's family wouldn't get into town until late night, early morning. Kevin stood. "You can talk to me."

"And how are you related?"

Kevin lied, "She's my fiancée."

"Come with me," the nurse said, extending her hand.

"Wait a minute." Jada quickly stood.

Wellington sat up straight. "Huh, what. What's going on?"

"I'm coming too," Jada insisted. "I'm her ex-mother-in-law."

The nurse ushered them. "Please, come quickly."

Following the nurse out the door, Jada said, "Wellington, you can go back to sleep. We're going to see about Ashlee."

The nurse led them to the burn unit. "They'll bring her to this room shortly. But I wanted to explain her injuries. Thanks to the brave young man, your son," the nurse touched Jada's hand, "she's alive. We need to keep her a while."

"What's a while?" Jada questioned.

"We're not sure. Maybe a week. Some patients heal faster than others. She has second-degree burns to the left side of her face as well as neck and back. Later she can decide if she wants dermabrasion or skin grafts. If you truly love her, sir," the nurse looked at Kevin, "she's going to need you now more than ever before. Her face won't ever look the same."

When the nurse displayed the photos, Kevin gasped. Jada gagged. One arm hugged her stomach, the other cupped her mouth. Jada raced into the bathroom.

"Oh, my gosh." Tears rolled down Kevin's face.

Ashlee's facial skin blended with flesh and blood. The nurse placed the pictures in her pocket and said, "Her back is slightly worse. She's heavily sedated so you can stay a few minutes and come back tomorrow."

"I'm not leaving," Kevin said, sitting in the chair.

"Kevin, don't," Jada said, drying her hands with a paper towel.

Kevin tightened his lips. His hands clamped then lay on his forehead. His head rested against the back of the chair. "I knew something was going to happen. I just didn't know what. If I had said something, maybe this wouldn't have happened."

Jada frowned at Kevin. "Kevin, what are you talking about?"

The nurse stared at Kevin. "What are you talking about? How could you have known something was going to happen?"

Kevin shook his head. "I don't know. I don't know what I know. All I know is . . . oh, my God!"

"What, Kevin? What do you know?" Jada asked.

"Darius . . ."

"Darius, what?" Jada stooped to Kevin's face level. "Look at me, Kevin."

The nurse said, "Darius is fine, Kevin. Amazing, but all Darius has are a few first-degree burns and minor bruises. Nothing serious. We're holding him for observation. He should be released tomorrow or at the latest the next day."

Kevin's eyes widened. "Darius knew someone was trying to kill Ashlee. He had tons of boxes in his storage room with threatening messages."

The nurse gasped, "We were advised this was an accident. But with that information, I have to report this to the authorities." The nurse quickly left the room.

"Kevin, why in the hell would you say something like that? You made her believe Darius was responsible for Ashlee's injuries."

"Well, he didn't say anything. Did he?"

Jada yelled, "You conniving bastard! Why would Darius risk his life? I never did trust you."

The nurse raced into the room. "I'm going to have to ask both of you to wait in the waiting room. The police are on their way to take a report."

"I'll be back," Kevin said, standing tall.

Jada yelled, "You'd better not tell the police Darius is responsible for this!"

Leaving the room, Kevin said, "Don't worry. I'll only tell them what I know."

Jada scurried by Kevin, then looked back. "Yeah, you do that and I'll tell them everything I know too. About you."

"You don't know nothin' about me, lady." Jada couldn't intimidate him. Kevin could lie to the officers and have Darius arrested. But how could Kevin avoid giving his statement in front of Darryl?

Kevin entered the unisex restroom and turned the latch. He dialed Ciara's number. "Yeah, Darius is going to be in the hospital a day or so. Have your attorney draw up the documents and I'll sign them. So by the time Darius is released, you'll have full ownership of both your companies."

Ciara asked, "How much do you want?"

"Your loyalty. That's all." Kevin hung up the phone, smiled, then opened the door. "What the hell?" Kevin braced himself then stepped backward.

Jada's ear was pressed against the door.

CHAPTER 44

"Wellington, go ahead without me, honey. I'll meet you at the hospital," Jada said, stuffing a tote bag with ointments, gauze, and tape for Darius to take home.

"Okay, ba. I'll see you there. You know this son of ours is always getting into something. This accident may be just what he needed to wake him up. I'm just sorry Ashlee was hurt in the process." Wellington kissed Jada's lips. "I love you."

"Yeah, me too. I mean about Darius. And I love you too, honey," Jada replied, inconspicuously gazing at the time on her watch. Her eyes trailed Wellington until he vanished beyond the doorway, down the stairs. He was still sexy. Handsome. Just like the night they'd met in San Francisco at the Will Downing concert. When Jada heard the front door close, she dialed Theo from the bedside cordless.

"Hey, babydoll. You're late. You were supposed to call me over an hour ago."

"I know. But I couldn't." Jada became silent. Nervous. Then said, "Okay, I'm listening."

"Well, your son is in serious trouble."

"Just tell me." Jada had enough worries. Nausea invaded her stomach.

"For starters, he's bankrupt and doesn't know it."

"Bankrupt! Darius is bankrupt!"

"Yup. There's a company named NyVek which is Kevin spelled backward with a *y* instead of an *i*. NyVek has embezzled almost all of Somebody's Gotta Be on Top revenue and falsified the financial records so on paper Darius thinks he has money. Darius has gained control over Ciara's companies. Monica, Ciara's sister has vowed revenge if Darius doesn't undo the legal mess he's created. Ciara's pregnant and in hiding. I've got to give it to her. Theo hasn't even found that broad. But I will. And . . . I hope you're sitting down. Ciara and Darius are legally married. So Ciara legally owns interest in Darius's company. And . . . I hope you're lying down for this one."

Jada sat on the edge of the bed.

"Some broad named Desire who lives in London is a part of the equation. She's six months pregnant, says it's Darius's baby, and when the baby is born she going to request a paternity test. Babydoll, you know what's next if the test comes back and Darius is the father. Mo' money."

"Stop! I can't take any more! Darius is bankrupt! Darius is married! Two women are pregnant!"

"I hate to interrupt you, babydoll but there's one more thing . . . Ciara and Monica are responsible for burning down Darius's office."

"Okay, I really can't handle any more right now. I gotta go."

"Don't you want to hear the good news?"

"No. I don't."

"Well, babydoll. Just so you'll know. I had my inside contact at the IRS freeze all of Kevin Williams's assets. So Theo will make sure that Darius eventually gets his money back. But if I were you, I'd make Darius sweat."

"Thanks, Theo. Bye." Jada hung up the phone, dried her tears, grabbed the tote, and bumped into Wellington who was holding the other cordless in his hand as she walked out of the bedroom. "Shit! You scared the hell out of me!"

"You care to tell me what that phone conversation was all about?" His eyes squinted so tight all Jada saw were Wellington's pupils.

"We'd better sit down and discuss this." Jada told Wellington how she'd hired Theo to follow Darius, Ciara, Kevin, and Candice. Candice was the only one on whom Theo had nothing to report. Jada reluctantly explained everything Theo had revealed.

Wellington shook his head. "I don't believe you." Wellington stood. Jada grasped his bicep.

Wellington whispered angrily, "Don't touch me." Pulling his arm away, Wellington walked out and slammed the door. Jada jumped. Tears poured. "What have I done?" Jada dried her eyes. "I don't have time to feel sorry for myself. Darius needs me."

On the drive to the hospital, Jada reflected on how she could have handled things differently. Why did she cover up so much from Wellington? Hopefully neither Wellington nor Lawrence would ever find out she had aborted Lawrence's child during their second year of marriage. Jada couldn't handle raising another child. Darius was almost in high school. Her business was thriving. Her body was tight. She didn't deserve Wellington. After his affair with Melanie, actually after their marriage, Wellington was faithful. No unexplained phone calls, numbers in his pocket, or questionable whereabouts.

When Jada arrived at the hospital, Wellington's car was parked in the hospital's garage. Jada parked opposite Wellington's Jaguar. "Lord, give me strength," Jada said, entering Darius's hospital room.

"Hi, Ashlee." She looked over at Darius. "Hi, honey. How are you?" Darius had requested to room with Ashlee. Jada patted Ashlee's hand then kissed Darius's forehead. Darius clung to Jada's embrace. For the first time since Ma Dear died, Darius had a tear in his eye.

"Tell him everything you know," Wellington insisted. "We have to work this out as a family."

Jada nodded toward Ashlee and said, "Wellington."

"She's family. Tell him now, Jada."

Jada told Darius what Theo discovered. Ashlee turned her back and wept.

"I'mma kill that connivin' muthafucka! I knew I couldn't trust him!" Darius limped around his bed. "Ashlee, you in on this shit? You knew about this? You giving my money away?! Huh! Answer me!"

Shaking his head, Wellington said, "Son, lay back down. This is not Ashlee's fault. The only thing you're going to do right now is listen to us. We've decided," Wellington looked at Jada, then at Darius, "that the money we loaned you must be repaid by the end of the year. And, since we already know you can't afford to repay us and you no longer have an office in Los Angeles, we're taking over your company. And you can't work for us, Son. You're going to have to get a job. Working for someone else."

"Oh, hell no!" Darius jumped up again. "Ma! You can't let him do this!"

Jada frowned at Wellington. His eyes met hers. Wellington didn't blink or speak to her.

Wellington continued, "Son, you don't respect your mother. You don't respect me. You don't respect your wife. You don't even respect yourself. So why should we contribute to you using other people? We won't. Never again. And if you don't get a job, we're taking your name out of our will. You'll inherit nothing."

"Man, this is bullshit!" Darius swung his fist in the air. "I don't need y'all! I'm going to the NBA!"

"And, if you curse one more time," Wellington harshly whispered, "I'll whup your ass and extend your hospital stay through the New Year. You can watch the NBA on television. But you won't play anywhere."

Darius shook his head. "Just go. Y'all need to get up out of my room."

"Boy, you are really pushing me." Wellington stood over Darius. "Shut up! And lay down! We leave when we get ready. And from the way things are right now, you won't even own a damn house to live in! I'll take those too!"

Darius stepped back and sat on the bed. "Why you always taking up for her?!" Darius pointed toward his mother.

What? For her. Jada was contemplating how she could help Darius and Darius was turning on her. Jada remained quiet. Tears poured again.

"Because I love your mother. I married your mother for better or for worse and I meant that. It's called commitment, Son. Something that you know nothing about."

When Darius's door opened, Jada, Wellington, and

Darius turned in unison. Lawrence stood in the doorway and said, "I came to see my daughter. I warned her not to come here. When she's released, I'm taking her back to Dallas."

Ashlee uncovered her head. "Daddy!" Her smile was tight due to the bandages. Ashlee stretched her arms. She couldn't reach far so Lawrence leaned over and kissed Ashlee.

Jada looked at Lawrence then at Wellington, grateful she hadn't given birth to Lawrence's child. The Lord knew Darius was more than enough. Jada glanced at Ashlee, then at Darius.

"Lawrence, man. Come in," Wellington said. "Darius, you owe Lawrence an apology for misleading Ashlee."

Darius looked at Wellington and said, "Maybe your wife owes him an apology for aborting his baby."

Chill bumps formed over Jada's body. Oh, no he didn't. The room suddenly became cold. Jada gasped for air. Everyone stared at Jada. Jada froze. How did Darius know? Her face dropped. Darryl? Candice? Damn. She did talk too much.

When Jada didn't respond, Wellington casually strolled out of the room shaking his head.

Lawrence stared in disgust. "Like mother. Like son. The only thing that will change your lying ways is death. But you're not keeping my daughter here with you."

Jada looked at Darius. Silence. Then Darius whispered, "Ma, he's right. I am just like you. I don't want to mess up other people's lives. But somehow I always do. I love you, Ma. But I hate you too."

Jada thought her mother's death had been the saddest day of her life. But hearing her only son say he hated her shattered her heart into a million pieces.

CHAPTER 45

Darius didn't need Wellington. Wellington could take back his money, the company, even his last name. Darius had Darryl. After all the cruel words Darius had spoken to his mother, shockingly, his mom continued supporting him. Jada made Wellington leave Darius's homes, cars, and personal bank accounts in Darius's name, saying, "Wellington, you can't strip Darius of everything he's worked for. You'll destroy him. And no, my child will not live in a shelter; he's going back to college." Darius had bet that Wellington, under the same circumstances, wouldn't have treated little Wellington the same. That spoiled brat tore up the entire house on visitation weekends and all Wellington did was laugh.

Darius drove his Bentley to what once was his office building to assess the damages. "Damn. Maybe that's what Ma Dear meant when she used to say, 'Is possession a form of ownership, if nothing lasts forever but everything has a price?'" Darius sat in his car. The front side of the building had collapsed. The back stair-

well, protected by the fire wall stood three stories high.
The perimeter was wrapped with yellow caution tape.
His records. Contracts. Furniture. Gone. He could replace the furniture. He'd request duplicate contracts
from his attorney. Some of his records were irreplace-
able. That's right, those were Wellington's records.
Wellington didn't know jack about the film industry so
sooner or later he'd have to rely on Darius.

Getting out the car, Darius leaned against the side.
Why would Ciara want to hurt Ashlee? When he did
come face-to-face with the Monroe sisters, they'd be
lucky if Darius didn't kill them. Why did bad things
happen to the women he loved?

A masculine voice from behind said, "I thought I'd
find you here."

Darius turned, paused. "Hey, old man. What's up?"

"Since when did I become an old man?" Darryl
asked, leaning on the car next to Darius. "You okay?"

"Don't know what to think right now. With my company gone and all." Darius was pleased Darryl had
found him. "I never expected this to happen. Why
would Ciara do something like this? Ashlee could've
died in that fire. And me too."

"Son, a woman scorned will do irrational things. A
business partner cheated or threatened will go to ex-
tremes. And accidents do happen. Pick one or all
three." Darryl walked toward the building. "How are
you so sure Ciara is the one who did this?"

Darius thought about the day Ciara and Monica
threatened him. Shaking his head Darius replied, "I'm
not sure."

"Well, you'd better keep thinking because this person may still come after you. Now for some good
news. Sixteen universities want you. You can start next

semester and you're guaranteed to walk on to any of those teams. We can tour your top five or six colleges together."

Darius smiled. For the first time in months Darius had a reason to be excited. "Whoa, are you serious?"

Darryl nodded then named the colleges. Darius smiled. Ma Dear must have saved him again.

"Son, if you have wronged anyone, I suggest you apologize and mean it. Because once you go pro, every skeleton you have will jump," Darryl leaped high in the air, "out at cha. Trust me."

"I have a few," Darius admitted. "You hungry, old man?"

"No, I'm going to Kevin's, packing my bags, and heading to the airport. Let me know what schools you're interested in in three days." Darryl opened his arms. For the first time, Darius embraced his father.

Darius sat in his car and dialed Ashlee's cell number. Darius drove behind Darryl until they went separate ways on the freeway.

"Hello," Lawrence answered.

Darius hung up. How could he apologize if he couldn't talk to Ashlee? Darius didn't know where Ciara was. Darius parked in his mother's driveway, then rang the doorbell.

The door opened. "Hi, honey. Why didn't you use your key?"

Darius was quiet. His arms wrapped around his mother's shoulders. Darius squeezed tighter. "I love you, Mom." Darius blinked, washing away his tears before his mother noticed.

"Oh, honey. You don't know how long I've waited to hear you speak those words." Jada sniffled as her body trembled.

"I apologize for hurting you, Mom. I'll never treat you like that again."

Breaking Darius's embrace, Jada looked up at Darius.

The tears Darius held for twenty-two years poured. Darius squatted to the floor. His mother sat in the foyer holding him in her arms.

Darius would apologize to Wellington tomorrow. Between sniffles and mucus, Darius mumbled, "Grandpa Robert is turning over in his grave right now calling me a sissy."

"Baby, everybody's gotta cry, sometimes."

CHAPTER 46

Kevin sat by Ashlee's bedside. Rubbing her hand. Making her laugh. While Ashlee wasn't as attractive on the outside, she was still perfectly beautiful on the inside. Her smile was slightly crooked, her eyes puffy and red. The nurse said that after the dermabrasion Ashlee's face would almost appear normal. And after the lawsuit that Kevin would help Ashlee to file against Darius, Ashlee would never have to work again.

Kevin reached into his pocket. A modest diamond ring, one and half carats, set in ten-karat gold, sparkled. Ashlee wasn't a flamboyant woman. She didn't need the riches to be happy. Kevin wanted to spoil Ashlee with money and love. First he'd have to convince Lawrence that, unlike Darius, he'd take good care of his daughter. Hopefully Kevin had made progress by visiting Ashlee each day.

"Ashlee Anderson." Kevin gently touched Ashlee's foot. The lower parts of her body weren't sensitive to pressure. "Will you marry me?"

Ashlee stared. She didn't frown or smile so Kevin waited for a response.

Shaking her head, Ashlee said, "You can't be serious."

The sensitivity in Kevin's heart softened the look in his eyes. "I'm very serious. I love you."

"You feel sorry for me. You don't love me. You're competing with Darius. I've had enough of your lies."

"Competing? What's that supposed to mean?"

"You're brothers. You're always in competition. For business. Women."

"Ashlee, I swear. I'm serious. I wouldn't lie to you about something like this." Kevin walked around the bed and knelt before Ashlee. He showed her the ring. "I would like an answer."

"Let me get out of the hospital. Get through rehab. Become as healthy as I can. So I can move as far away as possible from you and Darius. No, I will not marry you."

Kevin pressed two fingers against his lips, then pressed the same two fingers atop Ashlee's big toe.

Ashlee smiled then laughed. "You are so silly."

"Only with you, my love. Only with you. I'll be right back. In about thirty minutes."

Kevin raced to the lobby. Surprised to see Darius and Jada, Kevin ignored them and dialed Darryl's number.

"Hey, Dad. I have great news. Ashlee and I are getting married."

Darius stood over Kevin. "You are not going to marry Ashlee."

"Mein, step back. I'm not talking to you."

Darius moved closer. "Make me step back."

Jada bridged herself between Kevin and Darius.

"Break this mess up! Kevin, Darius is right. You will not marry Ashlee. You broke your lease in Harlem, and stole one million dollars from your brother's company, Somebody's Gotta Be on Top. I guess you thought that somebody was going to be you. Riding high off of someone else's wealth. Well, I've told Tony everything. And I've had all of your bank accounts frozen. You will repay my son every penny you owe him plus interest. Because you see we, my husband and I, loaned Darius a million dollars to start his business! And I'll be damned if you or anyone else is going to steal it from him! You are truly your daddy's child! Gimme that damn phone."

Jada snatched the phone from Kevin. "Darryl, you'd better come and get this child before the coroners have to. Kevin has stolen a million dollars from Darius. Darius's company nearly went bankrupt. And thanks to NyVek, Kevin's fictitious company, Wellington and I had to put money into Darius's account so his business wouldn't fold." Darius smiled as Jada handed the phone to Kevin. "Your daddy wants to talk to you. Darius, let's go." Jada looked back at Kevin and said, "If you lie to Ashlee, I'll tell her the truth. The whole truth."

Kevin squinted because he wanted to call Jada a bitch like his father had done years ago when he'd said, "All you bitches are just alike," but he couldn't. Because Ashlee was nothing like Jada. Nothing like any of the women he'd met.

Kevin exhaled, then said, "Yes, Dad."

"Is Jada telling the truth? You stole money from Darius?"

Kevin sighed. "Well, it was more like a loan."

"A loan my ass! A loan means someone gives you

the money. You're stealing if you take the money and only pay it back if they find out. So that's how you bought that house. The car. Boy, you wait until I see you. I'm not boarding this plane. I'm on my way to your house right now and you'd better be there when I get there."

"But, Dad. Some of the money I earned honestly from working for Darius."

"I knew you were up to no good when you moved to LA but I had no idea."

"I was tired of working, hustling, and still living in a one-bedroom apartment in the ghetto. I wanted to live rich like you. Like Darius."

"Boy, that's the stupidest thing I've heard. I work for the things I have. I have a job."

"Yeah, but you're working extra hard to get Darius into the NBA so you can quit your job."

"Kevin, that's not true."

"Dad, we're too much alike. I know you. It is true. You never helped me like that. Bye, Dad." Kevin hung up the phone.

How in the hell did Kevin's whole life fall apart in fifteen minutes? Kevin speed dialed the eight hundred number to his bank. He keyed in his ten-digit account number. "Please hold while we transfer you to an operator."

"Thank you for holding, may I help you?"

"I'd like the balance on my account number five dash. . . ."

After verifying the last four digits of Kevin's social security number and place of birth, the customer service representative replied, "Your balance is nine hundred fifty-seven thousand, six hundred eighty-two dollars and twenty-one cents."

"Yes!" Kevin balled his fist and jerked his arm alongside his leg which he lifted in the air. "I'm heading straight to the bank." Darryl would have to wait.

"Excuse me, Sir."

"Yes," Kevin cheerfully said.

"The IRS has frozen your assets. Your available balance is zero. On all of your accounts. Savings, checking, and credit cards."

Kevin hung up the phone. His direct deposit was just deposited yesterday. With five hundred dollars in his pocket, his mortgage and car note due, Kevin returned to Ashlee's bedside. He might need her a lot sooner than she'd need him. Ashlee had to have money. She lived with Darius a long time. Didn't have to pay rent. Darius insisted she charge all her meals to his expense account. Ashlee had to have a healthy bank account. Kevin had to stay close enough to Jada to prevent Jada from telling Ashlee the truth.

CHAPTER 47

It was two weeks before Christmas. Darius was relieved Ashlee was being released from the hospital. Their year started off joyfully. Darius reflected on holding Ashlee in his arms. He felt responsible for what had happened to Ashlee. Darius wasn't sure if he was standing outside Ashlee's hospital door because he felt guilty, or if he was still in love with Ashlee. Darius tapped on the door then opened it.

"Hey, you ready?" Usually when he spoke those words they were off on a trip. "I made plans for us to go to Paris for New Year's Eve." Darius wanted to apologize to Ashlee but not at the hospital.

"You shouldn't have. Yeah, I'm ready. Ready to get the hell away from you." The scar curved Ashlee's pinkish-brown lips into a half smile. "Oh, I almost forgot." Ashlee opened the drawer and removed her diamond ring.

Trying not to laugh, Darius smiled then lied, "Nice ring."

"Yeah, Kevin gave it to me when he proposed."

"What, I don't believe him. Ashlee, you cannot marry him. He—"

"I already know. He stole your money. I was in the bed next to you, remember? Anyway, I can't marry Kevin. Or you. Or anyone else right now. I'm resigning from your company. Your dad's company. Whoever owns it. And—"

"Ashlee, wait. I know a lot has happened. But don't make a hasty decision."

"You'll see Kevin before I do," Ashlee said, shoving the ring into Darius's hand. "Give it back to him for me."

A voice echoed from the doorway. "She's not making a hasty decision. I'm taking my daughter home. And hopefully she'll never contact you again." Lawrence picked up Ashlee's suitcase.

Darius looked at Ashlee. His eyes glazed with tears he refused to shed. "Is this what you want, Ashlee?"

"I told you—"

Darius turned to Lawrence and yelled, "I'm not talking to you!" Tears fell from his eyes. Darius looked at Ashlee. Closed his eyes. Opened them and said, "Ashlee, I need you. I love you. Please don't go."

Ashlee shrugged past Darius and said, "I think it's best that I do go. You ready, Daddy?"

Lawrence stepped aside and held the door. He looked at Darius and said, "Don't call her anymore. Please."

Darius watched Ashlee, the woman he loved, walk away, wondering if he'd ever see his best friend again. He sat and wept.

The nurse entered the room. "Are you okay?"

"I'm fine," Darius said, drying his eyes.

"I wanted to give this to Ashlee before she left," the

nurse said, handing Darius a brown paper bag. "Can you make sure she gets this? It's important."

"Sure," Darius said, happy he had a legitimate reason to run after Ashlee.

Darius crumbled the bag in his hands. A bottle was inside. He shook the bag. Tablets. Ashlee had forgotten her medication. Darius raced to the elevator. When the doors closed, he opened the bag and peeped inside. Darius read the label. Prenatal vitamins?

Darius raced toward Lawrence's rental car. "Wait! Ashlee! Wait!"

Lawrence turned, looked Darius in his eyes, and drove off.

CHAPTER 48

Three women. Three pregnancies. Hopefully the only child that was his was Ashlee's. But with Lawrence refusing to allow Darius to have contact with Ashlee, how would he know? Darius resented, in many ways, that he'd become just like Darryl. Well, almost. Darryl had four kids by two women. If Ciara, Ashlee, and Desire were pregnant by him, by the end of next year, Darius would have three kids by three different women. Maybe bad luck did come in threes. Not the children. The women. Darius could hire . . . no, actually he could no longer afford certain luxuries. But he was certain his mother would give him money for college expenses and enough cash to raise his kids.

Could a man drive a woman to the brink of insanity? After Darius discovered that Ciara was responsible for his office burning down, he realized the worst thing he could do was to report Ciara to the authorities. Monica had promised that if he reported Ciara, Monica and their father would avenge her.

On New Year's Eve, Darius lounged at his Oakland home, refusing to attend his parents' annual holiday party in Los Angeles. The invited guests knew Darius had to find a job until he went to college. Although Wellington said he wouldn't help Darius seek employment, Wellington had personally spoken to all his friends. Darius had already received several offers over the phone. One, as an office assistant. Another to house sit and landscape. No way. Darius was depending on his mother to support him and convince Wellington to give him back his company. Darius had grown to love working in the film industry.

Darius decided to complete his last three years of college at the University of California at Los Angeles and get his degree in Business Administration. UCLA was a feeder college for the NBA and Darryl had promised Darius would get into UCLA on a full scholarship and make the NBA draft before graduation. Wellington had to give Darius credit for returning to school because college was like a full-time job with benefits but no pay. Darius looked at his tuxedo. The phone interrupted his thoughts.

"Hello," Darius answered, lounging across his floating mattress.

"Hey, Darius. This is Theo."

"Theo?"

"Yeah, my man. Look, your mother asked me to facilitate a conversation between you and Ciara. Ciara is on three-way and only agreed to speak with you if I don't tell you where she's staying. So what you wanna do?"

Ciara said, "Hi, Darius."

"Hey—"

"The baby and I are doing well. I've had a lot of

time to think. I'll grant you your divorce if you give me thirty percent stock in your company. I won't ask for child support or alimony."

"We haven't been married long enough for you to get alimony."

"Oh, but we will be if you don't agree."

"Ciara, why are you doing this to me?"

"To you? Oh no, darlin'. You did this to yourself. I didn't ask for your hand in marriage. I didn't take over your companies. And I didn't call you a slut."

"Okay, okay," Darius said. "I'll give you back all the interest in your companies. But not in mine."

"I've already regained interest in my companies. Haven't you read your mail lately?"

Darius remained silent. The stack of mail that was forwarded to him while he was in the hospital, Kevin had read. *Fuck!* "We'll see," Darius replied. "But Ciara, I apologize. Where are you staying? You don't have to hide from me. I do want to do what's right."

"Well, I have to go now. Think about my offer and let Theo know. He knows how to get in touch with me. Take care of yourself, Darius. Bye." Ciara hung up the phone.

"Well, my man. If I were you, I'd give her what she wants. She has the upper hand. You can always dissolve the company and start another. Rich folk do that kind of stuff every day. Now, your mother also wanted you to speak with Desire. Desire is living in London."

Darius heard Theo pressing the buttons.

"What's your desire?" Desire answered, barely above a whisper.

"Desire? What the hell are you trying to do to me?"

Desire's tone became harsh. "Who is this?"

"Darius Jones."

"Oh." Desire laughed. "My baby's daddy. Well, it's good hearing from you."

Darius bit his bottom lip. "What do you want from me?"

"Desire, desires nothing from you sweetie."

"Then why did you trap me into getting you pregnant?"

"Trap you? You've got it backward. You were the one who pursued me. Remember?"

"So what? You know I wasn't trying to get you pregnant."

"Maybe that's true. And I wasn't trying to get pregnant. But I am. And you can afford to and will take care of your son."

"I knew it. All you bitches are just alike. Chasing a dollar."

"No, Darius. You've got it twisted. All you rich-ass, arrogant-ass, ignorant-ass, wealthy men think you can have any woman you want. Any way you want us. Whenever you want. Do whatever you like to us. With us. Then you want to dismiss us. I'm tired of your kind. I'm keeping the baby. So you think about how you're going to take care of him. And good luck at UCLA. I hope your daddy gets you into the NBA. I'll call you after our son is born. Bye." Desire hung up the phone.

Darius yelled, "Fuck, man! What am I supposed to do?"

"Think, so you won't end up in this situation again, man?" Theo said. "Well, Ashlee isn't telling who's the father of her child. And her father isn't letting you speak with her so we'll have to wait and see."

"Fine. I think I've heard enough for one day anyway. Thanks, man." Darius hung up the phone. Drawing back his arm, he hurled the cordless into his glass mirror. The mirror shattered to the floor. "Fuck this shit!"

Darius showered, put on his tuxedo, and then called his limousine driver. At least his mother had transferred enough money into his personal bank account for Darius to enjoy the New Year. Eleven o'clock at night. Darius wasn't feeling festive. The driver closed Darius's door, sat behind the wheel and asked, "Where to, Sir?"

"I've changed my mind. I'm not going to the party. Take me to church."

Darius stared out the dark tinted windows. His life felt the same. Dim. How did he get himself in this predicament? If Ma Dear were alive, none of this would've happened. Maybe Ma Dear would hear his prayers from the pew.

Before getting out of the limo, Darius told the driver, "Wait out here for me. I'll call you when I'm ready. And when I'm ready, I'm ready."

When Darius stepped inside, most of the pews were full. By request, the usher seated him near the back. That was best in case Darius wanted to leave early.

Pastor Tellings looked older but his Don King afro was the same. Lost in thought, Darius didn't hear the choir, or the preacher. He noticed a few familiar faces. None he wanted to see after service until he turned and noticed Fancy Taylor standing in the door of the church soaked in a sexy designer gown. Her weave hung dripping water to the floor. Darius motioned for Fancy to sit in the folding chair next to his pew.

Fancy tiptoed then squatted on the edge of the seat. When Pastor Tellings said, "Let us pray," Darius bowed his head.

"Lord, thank you for blessing this queen and bringing her home. If she has any burdens, Lord, I ask that you remove them from her heart . . ." Darius continued praying for Ma Dear. He missed her a lot. Then he prayed for Ashlee, Maxine, and his brothers. And fathers Wellington and Darryl. Darius said a special prayer for his mother. Silently Darius prayed for Ciara and Desire so Fancy wouldn't hear.

Church finally ended, so Darius stood and said, "Excuse me." If he weren't taking a break from women, he'd ask Fancy for her number.

Fancy stood but didn't move. She extended her hand and said, "Hi, I'm Fancy Taylor. Remember me?"

Of course. Who could forget? "Pleased to meet you. I'm Darius. Darius Jones."

"Why are the initials DL engraved on your handkerchief?"

Okay, she's persistent. "The DL is for Darius's Law. That's how I'm living. I make the rules. I don't follow them."

Fancy smiled, and then frowned as five people invaded her space. This was Darius's opportunity to leave but there was something about Fancy that made him wait.

Damn, was that little SaVoy all grown up? Darius hadn't seen her in a while but he'd heard she was still a virgin.

SaVoy smiled wide and bright, then said, "We're going to my house for appetizers and socializing, you guys care to join us?"

Darius nodded at SaVoy. When he opened his mouth, Fancy looked at him. "I can't. My car just broke down outside."

Some dude asked for Fancy's keys, offering to pick up her car tomorrow. Darius was not going to compete.

Darius looked at Fancy and said, "Looks like you need a ride, young lady. I can handle that for you if you can trust me." Darius flipped out his cell phone. "I'm ready." He hung up and said, "If you're rolling with me, let's go."

"Not so fast, mister," SaVoy said, grabbing Darius's arm. "Tell your mother I said hello."

So SaVoy was interested. Darius ignored SaVoy, looked at Fancy, and asked, "Ready?"

Darius waited for the chauffeur to open the door then said, "Don't slide over."

Fancy smiled. "I know."

Fancy was wet and gorgeous. Darius sat beside Fancy and waited for the driver to close his door then asked, "My place or yours?"

Fancy stared out the window. She turned to him. Her eyelids lowered, and lips curved down with her spirit. "Take me home. Please."

Darius held Fancy's hand until the driver parked in a circular driveway on Lake Merritt.

"Before you go, I'd like to see you again." Darius scratched through the business number and wrote his cellular number. "Here's my card. Call me if you'd like to have brunch later."

Darius didn't say go to brunch. If Fancy called, Darius would have the caterers serve their meals by the fireplace. Darius watched the doorman hold the car door for Fancy. Nice building. He hadn't noticed it before.

Darius stretched across the limo's side seats. Darius Jones was broke. But broke to a millionaire wasn't exactly the same as for someone who barely maintained the minimum balance in their checking account. Darius had enough clothes to dress like a millionaire. He still had his cars and houses and could commute to college from his Los Angeles home and he was still close to his mother's house. But would Fancy be interested in him when he told her he was no longer on top?

Darius's cellular rang, displaying Kevin's number. The audacity of Kevin to have called Darius at two o'clock New Year's morning. "Kevin, man I told you never to call me ag—"

"Darius! Wait! Darryl is dead!"

A Woman Without a Plan

A woman without a plan
Will definitely find herself without a man

And if she's fortunate enough to get a man
She usually can't figure out how to keep him
One second longer than he wanted to be kept

Unless he was in the midst of cumming
He definitely had someplace to go

Even if she cleaned like his mama
Cooked like his grandmamma
Stroked his ego
Rubbed his feet
Reared his kids
And sucked his dick

She still couldn't figure out how to keep him
One second longer than he wanted to be kept

A woman without a plan
Will definitely find herself without a man

I Make the Rules

I won't dignify that with a reply
You see—the life I live
Is not through your eyes

I make my own rules
I play my own games
So do I care
If you like my name

Not

I do not have to dignify that with a reply
Because I am neither memorized nor measured
By what you think is clever

While you dehumanize and strategize
To solidify and signify
That you are humanized and civilized

While you articulate and enunciate
To perpetuate and stimulate
And eradicate and eliminate

Wait!

Let me demonstrate and cultivate
While I evaluate and communicate
And educate and then dictate

Again and Again
I say unto You

I won't dignify that with a reply

You see—the life I live
Is not through your eyes

I make my own rules
I play my own games
So do I care
If you like my name

Not!

Wait!

I Make the Rules

My Kind of Woman

My kind of woman
is sexy and sassy
she's smart
she's classy
freaky and bold
behind closed doors

My kind of woman
knows how to please her man
and knows when her man is pleased
my kind of woman
is a natural born tease

Free as the wind
not afraid to sin
but refuse to shame
her man
she gives a damn
and at the same time
Not

Because she's cool
like that
Phat
like that
and above all
She's got it all

Beauty, brains, and
a pussy that's untamed
and at the same time
tamable

She's capable of pulling out her rabbit
just like that
Anytime
at the drop of a dime
It's mine

My kind of woman
is an extension of me
she's everything I want her to be
and at the same time
She's not

My kind of woman
Is a whole lot of women

And that's why
I could never
eat just one
keep just one
fuck just one
Or
love just one

My kind of woman
Baby
Is you
And you
And you
And you too

AUTHOR'S NOTE

In my writings, I don't make choices for my characters or my readers. I purposely develop the stories for you to intuitively and intellectually make your own decisions. If a person thinks any of my characters are brilliant, brave, or bad, it's not because I've stated that. Remember this: your deductive reasoning is rooted in your frame of references, not mine. So, in this message, as I offer you an intimate part of me—I don't seek compassion or understanding. I simply want to share with you an intimate potion, a dose, about the woman, about the writer.

I first discovered, at the age of seven, that I could control the movement of my vaginal muscles. Let me tell you, that was a liberating experience. I was excited beyond measure. Sitting on our pink porch, on the corner of First and Magnolia in New Orleans, I admired my fitted yellow knit shorts. Billy Ann and her girlfriend were engrossed in teenage conversation. I sat on the top step looking down at four stairs, thinking.

About what, I can't remember. Maybe just the fact that it was so hot that summer day. I do recall being happy that the older girls didn't leave or make me leave. Suddenly, my little kitty moved. I was amazed. I stared at her. Did I do that? Well, let's see. I tried to make her move again. She did! She moved again! I became so lost in my great discovery that the only thing that drew my attention was laughter. Billy Ann and her girlfriend were no longer laughing with one another. They were laughing at me so I stopped, got up, opened the screen door, and took my kitty inside. Today, I realize how beautiful my experience could've been if an older woman had explained how and why my little kitty had moved.

Ignorant of the sacredness my virginity held, I shared my virginity at the age of fourteen believing that would make him love me. I became pregnant and miscarried, one of the (if not the) most painful physical experiences of my life, at the tender age of fifteen. And, thankfully I had my first explosive orgasm at sixteen. You see, if someone hadn't—and actually no one had—told me about orgasms early in life, I would truly be a born-again virgin. Seriously. I was ready to quit having sex by the age of sixteen. Talk at home about sex was nonexistent. But talk on the streets made sex seem fun. To me, the boys were having all the fun. Did you hear me? I said, "All the fun." Most of them, in fact, *none* of the high school boys knew anything about how to make me reach my orgasmic peak.

A neighborhood friend of my family, and all the other families near Second and Loyola, who was also a boyfriend of someone I knew, started making advances toward me, after he'd broken up with her. He was fine, and much older (at sixteen, three or four years is much older). Let's just say at that time he was old enough to have committed statutory rape but not to have graduated from college. He was the one who introduced me to orgasmic oral copulation and my vagina has sung a happy tune ever since. Shortly afterward I learned how to have vaginal orgasms. At sixteen, I enjoyed sex as much as the boys.

An orgasm is a powerful healthy experience, especially for women. That's why my novel, *He's Just a Friend*, suggests that women should self-explore their bodies before sharing themselves and losing their virginity.

I can't say how many, but a lot of women have privately and openly told me that their parents never taught them about orgasms. As a result, we have generations of women who've had children but no orgasms. I hope my writings will aid in closing the gap. We, especially African-American women, need to explore our sexuality and talk openly with our children—particularly the girls—and one another. I say *we* because I am forever in a learning mode. I know a lot but I don't know everything there is to know about sex or about life. Never will. To keep my relationship exciting, I always initiate something new.

Since the age of fourteen, I've dated well into the hundreds of men. If you confuse dating with having sex, your mental scope is limited. Don't assume anything about anyone. Open your mind to reality. Ask questions. Lots of pointed and open-ended questions. Narrow-minded folk generally jump to conclusions. Trust me, every date isn't worth stripping off clothes for. Oh yeah, it does help if he's fine. However, if the kiss, touch, and eye contact aren't passionate, if there's no chemistry, and his conversation isn't thought-provoking, you ladies know what I mean . . . the *oh baby you so fine* lines . . . I won't invest time. "Nice to have met you. Good-bye. Next."

I could count the times I've been in love, but only if I stop and think. As with most journeys in my life, once I make a commitment, I give one hundred-plus percent. All or nothing at all. I don't like sleep-walking through life. Once I decided to become a writer, I quit my very good government job. If I'd stayed, my one hundred thousand dollar–plus a year salary couldn't surpass my gratification and fruits of being a writer. And thanks to each of you, my supporters—whom I hope have found your passion in life, for life—I'm still writing novels and starting to write screenplays.

Each time I've fallen in love, from my very first love—who happens to be my son's father, my ex-husband, and my very first lover—until now with the fine-ass man I'm dating, my heart is wide open. I'm not afraid to live. Not afraid to get hurt. Like many of you, I've been there. Again and again. Not afraid to start over. Not ashamed to cry. I do have a problem admitting when I'm wrong. I hate being wrong. But I'm surely, not afraid to fall in love. I'm proud to say that I can truly date better than any man I've dated. And ladies, you can too. There's only a shortage of men, if you think inside the box. That's another book I promise to write. In order to gain power, ladies you must know when to exhibit passion and when to show compassion. The key is never try to be the man. Men hate controlling women who make them feel unneeded. Ladies, be strong and be the wo-man.

At the start of this message some of you may have formed opinions about me. It's my life. I didn't start with this truth of being molested by my great-grandfather as a child. The stench of his ninety-something-year-old wrinkled uncircumcised, black foreskin, which when pulled back revealed a reddish-pink dick head with white mushy crust underneath the ridge, vividly lingers in my mind. Being raped while on my period on the filthy streets of my hometown, as we say, Nawlins', at the age of sixteen, and having been brutally battered by my ex-husband, I know many of you would've empathized and many more of you would've sympathized with me. I am not alone. You are not alone.

I don't know how I embraced God's amazing grace but my Daddy, may he rest in peace, used to say our family was anointed. I believe that. Through the toughest of times, sometimes with tears in my eyes, pain in my heart, no money in my pockets, and no goodness in sight, I've managed to reach for stars. No drugs. No alcohol. Stars. You see, none of the incidents I just mentioned were my fault. Even as a child I realized that I was not the one to blame. I was happy when my great-grandfather, with my white lace-trim panties in his trembling hand, folded my sleeveless summer dress above my head, tilted my booty doggie-style in the air, while my knees were embedded in the couch, and my head pressed against the wall, was finally caught with his dick in his hand. And stopped. He never molested me again.

After I was raped, I went to school and held my head high. After I was battered, I went to work and did not hide my black eye. How could I be ashamed of myself for someone else's actions? Would one feel ashamed if struck by lightning? Hit by a car? If you understood my Introduction at the beginning of this novel, this is an example of what I meant when I stated, "Emotions that are yours but at the same time, not." Far too often people allow others to dictate their emotions. I consider those "false feelings." If you don't think, you won't know how and why you truly feel a certain way as a result of a particular situation.

Each abusive situation could've been worse. When I was molested, I didn't lose my virginity. When I was raped, I wasn't a virgin. When my ex-husband used my face for a punching bag, I divorced him. Immediately. He cried. Begged. Pleaded. Promised never to hit me again. I refused to take him back. I'm from Louisiana. Deep down in The Dirty South and I can get downright ugly. I was scared. Not of him. But of what I would do to him if he ever raised his hand to hit me again.

He was twenty-three. I was twenty-one. But growing up witnessing my father chronically abuse my stepmother taught me that if a man strikes once and gets away with it, he'll probably hit again. I've had several marriage opportunities after my divorce, including one from my soul mate, but never remarried. If the relationship isn't right before I say "I do," then I won't stand before God at an altar taking vows I already know I won't keep. My loyalty and dedication does not lend to being in a marriage that is unevenly yoked or unevenly stroked. I have choices. You have choices, too.

I've started writing a book about my life. For each gentleman, I've decided to use first names only—a few I can't remember first or last names but baby, oh baby, I can tell you the stories. Each man has his own chapter. There are over fifty chapters that end with "Mary's comical moral of the story." The stories, some very humorous because I love laughter, unfold from a first-person point of view. I'm not sure if some of the intimate experiences, wild adventures, or ludicrous behavior I've exhibited—while mind-blowing even to me—can legally be in print but I'll find out. I'm serious. The readers who want to know have asked, "What part of your book is you?" After reading this book, you'll see no character parallels my life, but every character represents a part of me.

If you don't live, and I mean truly live—take risks, change your hairstyle, dance in the rain, start your own business, stop feeling guilty for every damn thing you didn't do to please somebody else and begin doing what makes you happy, learn your body medically and sexually, protect your health, lose weight for yourself, etc.—you're already decomposing. Live. Be happy. Smile. Tell someone you love them and mean it with all your heart. Your choice, good or not, is always yours. Don't blame others.

I'll end with one of my favorite sayings about life. "If I had to do it all over again, I'd do it all over again, and I wouldn't change a thing." I am who I am because I've done what I've done. I've had lots of fun and intend to keep having fun. I began my New Year praying. Giving thanks to God for everything and everyone. Partying with family and friends. And laughing with loved ones at the Oakland Paramount Theatre at one of my favorite comedians and all-around talented artists, Chris Rock, until my entire body ached and healed from the joy of laughter. Enjoy life. When you're feeling down, pray and reach for the stars. Just like God, the stars are always there. Even when we can't see them.

The other side of what I do that many are unaware of is I'm the Founder and President of **The RaW Advantage.**™ The RaW Advantage™ is a business dedicated to avid readers and aspiring writers. I conduct self-publishing workshops for writers and host author receptions for readers.

The RaW Advantage™ also encompasses The SHIFT Program and Who's Making Love workshops. I created The SHIFT (Supporting Healthy Inner Freedom for Teens) Program to help teenagers build self-esteem and make healthy relationship choices. Anyone who hasn't listened—I mean truly listened—to a teenager speak from the heart concerning their views on love, let me tell you, society has stripped away many of their hopes and dreams of having healthy relationships. I strive to show teenagers—especially young ladies who set the tone and establish the bar for relationships—how to use their inner strength to assist with their decisions. Decisions that parents, teachers, and friends can influence but cannot make for them.

I'm taking an additional step to provide references. The rest is up to you.

Spiritual Guidance	*Meditate and ask God or your spiritual leader*
SHIFT Program	*www.therawadvantage.com*
Free Testing for HIV/AIDS	*1-866-RAP-IT-UP*
Rape Crisis Hotline	*1-800-656-HOPE*
Pregnancy and Prevention	*1-800-BABY-999*

The following is a sample chapter from Mary B. Morrison's eagerly anticipated upcoming novel, WHEN SOMEBODY LOVES YOU BACK.

WHEN SOMEBODY LOVES YOU BACK will be available in August 2006 wherever hardcover books are sold.

ENJOY!

CHAPTER 1

Darius

A black woman did it all . . . because she had to. She did it all and she did it well, caring for others while neglecting herself. Four hundred and fifty years of birthing babies for white masters and black slaves sold off to the highest bidder, leaving her to raise her children alone. Four hundred fifty plus years struggling for freedom while black men died for what they seemingly couldn't live with today: dignity. Freedom came with a price and now that the black woman could choose her mate, her fate was the same, leaving her to take on more responsibility than she should, but not more than she could, so she carried on doing all she could do, the best she knew how.

Who would take care of the black woman while she sacrificed to raise her kids, pay the bills, and all too often, sleep alone at night, wondering if her direct deposit would post in time to keep the lights on, or balance her checkbook the day before payday, so she could restock the refrigerator before emptying the cabinets or feeding her children the last few slices of bread while she watched them eat?

The black woman didn't need anybody's sympathy. She was a survivor by nature. The Mother of Jesus. Many denied the undeniable, but what the black woman fell short of was epiphany: a lesson in how to love herself first. How to stop stressing about not knowing if her baby daddy—daddies—would ever show up at their children's event's and parent–teacher conferences, if he'd ever pay her child support. Ultimately, how to stop worrying about whom he had sex with when he wasn't loving her—that is, if he'd ever loved her.

Based on his mother's mistakes, Darius reluctantly admitted to himself that love, or the lack thereof, was what most men at some point in their lives experienced; he was terrified of two things: falling in love and failure. Either would render him vulnerable. Destroy his character. Ultimately strip him of his manhood.

A man in love was weak for his woman. Would do anything for his woman. The more he gave, the more control she wanted. Darius didn't want to be hard on women; he had to. The cold, callous, careless, arrogant, inconsiderate, selfish person ruling his existence, primarily with his dick, wasn't him. But if Darius didn't protect his heart, who would? Surely not the women who'd already emotionally broken him down. Like the one blabbering on the other end of his cell phone.

Sitting in the limousine, next to his fiancée, Darius regretted answering his phone. If it were up to him, he wouldn't have, but no Fancy had to insist, "Answer, it." Translation, "Put that bitch in check so I won't have to."

Darius was stuck again between the old and the new pussies.

Ashlee cried in his ear, "I'm sorry." No, she wasn't. "I never wanted to hurt you." *Yes, she did.* "And no matter what, I love you." That was probably the one truth. No woman could resist Darius or his big dick or the fact that he knew how to sling Slugger. "But you need to know."

Exhaling, Darius softly said, "Then tell me."

Crying, like most women did when they wanted sympathy, Ashlee said, "Our son, Darius Junior, died from HIV complications."

Whoa, that was some cold-blooded shit to drop on a brotha on his wedding day. "And you?" Darius whispered.

Sniffling, Ashlee said, "Positive."

The numbness in Darius's body caused the phone to slip from between his fingers.

Picking up the phone, Fancy questioned Ashlee. "What did you tell him?" Fancy looked at the phone, then said, "Hello? Hello?" Staring at Darius, Fancy began crying along with him. She muttered, "She hung up. Please tell me. What did she say?"

If Fancy had kept her damn mouth shut, he wouldn't be trippin'. Ignoring Fancy, Darius pressed a button lowering the divider window then instructed the driver, "Man, take me straight home."

"Oakland or Los Angeles?"

"Los Angeles," Darius said leaning against the back seat.

Holding her hair away from her face, Fancy placed her head in his lap. Instantly, Darius's dick expanded four times its size. Fancy rubbed the head, unzipped his pants, then licked the underside main vein. His hottest spot, next to the span from his asshole up to his balls.

"Ummm," Darius moaned, "that feels so damn good.

Lick him again." When the precum trickled out, Darius gripped Fancy's head and said, "Stop," desperately desiring to bust a nut or two. The sexual energy danced in his hands urging him to grab the back of Fancy's head and thrust his shaft down her throat. But what if he had . . . Fuck! Darius shouted in his mind, then said to Fancy, "Go to sleep."

"If you say so." Stretching her feet across the seat, Fancy's head weighed heavily on his thigh.

Darius wanted to sleep, too, but all kinds of shit ran through his head. Especially when Ashlee had the audacity to say, "I love you no matter what." Liar. Love didn't have a goddamn thing to do with what she'd said.

The driver was already cruising on Interstate 5 south, practically a straight shot to L.A., but hours away. Folding his limp dick in his pants, Darius closed his eyes trying to understand how a woman's need to be loved vastly differed from a man's desire to love a woman.

Perhaps his mother's need for love or her desire to be adored was the reason it took Darius Jones twenty years to discover her lie. After a paternity test confirmed the truth, Darius took back or should he say claimed his real name and irrespective of whether his mother was to blame he could never eradicate the pain or escape the shame of having to explain why, at twenty years of age, he'd changed his last name. From Jones to Williams.

With the exception of not marrying Fancy and losing his firstborn, the day his mother told him who his biological father was was the worst day of Darius's life. Darryl Williams. That was his real daddy's name, but how could Darius regain the years? Years lost. Not knowing the man he'd idolized growing up. His dad was a former NBA-star. Darryl was his college basketball coach when Darius played at Georgetown.

Darius's mother knowingly sent him to Georgetown, knowingly allowed him to play an entire season coached by his father, knowingly attended all of his high school games but never attended any of his college games, and knowingly never said a frickin' word until after she'd tricked Darius into quitting the team to accept the executive vice-president position at her company. To repay his mother, Darius fucked all four of her top-level executives the same way she'd screwed him, secretly.

Darius imagined what his mother might think now that a few years had passed since her confession. "I'm sorry I fucked up your life sweetie. Get over it. Move on. Be a man about it. Okay, if you won't forgive me then I'll just have to forgive myself and you'll have to get professional help."

Be a man about it! About what? Her emotional autopsy gutted his insides, ripped out his beating heart, then tagged his toe, "John Doe," like she'd done no harm. Suddenly, without cause, he'd become a heartless stranger to her. Women. They always wanted men to forget their mistakes, especially after they'd told their cure-all truth. If a man lied to his woman, she'd nag the hell out of him, reminding him every chance she got. That's why men had two choices. Bury the lie and never tell the truth or bury his soul for the rest of his life. A man in love eventually forgot his woman's errors but his subconscious never forgave her.

A tear sat on his left eyelid as Darius, disguised the bitterness in his voice instructing the limo driver, "Man drive faster." The ride from Oakland back to Los Angeles seemed a lot longer than the trip going.

For a moment, Darius chuckled at how neither Fancy nor he showed up at their wedding in Los Angeles. Instead both of them ended up at the pier in Berkeley, the first stop of their first date, forever their special place. Darius would never take another woman there. Yeah, Fancy was right. They were two of a kind. Over five hundred miles away from their matrimonial service, they'd stood on the planks overlooking the Pacific Ocean. Undoubtedly, Darius loved Fancy. Fancy excited him in every way imaginable. Challenged him. Confronted him on his lies.

In his heart, Darius also loved Ashlee. Only God knew how much he loved Ashlee. Ashlee, no matter what the circumstances, supported him. Every man needed a supportive woman. Ashlee shouldn't have had to carry his baby for nine months without him. Bury their son without him. Now that Ashlee needed him, she shouldn't have to deal with her illness without him. He'd already failed her several times.

Glancing down at Fancy while she slept, Darius thought, *Stop trippin' dog. Your commitment isn't to Ashlee. You've got the most beautiful woman in the world on your lap.*

Darius had already revealed more of his skeletons than he'd intended to Fancy, but how could he explain to his fiancée the phone call he'd received from Ashlee? He couldn't. Hopefully, things would work out and he wouldn't have to.

Quietly Darius leaned closer to Fancy making sure she was asleep. Then, he quietly dialed Ashlee's number.

"Hey, how are you?" Ashlee answered like she hadn't just given him the worse news of his life next to the day she'd told him their son died.

Angrily, Darius whispered, "How do you think I

am? Were you serious about what you said earlier or trying to fuck up my wedding?"

"I was at your wedding. You weren't."

Darius's lips tightened. "So what you sayin'? You was gonna drop that shit on me in front of over a thousand people?"

"You mean like the way you dropped me?"

Darius became quiet. Biting his bottom lip, his eyes automatically shifted to the corners whenever he lied or avoided telling the truth. He had no nonargumentative response, so he waited for Ashlee to say something.

"Darius, I need to see you."

"I don't think that's a good idea right now or ever," Darius replied, worrying how he'd feel about Ashlee if he did see her.

Firmly she asked, "Where are you?"

Darius whispered, "On my way home," checking on Fancy, praying she was still asleep.

"Which home?"

Lowering his voice more, Darius mumbled, "The Valley. Why? What's up with all the questions? You haven't called me in months."

"How close are you?"

Darius hissed, "Where are you?" then tightly ground his back teeth flinching his jaws.

"Close."

"To what? Ashlee, don't. Look, I can't ignore what you said earlier, but right now I gotta go. Don't call me. I'll call you later."

"I'm sick of being your fuckin' puppet!"

Widening his eyes, Darius's forehead tensed in disbelief giving him an instant headache as he continued listening.

"Ashlee, please move in with me. Ashlee please don't leave me. Ashlee I need you to work for me. Let me lick your pussy. Ashlee let me fuck you! Well, I'm tired of being fucked! Doing every damn thing your damn way just to make you happy when you obviously don't give a shit! About me! So I'mma tell you the fuck what!" Ashlee breathed heavily into his ear, then softly said, "Better yet, hurry your ass home. I'll talk to you when you get here."

Quick sharp puffs of air escaped Darius's flaming nostrils as he shut his eyes rolling his eyeballs to the top of the sockets. "Ashlee, you'd better not be at *my* house." Darius wanted to exceed her anger but said, "Fancy's carrying my baby and she doesn't need to deal with your nonsense."

Darius could've simply said Fancy was with him, but Ashlee already knew that and that wouldn't have convinced Ashlee to stay away from him. Damn, did he trust Ashlee wasn't daring enough to trespass on his property that he hadn't changed the locks? Fuck! How stupid.

"Our house. I love you Darius. I'll see you when you get home. Bye, baby."

Smothering his voice, Darius hissed, "Ashlee. Ashlee. Damnit," then sucked in all the oxygen he could before blowing the hot air out of his mouth.

A woman sure knew how to fuck with a man's head. Heads. Both of his were in pain: one from not getting enough pussy and the other from hearing too much bitchin'. Was any of the shit Ashlee said true?

How could Darius tell Fancy he couldn't make love to her? Not today. Not tomorrow. Maybe never again. He definitely didn't want Fancy to hear the bad news from Ashlee. Why, of all days, had Ashlee called him on his wedding day to fuck him up?

Interrupting his mental monologue, the limo driver said, "Mr. Williams, you're home," cruising into the driveway.

Darius lowered the rear tinted window staring at his house. The living room, dining room, and kitchen lights were on. Seconds later, all of the lights went out.